JACK OF HEARTS

JOSEPH HANSEN

JACK OF HEARTS

A DUTTON BOOK

DUTTON

Published by the Penguin Group
Penguin Books USA Inc., 375 Hudson Street, New York, New York 10014, U.S.A.
Penguin Books Ltd, 27 Wrights Lane, London W8 5TZ, England
Penguin Books Australia Ltd, Ringwood, Victoria, Australia
Penguin Books Canada Ltd, 10 Alcorn Avenue, Toronto, Ontario, Canada M4V 3B2
Penguin Books (N.Z.) Ltd, 182–190 Wairau Road, Auckland 10, New Zealand

Penguin Books Ltd, Registered Offices:
Harmondsworth, Middlesex, England

First published by Dutton, an imprint of Dutton Signet,
a division of Penguin Books USA Inc.
Distributed in Canada by McClelland & Stewart Inc.

First Printing, January, 1995
1 3 5 7 9 10 8 6 4 2

Copyright © Joseph Hansen, 1995
All rights reserved

 REGISTERED TRADEMARK—MARCA REGISTRADA

LIBRARY OF CONGRESS CATALOGING-IN-PUBLICATION DATA
Hansen, Joseph.
Jack of hearts / Joseph Hansen.
p.   cm.
ISBN 0-525-93924-5
I. Title.
PS3558.A513J3   1995
813'.54—dc20   94-3653
CIP

Printed in the United States of America
Set in Copperplate and Garamond No. 3
Designed by Steven N. Stathakis

For Paul & Mary Lou

JACK OF HEARTS

THE FIRST MONDAY OF January 1941 is fair and fine, so the windows and the door to the back porch stand open, but still, as it does every morning, the kitchen smells of burned toast. In her bathrobe, hair in curlers, Alma Reed sits at the table, where she has pushed aside her plate of charred crumbs to make room to lay out cards—not to play solitaire, but to learn what to expect from the day. A small, dark woman with lustrous, slightly bulging brown eyes, she studies Nathan now and smiles.

"You look nice," she says.

He has put on his best suit, a time-dulled blue hand-me-down of Frank's. He gets a cup from the cupboard, fills the cup from the pot on the stove, brings the cup to the table, and stirs sugar and milk into the coffee, using the spoon from his mother's saucer. "What's in the cards?" He sips at the hot coffee, sets the cup down, jumps up, and fetches from a cupboard a box of cornflakes. He fills a bowl, gets a spoon for himself, brings it to the table, sits down. "Gloom or sunshine?"

She sighs and holds the ace of spades out to him. "There's a disappointment." She tucks the card into the deck, tamps the edges of the deck on the tabletop, shuffles the cards. "I'll read them for you, shall I?"

She named him for Dr. Nathan Fuller, a white-goateed old charlatan back in Minneapolis who taught her all the nonsense she swears by. She hoped Nathan would grow up thinking as she does about the mysteries of life, but he didn't. For years, he felt guilty about this. No more. It's all rubbish—he just never says so. He loves her. Why hurt her feelings? He pours on milk, swallows a big mouthful of cornflakes, and tells her, "It's an important day for me."

"Hmm?" She lays the cards out, snap, snap, snap.

"It's a new year, and I'm through being a child."

She cries cheerfully, "Here you are!" and taps the jack of hearts; "and look what's surrounding you. A knave of diamonds on one side, a queen of hearts on the other, and the king of diamonds above. Oh, sweetheart"—she sits back on the kitchen chair and gives him that ever hopeful smile of hers—"you've picked the perfect day."

He nods at the cards. "That's the jack of clubs."

"Oh"—she waves a dismissive hand—"but at your feet. If he tries to harm you, you can do what you like with him. He doesn't matter. You're going to meet wonderful people who will be your friends and help you, sweetheart."

Frank appears in the kitchen doorway. "I hope there's fodder for the old horse. Heavy day in the shafts ahead." A rawboned man of sixty, with a slight stoop to his broad shoulders, he wears worn blue work clothes. He blinks at his seventeen-year-old son in amazement that never dies. Nathan came along when he was forty-three, when Alma was forty-one. An unexpected pleasure is how he puts it. Until then, Alma had thought she was barren, Frank had thought he was sterile. "You look nice," he says, pulls open the door of a palsied old refrigerator, bends to peer inside. "Fancy doings, schoolside?"

"I want to write for the paper," Nathan says.

"You said they wouldn't let you"—Frank carries bacon to the stove—"till next fall."

"That's too far off," Nathan says. "I can't wait."

Alma says, "I've read his cards. He'll get his wish."

"You've done a lot of typing this vacation." Frank lays bacon in a pan. "You going to show them your play?"

"It's not ready." In fact, he hasn't yet finished act one. "No—other stuff, sketches. Of school life. Just dialogue, the way the kids talk to each other."

"Fit to print?" Frank cuts butter into a second skillet. "I pass there with the truck, you know. Some of the language I hear from the football field is pretty rank."

"Would I know people who talk like that?" Nathan pushes back his chair, drinks the last of his coffee, takes the cup and his bowl and spoon to the sink, washes them, and lays them on the drainboard. If he doesn't do these things, they'll be here to wash when he gets home. Alma is no housekeeper. "I have to go," he says. Frank is peeling a potato. Nathan pecks his beard-stubbly cheek, kisses Alma's steel curlers, and pushes out the swing door.

AT THE FAR END OF A LONG BROWN CORRIDOR, a classroom has been made into the office of the Fair Oaks Junior College *Monitor*. The paper is off-limits to lower-division students—lower division means the last two years of high school, upper division the first two years of college—but a few weeks ago, very late in the day, when the sunlight was red and murky and no one was around, Nathan, with a thumping heart, edged inside. Peeling yellow oak desks held old Underwood typewriters. A half-circle copy desk strewn with pasteups stood against a wall. Brown metal wastebaskets overflowed. Strips of galley proof hung off wire hooks by the door to the printshop. Standing there in the silence, he got tears in his eyes. He ached to work in that room.

This morning, he approaches it from outdoors. It is absurdly early. No one is around. Because of the fine weather, the windows, with their crooked venetian blinds, stand open. He takes his neatly typed sketches out of his jacket, warm and a little damp from sweat. He thinks he will just toss the pages through the window. Someone will pick them up, see how good they are, and print them, not knowing Nathan Reed's age, nor caring. That would be best, wouldn't it? He stands on tiptoe, stretches his arm, and behind him someone says:

"What are you doing?"

He turns around, hiding the pages behind his back. A youth in a wheelchair smiles up at him, head tilted in amiable curiosity. Nathan knows who this is—Buddy Challis. His arms and legs are shrunken from childhood polio, his small hands twisted and gnarled. He is about the size of a ten-year-old boy, but he is twenty, said to be very bright; he's a writer, a jazz trumpeter, and, most glamorously to Nathan, he is features editor of the *Monitor*. Nathan's face feels hot. His mouth is dry. He tries to speak, but he can't.

"What's on the papers?" Buddy Challis says.

"What papers?" Nathan's voice cracks.

"The ones you're hiding behind your back."

"Oh, these?" Nathan flaps them forlornly. "Oh, just—just something I wrote."

"You were going to toss them through the window?"

"Yes, well, I thought—you might—want to—print them."

Challis smiles gently. "The office has doors. You know doors? They're not hard to work. Not even for me."

"I'm lower division," Nathan says. "I thought I wasn't allowed in."

Challis holds out a hand. This means he lets go one of the wheels of his chair, and it rolls on the uneven tarmac, turning him slightly away. "Let's see."

Nathan gulps and hands him the pages.

———

MOON'S IS A WOODEN SHACK with flaking white paint, wavy glass windows along the front, and a sign on the roof with red neon letters and a white crescent moon. Nathan has never been inside. He has regarded it as special, not for mere mortals, a Mermaid Tavern. Now he wheels Buddy into a noisy room of cheap veneer paneling, hand-lettered signs, small tables, bentwood chairs, smells of coffee and bacon. A listless old wood-frame screen door flaps shut behind them.

"Hey, Buddy!" someone shouts.

Nathan peers. He can't make out who called. The place is full. Boys and girls gobble corned beef hash, flapjacks, and ham and eggs, and wash them down with coffee and Cokes. And they are all talking at the tops of their voices, laughing, quarreling, clattering knives and forks. Then an arm waves in a far corner.

Buddy calls, "Good morning."

And Nathan steers him between the tables. The table they want is at the front, beside a window where the sun comes in hot, and a little neon sign hangs: Acme Beer. The group at the table shift their chairs to make room for Buddy's. Buddy says, "This is Nathan Reed. He's a very good writer."

He introduces the people at the table. Charlie Vorak, a fat fellow with crinkly, close-cut red hair, is editor of the *Monitor*. He must be as prosperous as Nathan—his jacket has moth holes. He grins and shakes Nathan's hand. He is standing behind the chair of a handsome, slightly cross-eyed young woman with dark roses in her cheeks and a cloud of black hair. "Peg Decatur," Buddy says. She gives Nathan a smile that melts him. Buddy says, "Donald Donald." This is a straw-haired boy of Nathan's age, with pimples, crooked teeth, and blue lips that make him look sick. He is smoking a cigarette. His smile is more like a snarl. He doesn't offer to shake hands.

"This is Donald's shining hour," Wayne Hotchkiss says. Hotchkiss is the fabled journalism instructor, said to be writing a novel, an idea that awes Nathan. But Hotchkiss looks all too mortal—a thin man of forty with pouchy cheeks that need a shave. His gray suit is rumpled, shirt collar crushed, necktie knotted too tight and twisted to the side. His eyes are bloodshot, with bags under them. Coffee has slopped from his cup into the saucer and the saucer is choked with wet cigarette butts. With a trembling hand, he lights another cigarette. "His design for the *Monitor* won."

"Hey, wonderful," Buddy says. "Congratulations."

"You get fifty dollars, right?" Vorak says.

Donald doesn't answer. Hotchkiss does:

"To be presented in a small ceremony in Dean Staat's office this noon. Among the participants, the head of the art department, and myself representing the journalism department. There'll be a photographer from the *Independent*." He touches his face. "Christ, and I forgot to shave." He has fastened the cigarette in a corner of his mouth, and the smoke trickles up into his eye. He squints at Nathan. "A good writer, huh? We can use you."

Charlie Vorak and Peg Decatur say, "Can we ever."

"Listen to this." Buddy has Nathan's pages in his twisted little hands. He reads the first sketch aloud. It is about the misadventures of a kid with a nickel trying to cadge another so he can buy a hamburger. At the end, everyone laughs and claps. Nathan smiles and gives a little comic bow, and feels a savage sting on the back of his hand. He jerks the hand up to his mouth.

"Oh, I'm sorry," Donald Donald says, acting surprised and innocent. "Did I burn you?"

"It's nothing," Nathan says. It hurts like hell.

"Here." A long, thin arm reaches past him, long, bony fingers pick up a wrapped butter pat from a saucer in the middle of the table where the sugar, salt and pepper, ketchup, and mustard stand. "I know just what to do for that." The fingers unwrap the butter, take Nathan's hand, smear butter on the red, angry burn. The owner of the fingers is a tall, skinny young man wearing a long, white wraparound apron. Nathan has noticed him getting plates from the service window at the back of the room and weaving between the tables with them, backchatting with the kids. "There." He smiles. "It will stop hurting in a minute. And it won't leave a scar." He looks Nathan quickly up and down. "We wouldn't want to leave a scar, would we?" He turns away murmuring, "Dear God, can it be real?" and sways, limp-wristed, toward the kitchen.

Someone shouts at him, "Where's the jukebox?"

"You want music?" he says. "You shall have music." He bangs through the kitchen swing door. "Sing for the customers, Moon, darling."

A round red face topped by wild red hair appears at the service window and bawls out, " 'Did your mother come from Ireland, 'cause there's something 'bout you Irish, 'tis the hint of Irish laughter in your sm-i-i-i-le. . . ,' " Groans and howls rise from the tables. Moon looks amazed and hurt. "Ah, you're all tone-deaf. You don't know beauty when you hear it." She turns away in mock disgust.

Donald Donald reads his watch. "Have to get to class." He hikes his chair back, planting one of its legs on Nathan's foot. He knows it. He looks up into Nathan's face. "Jesus, I'm clumsy this morning, aren't I?" Then and only then does he get off the chair. "Well, anyway, now you can sit down. Good-bye, all." He walks off. Nathan sits. The long, thin arm is there again. It sets coffee in front of him. He looks up. "Oh, no. I don't have any money."

"It's on the house," the tall young man says. "I'm Travers Jones. What's your name?" Nathan tells him, and he looks surprised. "You don't look Jewish."

"That's about all I'm not. My father's English-Scotch-Irish, my mother's French and Chippewa. A little."

"I'll tell Moon the Irish part," Travers Jones says. "There'll be free drinks all around."

"Jones isn't Irish," Nathan says. "It's Welsh."

"Mr. Jones was just a passing fancy," Travers says, and drifts away to ring the cash register, fetch a metal bin, and begin to make a clatter, clearing tables.

"What's the matter with Donald?" Charlie Vorak says.

"I guess you'd call him a sore winner," Hotchkiss says. "That's a funny piece, Nathan. It breaks my heart. Have you got some time you can give us?"

Nathan struggles with his conscience. Buddy looks at him. Buddy tells Hotchkiss, "He's lower division."

Hotchkiss winces, gives his head a shake, wiggles a finger in his ear. "What did you say? Something's gone wrong with my hearing."

"He didn't say anything," Charlie Vorak says.

"Not a word," Peg Decatur says.

"I didn't think I said anything," Buddy says.

Nathan is so happy he's afraid he is going to cry. "Excuse me," he says, and heads for the washroom.

IT IS NEXT TO THE KITCHEN. While he splashes his face with cold water and dries it with stiff brown paper towels, he hears Moon's voice through the partition.

"You'll never be able to pay it back."

Travers says, "So what if I can't? It's art we're talking about here, and intelligence, enriching people's lives, making them think, making them feel. Good God, Mother, what's two hundred dollars? You drink that up in a month."

"And that," Moon says, "enriches my life, you silly gaboon. Two hundred dollars is a fortune. You don't know. You never had to work for pay a day in your life."

"No, I have to work here," Travers says, "for no pay. All right? What about that? Suppose we don't call it a loan? Suppose we call it a start on seven years' back wages."

"You've a bed to sleep in, a roof over your head, and three square meals a day. A lot of men in this country would count themselves lucky to be in your shoes."

"I want a theater," Travers wails. "I'm dying for a theater. Don't you know what it means to love something so much that living without it is sheer hell?"

"I'm too busy in my own hell," Moon says, "cooking and washing dishes for the world."

"I'm not asking to rent the Pantages," Travers cries. "Just some storefront, some abandoned church—anyplace where we can have a few lights, some rags for costumes, a cracked mirror to make up in, a few splintery boards for a stage."

"Dear God," Moon says, "you wear your mother out."

"I hope so," Travers says. "You mean I can have it?"

"I'm tired of hearing about it," Moon says. "Oof! What are you doing? Take your bony arms from around me. Don't slobber me with kisses. I didn't promise anything. I have to think about it."

"I'll start talking again," Travers threatens.

"Ye can have the two hundred," she says, "but that's the limit, understand? Don't come plaguing me for more. There isn't any more. I want your word on that."

"We'll call it the Harlequin," Travers says.

"Why not the Abbey? The greatest theater in the world."

"People will think we're conducting masses," Travers says. "I never did understand that name."

"Well, the Sean O'Casey, then," Moon says. "The Lady Gregory, the W. B. Yeats, the J. M. Synge."

"Mother—this is not Dublin."

"Arragh," she says, and bangs pans. "I wish it was."

WHEN NATHAN GETS BACK TO THE TABLE, a big, olive-skinned young man is sitting in his chair, twiddling a cigarette, chatting and chortling. This is Dan Munroe. Nathan goes to all the school plays. He has seen Munroe looking stalwart in kilts and tartan in *The Drums of Oudh*, and sophisticated in white tie and tails in a Philip Barry play. He is saying, in his rich, amused voice, " 'All his daughters were lying out in the graveyard, though only one of them was dead.' " He laughs, Wayne Hotchkiss laughs, Peg Decatur laughs, Buddy Challis laughs, but Charlie Vorak doesn't laugh. He scowls. He taps Peg's shoulder and starts to move off.

"Come on, Peg," he says. "Quarter to eight."

"You go ahead," she says, not looking at him, still smiling at Munroe. "Dan will take me in his car."

"You're sitting in Nathan's chair," Charlie tells Dan.

"Who?" Dan looks around. "Ah. You're Nathan." He gets up off the chair, merrily shakes Nathan's hand. "The genius. Buddy's literary discovery of the new year."

"Keep the chair," Nathan says. "I have a class."

"Are you coming or not?" Charlie asks Peg.

"I told you," she says, "Dan will drive me."

"I'd take you too, Charlie," Dan says, "but my car is only a coupe. It's a question of chivalry."

Charlie grunts at him. He gives Peg a look of longing and despair. And bad temper. "See you later, Wayne," he says. "See you later, Buddy. We have to talk about those headings Donald designed. We'll want one for Nathan's column. We have to decide what to call it."

"Column?" Nathan feels dizzy.

Charlie nods. "One a week. Like the piece Buddy read us. You can do more of those, can't you?"

"I—I guess so." Nathan gropes for the chair and sits on it. "I mean, yes, sure, Charlie."

"Good." Charlie nods happily. "See you later, then."

"Wait." Hotchkiss unfolds from his chair. "I'm coming with you." His joints seem rusty. He moans feebly. "I'll be glad when it's summer. Winter, damn kids are always sick. What a night." He gives Buddy a pat on the shoulder, throws Nathan a wink, and hobbles off after Charlie, clothes flapping, cigarette smoke curling around his uncombed head.

Munroe smiles after him. "The wounded scarecrow."

"It wasn't the kids that kept him up," Peg says. "It was scotch. At two A.M., Charlie and I saw him and Ken Stone come staggering out of Laughing Jack's and down Sierra Street, yelling limericks to the night."

Munroe tells Peg, "Excuse me a minute. Have to talk to Travers. Urgent business. The wicked stage." He heads for the cash register and Travers. "Then I'll whisk you to the campus in my chariot of fire."

"They'll talk forever," Peg says to Buddy. "About how to start a theater without money. So . . ." She sighs, stands, and picks up a load of books from the window ledge. "I can lose a pound, walking. You ready to go?"

"Nathan?" Buddy backs and turns his chair.

"I don't think they'll talk forever," Nathan says.

Peg says, "You don't know them. I do."

"Travers just got the money," Nathan says.

Peg's jaw drops. "Honest? How do you know?"

"It's a reporter's job to know," Nathan says. "He's going to call it the Harlequin."

Buddy grins. "Didn't I say this kid was a genius?"

Nathan tells Peg, "I was in the washroom, and I overheard Travers and Moon talking in the kitchen. I wasn't eavesdropping. The wall is thin as paper."

Buddy begins to wheel himself between the tables toward the door. "Congratulations, Travers," he calls.

"What?" Travers almost falls off his cashier's stool. "How did you know?"

Buddy laughs. "It's a reporter's job to know."

THAT AFTERNOON, WHEN NATHAN reaches the gap-toothed fence, the yard of dark old magnolia trees, and the gaunt, scallop-shingled house with its spindle-work verandas and touches of stained glass, the gruff notes of Bach's C Major Suite for Unaccompanied Cello drift down from open attic windows. He doesn't look up. He looks for the water tank truck it's Frank's job to drive. Overgrown as the driveway is by untrimmed shrubbery, he could still see the truck if it were there, and it is not there.

He sighs and climbs the steep porch steps. He hates this place sometimes. If old Aunt Bessie Dupree, the last occupant of the house, hadn't left it as a legacy to little Alma, her favorite niece long ago when Alma was a child with braids and an enormous hair ribbon, things would be better. Sure, they have a lot more room here than in any of their bleak Minneapolis flats where frost-crusty window-panes kept out the snow but not the cold. But for those the rent came due every month. And that crass reality and the bad weather in the streets kept Frank working—unhappy, droning away at hymn tunes on a wheezy organ in the icy loft of some backstreet Presby-terian church, but working. Here, there is no rent to pay—only the tax bill, which arrives so rarely Frank forgets all about it in a day or two.

The minute Nathan steps indoors, he knows Alma isn't home. She didn't tell him she was going out today, but she often forgets. Her mind is on higher things, the great invisible world of the lonely and desperate dead, of the as yet unborn, of reincarnation and karma, of prophecies and portents, of cups and swords and toppling towers, of auras and vibrations, dreams, visions, lodestones, black cats, pol-tergeists, and the serenely smiling, all-wise Masters of the World, who dwell forever, high on the snowy slopes of Mount Shasta in the state of Washington. Of course, she's not home. If she were, Frank wouldn't be.

Nathan climbs to the attic. Like all attics in big old houses where generations of the same family have lived and died, it is filled with forgotten furniture, toys, photographs, barrels of chinaware, crates of linens, trunks of clothes. Dusty, cobwebby, and sad. But here the windup phonograph works. And musical instruments are everywhere, some in scuffed black cases, some glinting metallic from random horizontal surfaces, some hanging from nails. Every family of the orchestra is here: brasses, reeds, strings, even some percussion, including a xylophone, a snare drum, cymbals, gongs. An upright piano blocks off light from one of the dormer windows, stacks of music turning yellow on top of it, paper-weighted by a tarnished baritone horn.

The cello leans against a chair, now, and Frank, bow hanging from his hand, stands staring out one of the open windows into the treetops. Without turning, he asks: "How did it go? They make you editor in chief?"

"They're going to print the pieces I wrote."

Frank turns. And smiles. "That's wonderful." He comes and shakes Nathan's hand. "Congratulations."

They have not shaken hands often. There is something formal about it. It reminds him that he is now living in a man's body, and he feels an unaccountable pang of regret. Frank would have hugged him, not so long ago, and maybe kissed the top of his head, and playfully shaken him up. But everything is changing now. A handshake is the correct thing between men. It means more to him than the approval of Hotchkiss, Buddy, Charlie together, does Frank's approval.

"They want new ones from me," he says, "every week. But I can't do that. I can't stay in school."

"What? Why not?"

A happy thought comes to Nathan. "Did the truck break down? Is that why you're home early?"

Frank's cheerfulness departs. "That son of a bitch Ridpath wanted me to cut up a tree. Some estate down on Old Mill Road, someplace like that." He shifts the cello aside and drops into a worn velvet chair, its carved woodwork scratched and scarred. "That wasn't what he hired me for. He hired me to haul water to those damned vegetable plots of his all over town, and irrigate them with that damn leaky secondhand fire hose. He never said anything about sawing up trees." Frank's white hair needs cutting. He peers up at Nathan through the thatch that's fallen over his forehead. "I never did hard physical labor in my life. I can't start at my age. I'll keel over from a heart attack."

"Did he pay you what he owes you?"

"He didn't owe me anything." Frank takes up the cello and rubs the bow lightly across the strings. "I'd borrowed ahead. I owed him." He snorts, and angrily runs the C scale from top to bottom. "But sawing up trees?"

Nathan says, "I just stopped at the store for cornflakes. Mr.

Baumgartner's cut off our credit. We owe him twenty-seven dollars. Alma promised to pay him today, but she didn't. I don't know how she could. Her ladies won't come since she got arrested."

"That's called having the courage of your convictions," Frank says sourly.

"If they just hadn't printed it in the paper," Nathan says. " 'If Alma Reed can fortell the future, why didn't she know the police were coming?' Ha-ha."

"Newspapers operate on the principle rational people drop about age five—tell everything you know to everybody."

"So," Nathan says, "I told Baumgartner we'd pay him Friday, but now you're not going to get paid on Friday, so I can't afford to go to school. I have to find a job."

"You get your education," Frank says strictly. "In my time it wasn't so important, but a diploma is all anybody respects nowadays." He saws at the cello strings again. For eight flashy measures. Then stops. "I'll get a job, Nathan. A lot of funeral parlors still want me."

"You never stay. You always play what you want, and the bereaved get sore, and you get fired."

"They pick such trashy music to waft their loved ones to heaven on. You'd think people of taste and discernment never died. Their mortal remains sure as hell never show up at funeral parlors—not the ones that hire Frank Reed."

"The aircraft factories are crying for workers," Nathan says, "but you have to be eighteen. Maybe in the meantime I can drive the water truck."

"Not on your life," Frank says. "Joe Ridpath is not going to make slaves of the entire Reed family. I mean it. Don't you go near him, understand?" He holds Nathan with a stern look for a long moment, then bends over the cello and takes up the Bach suite again. "You let me worry about earning the living for this family. You're still a boy. You enjoy that while you can."

"Sure, Frank." Nathan goes back down the stairs.

HE TRUDGES UP ARROYO AVENUE. He left the house at sunup and the mountains were gray then. Now they've turned their natural winter brown, capped with snow. Maybe his aunt Marie was right —it's a wonder Nathan survived. Frank and Alma weren't fit to raise a child. They were just overgrown children themselves. This puzzled him to hear when he was small, but he knows now it is true. After all, though he was reading grown-up books when he was five, playing the piano like a little Mozart, working high school math problems in his head, he still ate with his fingers.

Aunt Marie felt duty bound to step in and teach him to use a fork, knife, and spoon, as God meant little boys to do. He was grubby, and she taught him to wash himself once in a while, brush his teeth, comb his hair. She taught him to button his buttons and tie his shoelaces. Off in her world of divine mysteries, Alma couldn't be counted on to load up the Maytag in the basement every time Monday rolled around. Aunt Marie pursed her lips, sighed, and saw to it that everyone, including Nathan, had clean clothes to wear.

She was strict and humorless, but he misses her. Life has been full of hazards since Alma inherited the old Dupree house, and she and Frank brought Nathan west, leaving Aunt Marie behind in Minneapolis. Commonsense Marie kept things from falling apart. They all three begged her, but she wouldn't come to California. She is seventy, and feeling poorly, and doesn't want to leave her church and her friends—those still alive. But things are slipping out of control here. Aunt Marie telegraphed bail for Alma after her arrest. But she's on a pension. She can't support the Reeds. It's up to Nathan, isn't it?

HERE IS JOE RIDPATH'S NURSERY. Nathan wanders in the long, slatted shadows of the lath houses, breathing in the smells of damp soil and fertilizers, hearing the trickle of water here and there.

At the back of the lot is a dooryard of roses and wheelbarrows and the scruffy frame cottage where Joe Ridpath lives. Nathan raps the screen door. A dog barks and claws the closed wooden door beyond it. A voice shouts at the dog to shut up. The dog keeps on barking. Nathan waits. At last, the door opens.

The dog claws the screen and jumps, still barking. Joe Ridpath swears at it and knocks it aside with a bare, dirt-crusted foot. The dog dodges away, ears laid back, tail between its legs. Ridpath buttons up a pair of filthy work pants. He is in his undershirt, a scraggy man, dirt in the deep wrinkles of his face, eyes black and sunken in their sockets, mouth wide and slack. "Cain't you read?" he says. "Sign out there says 'Closed.' Don't it, don't it?"

"Yes, but I came to ask for work," Nathan says.

Ridpath squints. "You got a driver's license?"

"No, but I heard you have a tree you want cut up."

Ridpath grunts, unhooks the screen, comes outside. He smells of old sweat. He studies Nathan, scratches his ribs, scratches his head where the hair is thick and Indian black. "Five dollars," he says.

"I'll need a saw," Nathan says.

Ridpath scratches an armpit. "Who says you won't go off from here and sell it?"

"I'm not a tramp. I'm a student." Nathan takes out his wallet and shows Ridpath his identification card.

"Reed?" Ridpath snorts. "You belong to Frank Reed? He your grandfather?"

"Never heard of him," Nathan says.

"I guess that's a lie," Ridpath says, and hands back the card. "You got the same address. Crazy as hell, you know that don't you?"

"He's not my grandfather," Nathan says. "He's my father, and he's not crazy. He's a musician. And he's too old for heavy work. That's why I'm here. Anyway, who could get five dollars for a secondhand saw?"

Ridpath barks a laugh. "Come along with me." He takes Nathan's arm in pincer fingers and leads him around the side of the house, past the water truck, into a shed. He pulls a dirty tarpaulin off an object on a workbench. "That there'd fetch a lot more'n five dollars, now wouldn't it?"

Nathan stares. He's never seen such a thing. "I guess so. What is it?"

"Power saw. This here's the blade." It looks like a bicycle chain with teeth. "And this here's the gasoline motor that turns it." He lifts the machine by a steel tube handle. "Hell, that's a big, ol' tree—thicker'n you are. Couldn't cut a tree like that with no hand saw." He cackles derision, then scowls. "You got brains enough to run it?"

"Just show me how."

Ridpath yanks a cord, and the motor snarls to life. Ridpath brandishes the saw, laughing evilly, mouth full of wicked-looking teeth. "You ain't *skeered* of it, are you?" He kills the motor, lays the saw down, finds a red can. He leers at Nathan. "Cain't cut off but one of your legs at a time." He unscrews a cap and fills the saw's gas tank, then glances at Nathan. "Naw, I'm just funnin'. There's a safety catch, right here, see? Just flip it with your thumb, it'll stop her dead, all right?"

"I'm not scared," Nathan lies. He picks up the saw. It is heavy, and a clumsy shape. "But how do I get it to Old Mill Road? I was going to walk."

"Walk!" Ridpath wags his head, turns, and walks out of the shed. "Drop her in the back of the pickup truck," he calls. "I'll put on my shirt and drive you there." The screen door of the house flaps shut, the dog barks joyously.

NATHAN STOPS THE RANTING OF THE SAW, lays it down, squints up at the sun through the tops of big dark trees like this one that have not fallen. It must be past four o'clock. He trudges to a stucco gardener's shed, turns the gritty handle of an outdoor water tap there, kneels, drinks, ducks his head under the flow to cool him. He splashes water on his naked chest and belly, shakes his head to get the water out of his hair, and rakes the hair back with his fingers.

He has alternated sawing up the tree—branches first, then the thick trunk with its splintery soft white wood—and carrying the chunks to a stone woodshed. He does some carrying and stowing now. Then takes up the saw again. He's been here nine hours. How long is it going to take him to finish? He bends, tugs the greasy starter rope, and the motor raves to life. Coughing in the gas fumes, Nathan goes to work, goes at it as hard and fast as he can. The toothed chain screams. Sawdust flies. Sweat pours off him. His arms, shoulders, back ache. His legs tremble. But he doesn't want to have to return tomorrow.

A shadow falls across him. He finishes a cut. The section falls on his foot. He looks up. Dan Munroe stands blinking at him in surprise. The tall, dark youth wears white, and looks as if he never sweats. He smiles a bewildered smile, and speaks, but the saw is too loud. Nathan stops it so he can hear. He lays the saw down on a section of trunk. Brushing at the sawdust stuck to the sweat of his face, arms, chest, he asks Munroe:

"What are you doing here?"

"I asked you first."

Nathan motions at the wreckage of the tree. It doesn't seem to him words are needed.

"Yes, but, I mean—why you? We expected you at Moon's this morning, at the *Monitor* office."

"I should have telephoned," Nathan says, "but it was too early." He doesn't add that the Reeds have no phone, and he hasn't a nickel for a pay phone. "Mr. Hotchkiss, Charlie, Buddy—they're not sore at me, are they?"

"Only mystified," Munroe says. "No one knows you, after all. We made all kinds of guesses about what had happened to you, but we never guessed you worked. And for Bathless Joe Ridpath, of all people."

"Yup." Nathan sits on an upended section of tree trunk. "Now—what are you doing here?"

"I live here," Dan Munroe says.

Nathan looks at the great, handsome house, its yellow-washed walls glowing in the light of the downing sun. He looks off at the rolling lawns, flower beds, tennis courts, swimming pool. "Why aren't you going to a good college?"

"Because I'm irresponsible," Munroe says cheerfully. "I was at Stanford. It was a disaster. They assume I'll go to classes and hit the books if I'm under the family roof. But I doubt it." He gives his rich laugh. "I don't think I'll ever grow up."

"Like my father," Nathan says.

"You mean he says that about you?"

"That's not what I mean." Nathan turns and picks up the saw again. But before he can pull the starter rope, Munroe catches his arm. "You've been here since morning?"

Nathan nods wearily. "Seven o'clock."

"Working all that time? No lunch?"

"If you eat oatmeal for breakfast," Nathan says, "you don't need lunch."

"Come into the kitchen." Munroe starts for the house, his white shoes crackling leaves and twigs. "I make a mean Welsh rarebit." He waggles his eyebrows. "With beer."

"Thanks, but I have to get this finished." Nathan pulls the cord and starts the saw. Munroe blinks at him, offended for a second. Then he takes off his jacket and rolls up his sleeves. He shouts over the racket of the saw, "All right. I'll help you!" He squats and clumsily loads his arms with wedges of tree trunk to carry to the woodshed.

NATHAN RETURNS THE SAW AND GASOLINE CAN to Joe Ridpath, and between the nursery and home he falls asleep on the deep leather cushion of Munroe's Packard convertible. He stumbles out groggily in the thickening dusk and makes an awkward job of closing the car's long, heavy door. He is so tired, he can hardly speak. "Thank you for helping me," he croaks, tries for a smile, touches his forehead in a salute. "And for bringing me home. Appreciate it."

"See you tomorrow at Moon's." Munroe drives off.

Nathan doesn't want to think about tomorrow. He limps through the gap in the fence where a gate is supposed to hang, cuts across under one of the big magnolias, and, brushed by untrimmed shrubbery, takes the narrow path along the side of the house, heading for the back door. Above his head, the kitchen window glows. It's open, and out of it drift smells of frying liver and onions. His stomach turns. He fingers the crumpled dollar bills in his pocket. He has pictured himself strolling into the kitchen and laying them on the table for Frank and Alma to admire. Now he can't face it. An old honeysuckle vine climbs a trellis at the back of the house. He takes a deep breath, and with aching muscles clambers up it to the second-story screened porch where he sleeps.

IN DIM LIGHT FROM THE HALLWAY, Frank bends over him, poking at his belly. He has taken off Nathan's shoes, and now he is unbuckling his belt. Nathan mumbles, " 'Sall right. I'll do it." His fingers are bruised and stiff, but he gets the buckle loose, hikes his butt, and strips off the dirty corduroys. "Time is it?"

"Eleven." Frank takes the pants, lays them on a chair. "When'd you get home? You've been gone all day. We didn't know you were here. Been worrying about you."

"I was tired. All I wanted was to sleep." It is still all he wants. "Go away, Frank. I'm okay."

Frank plucks at the grimy sweatshirt. "You didn't go to school in that."

"Not school—work. We need money, Frank."

"Rough work, it looks like."

"I cut up that tree for old man Ridpath."

Frank stands still for a long minute. Then he says, with a break in his voice, "Aw, Nathan—no."

Nathan reaches for his hand. "You were right. You couldn't have done it. It would have killed you."

Alma darkens the doorway. "Is he sick?"

Frank goes to her. "He worked. He's tired out."

"He didn't have any supper," she says.

"Let's let him sleep," Frank says, and shuts the door.

He sleeps till noon, soaks for half an hour in a tub of hot water and Epsom salts, and goes down to the kitchen to find the refrigerator full of food. He is blinking at it, stunned, when he hears voices, cheerful women's voices, calling out to each other at the far front of the house. Alma is saying good-bye to a client. There's a tone she gets with paying customers she never uses with anyone else. And in a minute he hears the front door close, and her footsteps coming through the vast dining room. She pushes open the kitchen swing door, still wearing her professional smile. She sees him, and the smile changes. It grows real.

"You're all right. Oh, thank God. I was so worried. You slept so hard. I was afraid you were sick."

"I'm all right." He nods at the refrigerator. "Where did all this come from?"

"Did I tell you about Mrs. Gregory? The medium? She wrote to me after the arrest was in the paper. To sympathize. Lovely woman. Well, at a séance at her house, on Monday afternoon, I met several very nice ladies."

"Who wanted their cards read," Nathan says. "What if one of them had worked for the police? You'd be in jail again, and we'd be running around trying to find the money to bail you out."

"Oh, Mrs. Gregory vouched for these ladies," Alma says, and pats his cheek. "You mustn't be so suspicious of everyone, darling. Learn to trust. Our fate is in the hands of higher powers. They are looking out for us, Nathan, truly they are." She edges him aside. "Look at this abundance. Can you believe it? Three ladies came yesterday—at twenty dollars apiece."

"This stuff didn't come from Baumgartner's," Nathan says. "I hope you paid him."

"I did, but we won't patronize him again. Oh, he's sorry for the way he treated us, but it's too late, isn't it?" She breathes a sad laugh. "Not a spiritual man. I pity him. So many difficult incarnations ahead."

"But this is all ours?" Nathan says. "Paid for?"

"And the gas and water and electricity as well." Alma bends and touches packages in the refrigerator. "Now, what shall I fix for your breakfast?"

"It's all right," Nathan says. "I'll fix it." He gauges from its shape that there's a ham inside that white butcher paper bundle, and takes it out, finds a fresh loaf in the bread box and a new bottle of mayonnaise in a cupboard. "Where's Frank?"

Her expression changes. "He's—taking a nap."

"You mean he's ashamed of himself." Nathan unwraps the ham, sets it on a plate, cuts thick slices from it. "And he plans to hide in bed forever."

She drops onto a chair at the table. "He feels terrible that you went and did that awful job he was too proud to do."

Nathan digs into a pocket and lays his five sorry dollars on the table. "That's what I earned. Pitiful, right?"

"Not pitiful, no." Tears in her eyes, she hands it back. "Heroic. Saintly. You're the best son any mother ever had. I can't tell you how grateful I am. But you earned it, and you keep it. Just one thing." She waits. He looks up from smearing mayonnaise on slices of bread. "No more cutting school, understood?"

"Understood." He pokes the money away. "Make you a sandwich too?"

She shakes her head. "I have another client coming in a few minutes." She gives him a smile. "Thank you anyway. You're a dear, good boy. Dr. Fuller would be so proud."

"Soon as I eat, I'll talk to Frank, but I'm starving."

She gets up, goes to a cupboard, sets a shiny new jar on the table. Mustard. He gives her a grin. The doorbell jangles. She goes to answer it, Nathan listening to her eager footsteps, hoping it's not a cop. She'll never learn.

He eats the sandwich, washing it down with cold milk. In the snow-crusted freezer of the refrigerator he finds two pints of chocolate ice cream. He eats one of these. From the carton. Dishes lie in the sink from last night's supper. He washes these, dries them, puts them away.

He climbs the stairs and knocks on the door of the bedroom Frank and Alma share. Frank mumbles something he takes to be permission to enter. He goes inside. The room smells stale, and he opens a window. He stands beside the General Grant bed. Frank is scrunched down on his side, covers hiding him completely. His words come muffled:

"I feel rotten about how I acted."

"Then why aren't you out canvassing those funeral parlors? You said I was supposed to let you earn the living."

Frank says from under the blankets, "I couldn't face you, after what I made you do."

"You didn't make me do it. We needed money. Cutting up Ridpath's tree was the only job I knew about." Nathan sits on the side of the bed and laughs ruefully. "I didn't know Alma was law-breaking again. Hell, she made sixty dollars. I only made five."

"What?" Frank throws off the covers and sits up, scowling. "That cheap redneck son of a bitch."

Nathan shrugs and takes the bills out of his pocket again. "That was the deal."

Frank jumps out of bed. His pajamas are wash-faded and have a rip in the seat. He flings them off. His clothes are strewn over a chair. He reaches for them. "Taking advantage of a child. He got fifty dollars for that job."

"What do you think you're doing?" Nathan asks.

"Going over there and get the twenty he owes you."

Nathan stands up. "What do you mean?"

"He offered me a fifty-fifty split." Frank is breathing hard. He flaps into his shirt and buttons it up crookedly with shaking hands. "Five dollars is an outrage and a crime." He kicks into his trousers. "How long did it take you?"

"Eleven hours."

"Christ." Frank tucks in his shirttails. "And you think that's fair?"

"Not really—but I agreed to it." Nathan feels like an idiot. "It was stupid of me. How far was five dollars going to go, the hole we were in?"

"You're not to blame." Frank buttons the trousers and buckles his belt. "He cheated you when you didn't know any better." Frank sits on the side of the bed to pull on socks and shoes. "No decent man would do that."

"It's too late now," Nathan says. "I agreed. I went ahead and did the job. I took the five dollars."

"I'll break his neck." Frank tugs angrily at a shoe lace, and it snaps. "Damnation."

"Don't go make trouble with him," Nathan says. "The cupboard isn't bare this morning, but who knows when the cops will close Alma down again? Joe Ridpath could have other jobs for me."

"Over my dead body," Frank says.

"Breaking necks isn't your style anyway," Nathan says. "Any more than driving that dumb water truck was your style. Now, will you please go do what you're meant to do?"

Frank groans. "Hodgkin and Lacey?"

"Walk in there and tell them you'll play what the customers want from now on and no funny stuff."

"If you knew how I hate the smell of cut flowers," Frank says. "Look at that shoelace. Can't walk into an elegant charnel house like Hodgkin and Lacey with my shoe coming off. Anyway, I haven't got bus fare." He rubs the white fuzz on the back of his neck. "I need a haircut—that's two bits right there." He plucks at his shirt cuffs. They are frayed. "Look at this."

Nathan holds out his five bills. "Get a new shirt."

"Absolutely not." Frank puts his hands behind his back. "You worked too hard for that. Half killed yourself. Look at your hands, all bunged up."

"Then ask Alma," Nathan says. "She's coining money."

Frank snorts. "Be serious. She'll feed me, but she won't give me a dime. You know that."

Nathan knows. It started when they got here to Fair Oaks. She tired quickly of being the breadwinner while Frank doodled with his instruments in the attic, day after day. She figured if she gave him money, he'd never go earn any for himself. Her policy has only half worked, but she can't think of a better one, so she sticks to it.

Nathan offers his five again. "You can pay me back."

"Well—" Frank takes one. "I guess that's right."

"New shirt—remember?" Nathan says.

"Dime store." Frank takes two more bills. And unexpectedly gives Nathan a bear hug. Nathan's arms, shoulders, and back are sore, so the hug hurts. But he is glad to get it. When Frank lets him go, he has tears in his eyes. "You're a very good boy, Nathan. I don't know where you got it. Not from me." He stands for a moment, beaming at his son, then breaks for the hallway. "Got to shave."

THE NEXT MORNING, BACK AT MOON'S, devil-may-care Nathan shoots fifty whole cents on a plate of crusty corned beef hash and poached eggs. Since all he reads about in magazines and newspapers are books, movies, plays, he doesn't understand the talk that washes around him as he douses his food with ketchup and shovels it down hungrily. The talkers are Wayne Hotchkiss, Charlie Vorak, and a stocky, sandy-haired, freckled, frog-mouthed man named Kenneth Stone, a newcomer to the teaching staff.

"The Luftwaffe can never come back." Hotchkiss lights a fresh cigarette from the stub of another and drops the stub into his saucer, where it hisses. "They kept at it too long, Ken. Didn't know when to quit. Now they haven't got England, and they haven't got an air force either. It's over, Ken. Hitler is finished."

Stone shakes his head. "Are you beaten, if you don't know you're beaten?" He watches the blond girl, who today is wrapped in Travers Jones's apron, fill their coffee cups. She smiles and goes away. Stone says, "It's a question that would have amused David Hume." He pushes back the cuff of his wrinkled tan whipcord jacket and blinks at his watch. His eyelashes are white, his eyes pale blue. "I'm off to scatter wisdom to the yahoos." He backs his chair, the legs stuttering on the linoleum, and stands. "Farewell, all." He nods at Nathan. "Nice to meet you, Reed." He stumps away.

Charlie Vorak frowns after him. "It doesn't make sense. What the hell is somebody with his brains, his background doing teaching freshmen and sophomores at pitiful Fair Oaks Junior College, for Christ's sake?"

Hotchkiss says, "You have real tact, Charlie."

Vorak gets red in the face and laughs. "Aw, shit, Wayne, you're only here because it beats newspapering."

"Joanie thinks it does, mainly because dissolute reporters don't swarm around me, tempting me to drink." Hotchkiss watches Stone go out the door. "It's his business, Charlie."

"Secrecy starts rumors," Charlie says. "Like, his clothes are made in Germany. People have read the labels. He gets mail from Germany. Ergo—he's a Nazi spy."

"With that corn belt accent?" Hotchkiss scoffs.

"They say it's a phony, too perfect. No, he's Hitler's eyes and ears in Fair Oaks. He's always skulking around Sierra Tech. Why? Trying to steal military secrets, obviously. Well, Sierra Tech does do a lot of government science stuff, Wayne."

Hotchkiss says, "Nathan, don't listen to this." And to Charlie, "He cuts through Sierra Tech on his way home. Charlie, don't repeat such bullshit. Please?"

"Give me credit for some common sense," Charlie says. "You're the only one I'm telling." His brow wrinkles. "All the same, if he'd be more outgoing, not keep to himself so much, the rumors would die down. You're his only friend. Where's he come from? What's he all about?"

"We're not friends, Charlie. We're drinking buddies. At Laughing Jack's. We've only met. I haven't asked, and he hasn't told me where he comes from. But what he's all about is loneliness." Hotchkiss drops his cigarette stub into his coffee and gets lamely to his feet. "I never knew a man so lonely in my life." He glances at Nathan. "Young Reed, you walking back with us?"

Nathan is mopping egg yolk and ketchup off his plate with a scrap of toast. He shakes his head. "I'm still hungry." He looks around for the aproned girl. "Unless you need me," he says anxiously. "Do you need me?"

"Eat." Hotchkiss laughs. "Dan Munroe says you're a mighty woodsman. I was surprised when you didn't order a wagonload of flapjacks." His skeletal frame seems to creak as he leans across to peer out the window. His eyebrows go up. "I'm even more surprised not to see a blue ox tied to Moon's hitching post."

"It was just an odd job," Nathan says. "I was broke."

Hotchkiss pats his shoulder as he turns to leave with Charlie Vorak. "I'm glad you're back."

HE AND CHARLIE PAY THEIR CHECKS and reach the door just as a fat young man and a surprisingly tall young woman burst in. The fat young man has heavy-lidded eyes, a big nose, and kinky hair. In a burnoose, he would make a perfect Arab. The tall young woman is handsome, with standout cheekbones and a strong jaw line. Hotchkiss, Charlie, and these two almost collide. There is laughter. They know one another. There is comic after-you-Alphonse bowing all around, then Hotchkiss and Charlie file out onto the sunlit sidewalk, and the fat young man and the very tall young woman, arms held out and uttering glad cries, sweep between the tables toward Travers Jones at the service window. Travers seems to be the cook this morning. Nathan hasn't seen a sign of Moon. Nor, more strangely, has he heard her.

Now the girl in the apron comes to take away the wreckage from the breakfasts of Hotchkiss, Vorak, and Stone, and Nathan asks her please to bring him two more eggs, bacon, and a new stack of toast. She picks up the jam jar and blinks at it. "You ate it all," she says.

"I hope there's more someplace," he says. "I feel as if I'm never going to get enough to eat."

"There's more." She gives him a smile and a wink. "For you." And she goes away, empty plates rattling.

Moon has arrived. She is yelling beyond the service window. "Get out, get out, all of you! How can I work with my kitchen full of actors, flotsam and jetsam, riffraff, scum of the earth? Out, out, out!" The kitchen swing door flies wide. The Arab, the tall girl, and Travers Jones duck out, shoulders hunched, hands over their heads, a broom waving in the air above them. They settle at an empty table, laughing and gasping. Travers fetches coffee, they light cigarettes, lean their heads close, and buzz with talk. Plainly something exciting has happened. Nathan wonders what it is. He yearns to be at that table.

Then his second breakfast arrives, and he forgets everything but his stomach. He has polished off eggs, bacon, toast, and half the new jar of jam, and is downing the last swallow of his coffee, when Travers and friends rise with much rattling of chairs. The tall girl and the Arab make for the door, but Travers veers to stand, poker-faced, at Nathan's table.

"Dan Munroe tells me you're physical," he says.

"I've eaten so much," Nathan says, "I don't think I can even walk."

"You can cut up mighty trees with ferocious saws," Travers says. "Can you measure lumber and nail things together, and paint, and the rest of it?"

"My uncle Chester"—Nathan belches, wipes his mouth with a paper napkin, stands up—"was a carpenter. I used to help him summers." He heads for the cash register, where the blond girl waits. "Just let me pay my check."

"Put your money away," Travers says, "and come with me." He steers Nathan to the door and outside.

"You've found a place for your theater, is that it?"

"Subject to approval by all and sundry. We'll see." Stork-legged, long hands flapping at the ends of bony wrists that stick out of shirt cuffs as frayed as Frank Reed's, Travers hastens around the side of the shacky café to a strip of rutted, bumpy hardpan where customers can park if they don't mind risking broken axles. A wooden-sided 1938 Ford station wagon stands there, the Arab at the wheel, the young woman beside him. Travers opens a door and lunges, all elbows and knees, into the rear.

"I'm bringing Nathan. He's a skilled carpenter." Nathan can hear his uncle Chester laugh at that. "We'll need him." Travers presses himself into a corner on the far side of the fake leather seat. Nathan climbs in and slams the wooden door. Traver says in a bored voice, "Abou Bekker? Nathan Reed. Alex Morgan? Nathan Reed." They turn their heads, smile at him, he smiles back at them, nods, says hello. Abou Bekker starts the car, and they jounce out of the parking lot and rattle westward out Sierra Street.

They pass the campus. No students amble the walks or sit on the lawns under trees. They are in classrooms, where they belong. So does Nathan, but he doesn't worry. He barged through the trigonometry textbook during Christmas vacation. It holds no challenges for him. Like music, it's a matter of patterns. He never has any trouble getting the hang of patterns.

Abou Bekker has a lilting tenor voice. Alex Morgan's rumbles like a man's. The two chatter away cheerfully in the front seat. But Travers says nothing. Nor does Nathan. He dreams out the window. Then a noise across the street makes him turn his head, and Travers Jones is making a hideous face at him. His eyes are crossed, he has pulled his chin back so his upper teeth stick out, his head is tilted goofily. The whole thing is goofy. And as soon as Nathan sees him, he stops doing it—so quickly that Nathan isn't sure he's really seen what he thought he saw. He gives Travers a weak smile and turns away. The fronts of the stores they pass gleam in the morning sun, still not open for business. He thinks about his play.

But he can't help it—he sneaks another look at Travers. And the skeletal youth is doing it again. This time, his mouth is stretched so all his teeth show. His tongue lolls, he rolls his eyes, like Satan in spasm. Again he stops at once, and his face becomes a bland mask. This time Nathan frowns puzzlement at him, and Travers shifts on the seat to stare out the window on his side of the car. It happens a third time—a different, sillier face than the others, cheeks sucked in, mouth like a pig's snout.

Then Abou Bekker halts the bang wagon at a grimy curb in front of a gray, vacant business building. This is a seedy part of town; grit and blown trash on the sidewalk crackle under their shoes. Trash has been piled by the wind in the doorway to which Travers leads them, digging a key from a pocket. The key crunches into the corroded lock of a door whose thick glass is cloudy with dust. The door opens on an upward flight of bare wooden stairs.

Travers advises Abou Bekker, "Take a deep breath, and pretend we're Little Women climbing the Delectable Mountains." He starts up the stairs, his worn-down heels banging the treads, the sound batting back off the faded walls. The fat youth follows, a springy climber. Alex Morgan starts after them. Nathan plucks at her sleeve.

"Can I ask you something?"

He is six feet tall. She is taller. She smiles down at him with glorious teeth. "Of course I'll marry you," she says. "Who needs long courtships?"

He feels his face go hot. "No. I mean, it's about Travers." He glances up the stairs, lowers his voice. "He kept making faces at me. All the way here. Horrible faces. What's the matter with him?"

"Oh, that." Alex laughs, pats his shoulder, and starts up the stairs. "Nothing, love. It only means he likes you."

"Really?" Nathan begins climbing after her. "How would he look if he hated me?"

Her only answer is a long, rich, baritone laugh.

TRAVERS STANDS IN THE MIDDLE of an enormous empty loft on the top floor, waving his skinny arms around, talking about stage left, stage right, seating, lighting. Alex goes and opens doors and peers through. "Lovely dressing room space," she says. Abou stands frowning, a pensive finger to one plump cheek. "I . . . don't know. It's awfully long and narrow, Travers. I'll have to block every scene in bas relief. The seats will have to run along that wall. People will have to crane to see what's happening way down there, or way up here."

"The rent is cheap," Travers says. "And the landlord doesn't care what we do with it, this side of total destruction. Every owner isn't going to let us paint their place black, you know."

"We can make it work," Alex says.

"Who's going to climb three flights of stairs to see a play?" Abou says. "We'd have to have a nurse on duty with oxygen. What happened to the vacant church?"

"They'd rather it stayed vacant than have a theater in it," Travers says. "The devil's workshop, they called it."

"That'd be a nice name," Alex says brightly.

Travers is severe. "The name is the Harlequin."

"If I fasten the seats on risers, in small units, they could be shifted around," Nathan says, "so you can use different acting areas for different plays if you want."

"Brilliant," Alex says.

Abou tilts his head. "You're not a carpenter. What are you?"

"There's nothing to building risers for a few theater seats," Nathan says. "Anybody can do it."

"Anybody but I." Abou smiles. "No, but I mean—what are you?"

"He's a writer," Travers snaps, and looks crossly at Nathan. "Buddy Challis says he's a genius."

Nathan's face grows hot again. "He likes my stuff because it's short," he says.

"A mark of excellence in a writer," Abou says. His soft brown eyes rest for a moment on Nathan. "But with your looks, you ought to be an actor."

Alex lights a cigarette. "I vote we take this place."

"All right." Abou has heard footsteps climbing the stairs. He pushes open the door and says, "Ah, it's you. Come see the devil's workshop." Dan Munroe comes in. He wears a seersucker suit today.

It looks new. He beams and chuckles. "Alex! Travers! Imagine find-ing you here. And you've met the radiant Nathan." He squeezes Nathan's arm. "They're low characters. Don't let them corrupt you."

"I'm just the carpenter," Nathan says.

Travers tells Munroe, "You're late, as usual."

Abou looks at his watch. "I have a nine o'clock class." He makes for the door again. "Anyone who wants a ride, step lively."

"Wait," Travers says. "We have to vote. Dan—is it all right with you? Nathan's going to build the seats so they can be shifted around and we can stage anyplace, front, back, along the sides."

"Lots of dressing room space," Alex says.

"If you're sold," Dan says, "I'm sold." He takes out a wallet. "Here's the hundred I winkled out of mother. With the solemn promise we won't produce anything shocking."

"Thank you." Travers pockets the money. He says to Abou, "I have to sign the lease at the bank, pay the first and last months' rent, and add this to Moon's and Alex's in the theater account. So you go ahead—I'll catch a bus back to Moon's." Travers doesn't often smile. He smiles now. All teeth and gums, it makes him look like a horse. "It's a dream come true. A wonderful day. The greatest day of my life. We're going to do beautiful things in this unlikely place." He holds out his arms. "Oh, friends." His voice breaks. Tears leak down his cheeks. He goes to each of them and gives them clumsy hugs. "Let's never forget this moment. Let's swear to remem-ber it all our lives."

"Travers," Alex says mildly, pushing him away. "I'm shocked. You've been drinking."

"Since two A.M., darling. Wouldn't you?" Travers dries his tears with a crumpled handkerchief. "I mean, sleep was out of the ques-tion. After what I've been through these past weeks? Begging for money, searching for a place." He blows his nose. "Wondering if you'd approve. Struggling toward this moment has made me a total nervous wreck." He pushes the handkerchief away and smiles wanly. "Think of it. A theater. A theater of our very own."

"I love the name," Munroe says. "The Devil's Workshop."

"No, no," Travers wails. "The Harlequin."

ON THE SCREENED PORCH, at a rickety old kitchen table, by the light of a goosenecked lamp, Nathan types away at his second act. Standing in that dusty loft this morning, he caught Travers's excitement. *We're going to do beautiful things in this unlikely place.* He wants the first beautiful thing they do to be his play. He can see it, the pitch dark of the enormous room, the hard beams of spotlights stabbing down; he can hear it, the actors' voices ricocheting off the walls. The vision makes his hands shake, so he hits wrong keys. And now here's Frank. He comes in and sits on Nathan's cot. It squeaks.

"Schoolwork finished?"

Nathan nods. "I was just working on my play." He turns on the stiff chair. "Alma gone to bed?"

"Tired these nights," Frank says. "Since she met that Gregory woman, she's got more fool females coming here every day than she can handle. Tarot cards, crystal ball, it's over when it's over, but the horoscopes take time."

Nathan can't help it. He turns to read the words he's just put on the page in the machine. Frank notices, and stands up. "Listen, I didn't mean to interrupt. Too early for me to hit the hay. Just wondered if you'd like a game of chess. We haven't played since we got to California." He wanders into the hallway. "Must be something about the perpetual sunshine. Bakes the brains."

Reluctantly, Nathan tears his gaze from the page. He has got going pretty well. He knows just what the next line should be. He hates to leave. But he gets up off the chair. "Good idea," he says, and switches off the lamp.

In the attic, Frank lays the chessboard on a crate and arranges the pieces. They sit in unraveling basket chairs. A weak, green-shaded lightbulb hangs on a twisted cord above them and casts their malformed shadows among the trunks and instruments. Nathan wins the draw and moves pawn to king four, when Frank instantly does something he's never done before. He advances his queen's rook's pawn to the fourth square. "Whoa." Nathan stares at him. "You been studying a book?" He squints into the shadows as if looking for it.

"It's original. I've been thinking up ways to flummox you. Take you down a peg. You're too smart by half. After all, it was me who taught you this game."

Chess is another pattern thing. Nathan learned it young and it wasn't long before he was beating Frank three times out of four. "It's not original," Nathan says, "but nobody plays it much." He sits frowning at it for a moment till he decides on a defense. And they play on in companionable silence for half an hour till Frank says:

"Checkmate."

Nathan blinks at the remaining pieces. "Congratulations," he says. "I'll be damned."

Frank grins. "You thought I wasn't right in the head, didn't you? Thought I couldn't bring it off."

"You brought it off, all right," Nathan says, and begins dropping the pieces into their wooden box. "Surprised hell out of me." He closes the box. "You going to be able to sleep now?"

Frank nods. Doubtfully. "Wish to hell I could get work. Greiner and Tuttle just hired that redheaded sissy-boy, Desmond Foley. He's rich. Doesn't even need the job."

"Too bad." Nathan detaches himself from the wicker snags of the basket chair and stands up. "Don't worry. Someplace else will have an opening."

Frank snorts. "Greiner and Tuttle will. Foley's kind don't last. They get into trouble, and they're out."

Nathan doesn't follow this. "Foley's kind?"

Frank clears his throat uncomfortably, shifts in his chair. "What would help a lot," he finally says, "is having a telephone. I give the number of Baumgartner's pay phone, and he says he'll take messages, but I don't think he bothers to answer it if he's busy."

"What kind of trouble?" Nathan says.

"Ah." Frank stands up. "You don't want to hear about it. Forget I said that." He walks into the shadows, picks up a violin, and begins tuning the strings, plucking them with his fingers. "It's the sort of remark that would prompt your aunt Marie to say, 'Frank, not in front of the child.' "

"I'm not a child anymore," Nathan says.

"Don't rush what comes next," Frank says. "There are things in life you'd be happier not knowing, no matter how old you are." He puts the violin to his chin and begins to play. Fritz Kreisler's "Caprice Viennoise." He plays it with exaggerated bowing, meaning to make it laughable.

"The sissies I've known," Nathan says, "would be the last to get into trouble. They're too nice."

"You're talking about little boys. Sissies don't stay little boys forever."

"And then?" Nathan says.

Frank lowers the violin. "Don't badger me, Nathan. Can't you see, I don't want to discuss it? Just keep away from them." He comes back into the lamplight and looks hard at Nathan. "Don't let it go to your head, but you're a good-looking boy—exactly the kind they love to get their hands on, so watch your step. Understand?"

Nathan understands Frank wants the subject changed. "Alma's going to get us a telephone soon," he says.

Frank snorts. "Doesn't mean she'll let me use it."

"If it's to find a job, she will." Nathan pretends to yawn. "I have to go to bed."

What he has to do is get back to his play, and he does get back to it, just as soon as he hears the toilet flush, hears Frank's heavy footsteps down the hall, hears the bedroom door close. He shuts the door to the screened porch, sits at the lame table again, switches on the lamp, and takes up where he left off. When he remembers to look up, headachy, blurry-eyed, the bent hands of his rackety alarm clock point at ten past two.

The night has grown cold. He shivers as he undresses, turns off the lamp, falls into bed. But he can't sleep. What will happen next in the play keeps speaking itself in his head—Aunt Marie's voice,

Alma's voice, Frank's voice, his own voice, as a little boy. He tosses and turns, and finally gets up and dresses again. He shrugs into Uncle Chester's old leather jacket, switches off the lamp, climbs out the window and down the honeysuckle trellis.

The town is familiar to him now. He has walked it many nights like this, trudged in his scuffed rubber soles north to the forested foothills of the hulking old Sierra Madres, west to the deep arroyo with its high-arched, lamp-lit bridge, east to the flat farmlands of Arcadia, south to where Dan Munroe lives in the broad-lawned enclaves of the fabled rich whose money built the town.

Except for the business streets, the streets at night are all dark in the shadows of big trees whose leafage, never changing, winter and summer, screens out the light of streetlamps. The low-roofed, broad-eaved houses crouch asleep, block after block. It is deeply pleasing to him that no one else is out, that he is all alone. It saddens him, and he devours the sadness greedily, like the man in Stephen Crane's poem eating his own heart.

HE IS FAR FROM HOME, up in the shacky section where Fair Oaks' few Negroes live. Chickens roost in a rusted-out automobile. An old tire hangs by a frayed rope from a front yard tree. Overgrown lantana, weighing down a broken fence, crowds him off the sidewalk. A dog barks somewhere. Somewhere a drowsy rooster crows. Suddenly he is dead tired. He turns back. Why has he come so far? What is this craziness? He sighs, shoves hands into pockets, and hikes homeward, street after empty street. His legs ache. His eyes keep falling shut. Sometimes he staggers.

Milk delivery trucks begin to jingle past. Shadowy boys on bicycles flit along sidewalks, flinging newspapers onto front porches. In the alleys back of Sierra Street, trash barrels empty noisily into trucks. He crosses the empty boulevard and is in the darkness of a side street again. Then here is the campus of Sierra Tech. So he's nearly home. And none too soon. Gray light is creeping into the sky over the brushy black treetops. Alma sleeps like a child, not a worry in the world, eight perfect hours every night of her life. But sleep isn't Frank's friend. Frank could get up early. It happens. He wouldn't look for Nathan, would he? Hell, he might. He seems these days to worry about Nathan more than he used to. And how would Nathan explain his night walking to Frank? He can't explain it to himself.

He cuts through the campus to save steps. It is empty and eerily quiet. He follows a pathway overarched by trees. Ivy climbs the rough gray stucco walls of the buildings, so they look like huge, shaggy animals asleep. Beyond one wide, high window, lightning flashes silently from one great iridescent metal ball to another. He has often stood watching this, fascinated, but there's no time now. He makes for an archway between the laboratory and another building, then halts.

A man is coming toward him, in and out of the leaf-shadowy circles of light thrown by the lamps that line the path. He's a square-built man, strands of his thin, pale hair stirring in the chilly breeze that has risen with the coming of dawn. Nathan resents all other night walkers. They shatter his cherished sense of aloneness in the world. And whenever he sights one, he hides. He knows this makes him look guilty of something, and he's not guilty of anything, but if others exist in his empty night world, he does not want to exist. So now he steps quickly back into a clump of tall shrubbery, out of sight.

The man nears. It's Kenneth Stone. His head is bowed, the collar of his jacket is turned up, his hands are thrust into the pockets of his rumpled tan suit. *A Nazi spy. He skulks around the campus of Sierra Tech.* Nathan feels a chill. Stone passes. Tears shine on his face. There's a smell of whiskey. He mutters to himself. Nathan can't make out the words—but they're English, not German. For years he's listened to the Saturday broadcasts of the Metropolitan Opera. He knows German when he hears it. He laughs wryly to himself. The stupid, cruel things people make up. *What's he about? Loneliness.*

I never knew a man so lonely in my life. Nathan looks after him until he vanishes in the shadows.

Then he hikes bleakly home to bed.

IT IS SATURDAY MORNING, COLD AND GRAY. Nathan is tired of waiting on the root-humpy sidewalk of Oleander Street outside the broken picket fence. Hands stuffed into the pockets of his worn-out corduroys, shoulders hunched inside the old leather jacket, he finally decides they aren't coming, and starts back up the path to the gingerbread front porch. Tires squeal against the curb, a horn toots, and he turns to find Travers Jones making a face at him, and Abou Bekker climbing out the driver's side of the wooden station wagon. Nathan grins, gives them a wave of his hand, and trots to them. Abou is gazing delightedly up at the shabby old mansion behind its gloomy trees.

"What a wonderful house," he says. "Pure American Gothic. Aren't you lucky?"

"It's collapsing," Nathan says, "like the House of Usher." New two-by-fours are lashed with clothesline to the roof of the car. Nathan touches them, gratefully breathes in their piney smell. His uncle Chester says, *No perfume like it in the world.* He takes hold of the door handle.

"I'm afraid it's roped shut," Abou apologizes.

"You're shivering." Travers opens his door and starts to get out. "Sit between us. We'll keep you warm."

"Forgive me, but no." Abou smiles pleadingly at Nathan. "I am not the world's most gifted driver. If I get hold of your knee, we could end up in a storm drain."

"A mere knee?" Travers says.

"It's okay." Nathan crawls through the rear window. He is surprised again by his size, makes a clumsy job of it, bangs elbows and knees, and lands folded on the floor. He struggles, laughing, and at last is sitting upright on the seat. He combs his hair back with his fingers and gives them a grin. "See, who needs refinements like doors?"

"A man of infinite resource." Abou gets in, starts the engine, and they roll off down Oleander Street.

By noon, after much clambering up and down a tall, wobbly, paint-drizzled stepladder, measuring this area, then that area instead because Abou and Travers argue and change their own and each other's minds three or four times—after marking the sweet-smelling studs with a carpenter's square brought by Dan Munroe, and cutting them with a saw and miter box Peg Decatur sneaked from a neighbor's garage, and nailing the sections together with Abou's hammer, and screwing steel corner braces to them with Travers's dull old screwdriver, Nathan has completed a framework to hold spotlights above the acting area. He has been crouching some of the time, but much of the time he has been on hands and knees. Now he totters to his feet, and everyone applauds. Wiping grimy hands on his corduroys, he grins, but he is hungry.

"May I go eat now, please?" he asks Travers.

"Go?" Travers is appalled. "Where?" He looks around him in bewilderment. "Stand in line with the hobos at the Rescue Mission for a bowl of shoe-leather soup?"

"Anything." Nathan heads for the door. "I'm starving."

"Wait." Peg Decatur picks up her big soft leather shoulder bag. "There's no place to eat in this neighborhood. Let's all pile in Abou's car and go to the drive-in."

"Halt." Travers stations himself in front of the door, arms spread. "No one leaves this room. What do you want to do—break my poor old mother's heart?"

"What's Moon's heart got to do with it?" Abou asks. "Moon's isn't open on weekends. Anyway, I didn't know she had a heart. You never mentioned it before."

Travers looks stricken. "Ah, what a miserable son I am, to be sure. Her heart's as big as all county Cork."

Dan Munroe's raveled sweater and shapeless flannel trousers

look as if he'd picked them like a costume from a secondhand cloth-
ing store. He's topped the outfit off with a battered felt hat that he
wears at a rakish angle. Are there no old clothes in the closets of the
Munroe mansion? In the Reed mansion, that's all there are. Dan
should have asked Nathan to outfit him. Dan says, "Do you mean
Moon is bringing us food? From the café? Here?"

"Corned beef and cabbage and soda bread with currants," Travers says. "Any minute now."

"I hope so," Nathan says. "And just to keep me from thinking
about it"—he returns to the framework lying on the floor—"can we
get this thing in place?" Ropes hang from pulleys he has screwed
into the ceiling. Now he ties each of these ropes to big screw eyes
at the corners of the framework. "All four corners have to go up at
once. I'll have to be up the ladder, to read the spirit level." He drags
the ladder into place and climbs it. "Places, please."

Dan takes a rope. Travers takes a rope. Peg takes a rope. Abou
stands. Nathan raises eyebrows at him.

He is aghast. "Are you proposing I do physical labor?"

"Into each life some rain must fall," Nathan says.

Peg laughs. "We promise not to tell."

"If Moon comes in while I'm hauling on a rope," Abou says,
"it'll be all over town." He begs with his eyes, but the others remain
stony, and he sighs, steps up, and takes the fourth rope. Gingerly.
He lets it go. "Haven't you got a wig or a false beard or something.
This could ruin me."

"Let's be serious," Travers says, and wraps a loop of his rope
around his knuckly fists. "We're making a dream come true here."
He plants his feet, squares his shoulders. Dan and Peg do the same.
Abou fidgets and fusses.

Nathan says, "Everybody set? Okay. On the count of three.
Hand over hand. Slowly, not too hard. One. Two. Three."

Creaking and tilting, first this way, then that way, the framework jerkily rises toward the high, rain-stained ceiling. Four feet
short of it, measuring by eye, Nathan tells them to stop. He sets

the spirit level on the framework and gives directions first to Peg, then Dan, then Travers, then Abou, until the rack is level.

"Now, try to hold it steady." He scrambles down the ladder, goes to each rope in turn, and gives it a jerk to the side so as to lock it in the pulley wheel. "Okay. You can let go now. Thanks." He scrambles up the ladder again and puts cinch knots in one rope, climbs down, moves the ladder, climbs up, and cinches the next rope. He doesn't cut the extra lengths of rope, but bundles them and lets the bundles hang up there, against the day when Travers or Abou wants the framework shifted. He starts down the ladder the last time, muscles aching.

"Oh, God," Travers wails.

Nathan peers down at him. "What's wrong?"

"We forgot to paint it," Travers says. "Black."

"If Michelangelo could paint above his head," Dan says, "I guess I can."

"We'll get you a very lightweight brush," Abou says. "So you don't hurt your wrist."

And far below, the street door bangs. Moon's voice comes keening up the stairwell. "Jesus, Mary, and Joseph. Is no one going to help me, for the love of God and all his angels? I can't carry this great feast all by meself."

"Food." Nathan's foot slips, he almost falls.

"Coming!" Dan and Peg dash for the doors.

Travers and Abou have had their heads together much of the morning while Nathan worked, with occasional clumsy help from Dan and Peg. Now the skinny youth and the fat youth return to the place under the windows where they sat before, studying a thick, paperbound book. Nathan goes to them.

"What's that?"

"A play catalog," Travers says. "We've got to start rehearsals. We absolutely must open in four weeks."

"I say *Hedda Gabler*," Abou says.

"And I say it's got to be a comedy"—Travers snatches the

catalog and leafs the pages over frantically—"or a thriller. We can go highbrow later, when people have found out we're here."

Abou lays a hand on the catalog to keep it open. He pokes the page with a finger. "That's it—*Ah, Wilderness.*"

"Eugene O'Neill is out of fashion," Travers says; he pulls the book away, turns more pages, and says with finality, "Here. I've found it. *An Inspector Calls.*"

Abou looks up. "Maybe Nathan has a suggestion."

"Fine." Travers keeps his nose in the book. "But remember, the royalty must be very, very cheap."

Nathan opens his mouth to say they can have his play for nothing. But it isn't finished, is it? He doesn't even know if he can finish it. He's never tried anything so long before. It could take forever. He closes his mouth.

Travers looks at him. "You were going to say—?"

"Nothing." Nathan shakes his head.

THE FIRST ISSUE OF THE *MONITOR* has come out this morning. Everyone at Moon's has a copy. Tabloid size, the paper looks crisp, jaunty, professional. Donald's carefree script lettering of the masthead and the titles of departments—white, dropped out of a screened blue background—gives it panache. The word is Kenneth Stone's. Donald has a seat of honor with Hotchkiss, Vorak, and Buddy at the table under the beer sign. Stone, Peg, little Tom Dawes, the sports editor, and Nathan sit at the next table. In turning the pages of the paper above his plate, Stone nudges Nathan's elbow while Nathan has a fork full of fried potatoes on the way to his mouth. The potatoes scatter, and Nathan gives Stone a glance. He is frowning.

"Something the matter?" Nathan says.

Stone blinks at him. "What?"

"What's bothering you?" Nathan spears bits of potato up off the table. "What is it you don't like?"

"Nothing, nothing," Stone says quickly, folds the paper shut, lays it beside his plate. He glances over his shoulder at the other table and leans next to Nathan's ear. "There's something familiar about Donald's design. I'd almost swear I've seen it before. But damned if I can remember where."

"It's very professional," Nathan says, "don't you think?"

Stone shrugs. "Stylish. There's nothing to that. He'll learn in time that a child who can perform like an adult is no better than a monkey. To be an adult who can perform like an adult—now that's something else." He laughs at his own paradox, then gravely turns those pale blue eyes of his on Nathan. "No, there's originality in here"—he taps the paper—"but it's yours, not his."

Pleased, embarrassed, Nathan ducks his head over his plate, forks in food, says with his mouth full, "It's just a sketch. There's nothing to it."

"It's honest, and it's all yours—nothing borrowed. Somewhere, you've learned two important lessons. To speak plainly, and to be yourself."

Nathan laughs. "That doesn't sound like much. Can we help it? Aren't we all ourselves?"

"We are—but not many of us ever make our own acquaintance." Stone tastes his coffee. It is cold, and he makes a face and sets the cup down. "For the common run of mankind, that doesn't much matter. But for a writer, an artist of any kind, it's fatal. His work will always be second rate."

Again he glances at the next table, where the party is breaking up. "Like Donald's, facile and meaningless."

Talking excitedly about the *Monitor*, Charlie Vorak pushes Buddy past in the wheelchair. Donald is deep in discussion with Travers at the cash register. Wayne Hotchkiss, necktie crooked, shirt creased as if he'd slept in it, bends over Stone. "I believe you have a nine o'clock class."

Stone gives a start and reads his watch. "Unbelievable." He pats Peg's hand, gives Tom Dawes a nod, lays down his napkin, pushes back his chair, rises, picks up the paper. "Thanks for the company." He trails after the hobbling Hotchkiss to pay his check, then detours back to say to Nathan, "You walk a lot at night. I've seen you."

"Sometimes I can't sleep. It's just to make me tired."

"Ever do any hiking?" Stone asks. "Great canyons in these mountains of yours. Ever climbed up there?"

"I never thought of it," Nathan says.

"Think of it," Stone says. "I go every weekend. Wayne isn't up to it. Got too much family, anyway. You want to come along, sometime, I'd like the company."

"Well—I don't know," Nathan says. "I guess so, sometime, sure." The disappointment in Stone's eyes is plain, and Nathan feels sorry for him, forces a smile, and says, "Yes, I'd like that very much."

Stone looks relieved. "We'll do it, then?"

"Anytime you say," Nathan says.

"Soon," Stone says, and heads off down the long, noisy room to where Hotchkiss waits for him by the door.

Peg says, "He's really impressed with you, Nathan. He made Buddy show him your other two pieces too."

"No offense"—Tom Dawes gathers up his books—"but I wish he didn't give me the creeps."

ALMA COMES BACK INTO THE KITCHEN, looking disappointed. She picks up the apron she's discarded and puts it on again so she won't get anything on her good dress. She sits down grumpily and tells Nathan, "It's people for you. A very thin boy. His mother ought to feed him."

Nathan stands up, surprised. It's suppertime. He's barely started on his roast beef, mashed potatoes, and creamed peas. "His mother owns a restaurant," he tells Alma, "and he works there. He could eat all day if he wanted to."

"The other one is too fat," she says. "He looks foreign. A Jew or a Greek or something."

"Arab," Nathan says, and starts for the swing door.

"You haven't finished your supper," Frank says. "Tell them to wait."

"I'll just see what they want."

Nathan finds them standing in the gloomy parlor, gazing spellbound at the round, black-velvet-covered table with the crystal ball and the tarot cards under the hanging, red-shaded lamp. "What's up?"

"We've got the seats. Free. No charge," Travers says. "But we have to pick them up tonight. Tomorrow morning, the wreckers come to tear down the building."

"The Jewel Box Theater," Abou says, touching the cards. "What's all this?"

Nathan's never heard of the Jewel Box. "It's not here in Fair Oaks," he says.

"Hollywood," Travers says. "Help us, Nathan. We need every hand we can get."

"Reed," Abou exclaims in sudden recognition. "Alma Reed. The fortune-teller. She was arrested. It was in the papers."

"She's my mother," Nathan says.

"You're full of surprises," Abou says.

"We've borrowed a moving van from Alex's father," Travers interrupts. "We have to detach the seats, load them, get them back to the Harlequin, and return the truck—all before six A.M. You drive. Abou's simply too dainty."

"Sixty seats?" Nathan says. "It must be a jewel box."

"There are three hundred," Travers says, "but sixty is all the fire department will let us use."

"Did you say free?" Nathan says.

"They couldn't find a buyer," Travers says. "Thespis is smiling on us. You won't believe the prices people were asking. I made the mistake of telling Moon about the cheapest. She screamed like a banshee."

"We'd better get going," Abou says.

"I have to finish my supper," Nathan says.

Travers moans. "I'll buy you breakfast."

"If I don't eat," Nathan says, "my father won't let me go. It won't take long. I'm a fast eater."

"We'll wait in the truck," Travers says, glancing uneasily around. "This place is spooky."

"The spirits of the dear departed love it," Nathan says.

Travers hurries like a ruffled stork for the hall, the entryway, the front door. "Coming, Abou?"

Abou studies Nathan. "The dear departed—really?"

"Not really," Nathan says. "She's not a medium."

"Eat your supper," Abou says with a smile. "I'll go hold Travers's hand."

A PARLOR IS ACROSS THE HALL FROM THE LIVING ROOM behind sliding doors. This is where Alma and Frank spend their evenings together, listening to the radio—Alma prefers the "Lux Theatre," Frank anything that will make him laugh—in a pair of scuffed leather wing chairs under floor lamps with orange silk shades and long gold fringe. The room can't be called snug—the ceiling's too high for that—but it's not Mammoth Cave, either, and on those rare nights when Fair Oaks is cold, the hissing fireplace gas heater, fashioned to look like logs in a grate, keeps it warm.

The sitting room is where the books are—crowded into golden oak bookcases with cloudy glass doors. Lifting one after another of these doors, Nathan smiles to himself. The books came with them from Minneapolis. The spines bear titles he's known all his life. Old friends—he's glad they're here. *Lessons of the Masters* jostles *The Call of the Wild*. *Reincarnation and Karma* stands beside *A Son of the Middle Border*. *Huckleberry Finn* is sandwiched between *Isis Unveiled* and *True Mediumship*.

But what he's looking for is a hefty book with red-edged pages and flexible black covers that was Uncle Chester's. Tomorrow is Saturday, and Nathan is nervous about building those risers. He told Abou anybody could do it, but he was showing off. He has to read up on how to build steps, which is basically what the risers for those moldy, loose-hinged old seats from the Jewel Box will be. He thinks he knows, but he mustn't waste expensive lumber. And he doesn't want to look like a fool.

Frank comes in. "If you're looking for the fabulous Reed diamond necklace," he says, "you're on the wrong scent, Buddy. You jewel thieves these days——." He stops, rears back, ham-acts surprise. "Why, Nathan—it's you. I thought you were Jimmy Valentine."

Nathan closes the bookcase and gets up off his knees. "Where's Uncle Chester's carpentry book? Did Aunt Marie keep it? I wanted that."

"Try the attic." Frank sits down in his chair and rattles open the *Independent*. "There's cartons of books up there that never got unpacked." He glances at the bookcases. "No place to put 'em."

"I forgot," Nathan says, and starts out of the room.

"You're not going to try to fix this old barn up, I hope," Frank says. "Losing battle."

Nathan tells him about the theater.

Frank asks, "They going to put on your play?"

"Maybe. When I finish it. I hope so. But that's not why I'm helping them. They're my friends. I enjoy being with them."

Frank grunts. "You don't know them very well yet. They're older than you. Don't let them exploit you, Son."

"They wouldn't do that," Nathan says. "They like me. They're intelligent and funny and they're good to me. I'm glad I found them. I never had any friends like them before. You're right—they are older than me. That's why it's exciting to be with them."

"Yup—well, while you're hammering and sawing and painting and heaving seats around for them, what happens to your homework——"

"You know I always do my homework, Frank."

"—All right then. What about your writing?"

"I'll get back to it," Nathan says. "After the seats are finished, there won't be anything for me to do. They're rehearsing the first play already."

Frank is leafing through the paper, running his gaze over columns, pictures, ads. "I expect writing's a lot like music. If you're going to be good at it, there's not much time for anything else."

"Maybe, but you were the one who said I was still a boy and I ought to enjoy it while I could—remember?"

Frank throws him a brief smile. "You do what makes you happy, but don't forget that every hour you spend as dogsbody for your little-theater friends is an hour you can't spend writing that play. It's a fact of life."

Nathan sighs. "You're right. And Charlie keeps assigning me more and more news stories. And I can't drop the sketches. Buddy says they're the best thing in the paper."

"Buddy is right," Frank says. "You see the tragic side of comedy. That's surprising in somebody your age."

" 'Even though your heart is breaking' "—Nathan lays a dramatic hand on his chest and sings in a sobbing voice—" 'laugh, clown, laugh.' " He leaves the room for the staircase. "I have to find that book."

THIS MORNING, THEY ARE REALLY LATE. It is cold and gray again. A thin, misty rain falls. Gulls circle overhead, complaining in their creaky voices. He watches them awhile, then decides something's wrong and hikes over to Baumgartner's grocery store to use the pay phone.

"Oh, he's gone to the theater," Abou's mother says. "They're working day and night to get ready for the opening."

"I know. I'm the carpenter. He was supposed to pick me up at my house at seven."

"Oh, no. You must have misunderstood."

"Have they got the phone in at the Harlequin yet?"

"They expect it Monday," she says. "That will make things easier, won't it?"

"Not today," Nathan says.

He hikes under the big old dripping trees down to Sierra Street, where he waits under a shop awning until a bus comes creaking and rumbling, and he climbs aboard and drops a dime into the glass-sided fare box. A neon-circled clock above the barred door of a pawn-shop opposite the gray building that houses the theater reads ten of nine when he gets off the bus. There's no traffic. He trots across the street.

At the curb are Abou's station wagon, Dan Munroe's Packard with the top up, Alex Morgan's sharp new black-and-white Stude-baker, and Charlie Vorak's 1932 Chevy, probably driven here on a teaspoon of gasoline by Peg. Whom the long sleek black La Salle belongs to he doesn't know. The same for the honest-to-God Model T Ford, with which he immediately falls in love. He crosses the sidewalk, opens the building door, and down the staircase come sounds of hammering and sawing. He scowls. What's going on?

He takes all three flights of stairs two at a time, bats open the doors to the loft, and stops in his tracks. Under his light rack, a stage is being built. Half the fabric of its supports is already in place. A balding, middle-aged man in glasses and a toothbrush mustache has rolled up his shirtsleeves and is sawing two-by-fours to make the rest of the supports. A boy about fourteen is cutting one of these short lengths on the bias. An older boy, on hands and knees inside the maze of the support structure, is hammering the struts into place. Large squares of plywood lie nearby to make the flooring. Nathan goes to the man.

"There wasn't supposed to be any stage," he says. "The seats were going to be on risers." He spent half the night with Uncle Chester's book, making drawings to guide him in building those risers. He yanks the drawings, limp from the rain, from his pocket and pushes them under the man's nose. "See? So they could be shifted around. That way, the plays could be staged in any part of the room. Flexibility? You know?"

The man stops sawing, lays down the saw, takes off his glasses, and blows the sawdust off them. "Who are you? Let me guess." He grins. "An actor. With those good looks—"

"Nathan Reed," Nathan says. "I'm the carpenter. I was." He

points to the rack, now painted black, with boxy little black spotlights clamped to it, and black wires snaking over it. "I made that."
"Ah." The man puts on his glasses and looks up. "Nice job.
Nathan? I'm Dr. Dick Schwiller." He takes Nathan's hand and
shakes it. "I panic the world with a dentist's drill four days a week,
but carpentry's my hobby, and the theater is my first love." He
waves a hand. "These are my boys, Dick, Junior, and Lawrence—
Larry." They look up at hearing their names. Nathan nods to them.
They go back to work. "This is a rush job. Needed all hands."

"I guess not quite." Nathan pushes through the doors to the
dressing rooms. He passes these and barges into the office. Travers
is there, with Abou, Dan, Alex, Peg, and Donald Donald. They lean
on their arms over a battered desk under a window, looking at drawings. Beyond them, damp pigeons huddle miserably on the window
ledge. When Nathan storms in, the humans raise their heads and
look at him. "I thought you were picking me up," he says.

Travers looks quickly at Dan. Dan's eyes open wide, he covers
his mouth with a hand for a guilty moment. "Oh, Nathan, I'm sorry.
I was supposed to tell you. I forgot."

"To tell me what?" Nathan glares at them all. "That I wasn't
needed anymore? Good-bye? It was nice knowing you?"

"Oh, Nathan." Travers shoots Dan a look of pure fury. "No, of
course not. Don't even think it." The others all pull shocked faces
at Nathan, and croon denials. Travers comes to him, puts hands on
his shoulders, looks into his eyes. "You are loved and cherished here.
You are an important part of the Harlequin, and you always will
be." He tries to give Nathan a hug, but Nathan steps away.

"Then why didn't you tell me you wanted a stage? I could have
built you a stage."

"They didn't want a stage." Donald Donald has been silent,
sullen, first shuffling the drawings on the desk, pretending to ex-
amine them, then tapping on the dirty window glass, hoping to
disturb the pigeons. Now he turns back. "Alex brought her dentist
around, didn't she? And he told them people wouldn't consider it a
real theater if it didn't have a stage. And he would pay for the lumber

for a stage. And invest five hundred dollars in the Harlequin to help get it on its way. Could you have done those things?"

Travers looks everywhere but at Nathan.

Donald grins. "I guess the answer is no, isn't it?"

Nathan says to Abou, "I could still have helped."

"He wants his sons to have the experience," Abou says.

Alex says, "Dan was supposed let you know all this."

"I told you I was irresponsible," Dan says.

"You should have told Abou and Travers," Nathan says.

"He has to outgrow it sometime," Abou says.

"Peter Pan never did," Dan says cheerfully, "and look what a long run he's had."

"It's all right, forget it." Nathan goes to the desk and looks at the drawings. Pale pinks and greens have been washed into them. Harlequins. Old, young, thin, fat, two or three to a page. He looks at Donald. "Did you do these?"

"You're not the only genius around here," Donald says.

"The La Salle downstairs has to be Dr. Dick's," Nathan says. "Is the Model T yours? It's beautiful."

"It's Malcolm's, my kid brother's," Donald says. "He can't drive it. He's too young to get a license. But will he let me drive it? Hell, no. Today, however, I found the key." Donald's evil, blue-lipped grin is back. "He'll have a fit when he learns I let it sit out in the rain."

"He'll kill you," Peg says.

Donald gives her an odd look. "No. He knows there's no need for that." Donald turns back to the window and raps it sharply with his knuckles. "Fly, you filthy sons of bitches. Fly in the rain and crash."

The pigeons huddle down and stay.

UP IN THE NIGHT ATTIC, rain sifting on the shingles, Frank has moved the plush carved chair close to the phonograph, stuffed a mute into the bell of a trumpet, and sits playing quietly along with a jazz record. His foot taps, his shoulders move to the rhythm. He is turned so he doesn't see Nathan, who goes into deep shadows, finds the carton, opens it, and lays Uncle Chester's book back inside. The dusty flaps don't want to stay closed, so he lifts a euphonium down from its nail in a rafter and lays it on the flaps. He edges out from among the crates, trunks, boxes, and the record is finished. The needle scuffs in the end grooves. Frank stands to fold back the pickup arm, and sees Nathan.

"Grab that tuba." He waves a hand toward the big instrument gleaming dully in a corner. "Can't get decent bass out of this grindola. When I get work, I'm going to buy an electric phonograph. They sound great."

Nathan doesn't feel like making music, but if he says so, Frank will ask why, and he knows himself. He'll end up telling Frank, and Frank will say something like they weren't his friends, anyway, they're too old for him, and it's just as well he found out early. Stuff Nathan doesn't want to hear—not tonight. Frank is happily sorting through records. Nathan heaves the tuba off the floor, parks himself on a straight chair, wipes dust out of the tuba's mouthpiece with his shirttail, and blows a few tryout notes into the instrument to find his lip, if he still has one. He runs spluttery scales while, out of the corner of his eye, he watches a spider drop on a strand from the lip of the tuba's bell to the floor.

"Pick something slow," he says. "I'm rusty."

"Okay." Frank peers at labels in the poor light. "How about this one—'At Sundown'?"

He gets a nod from Nathan, and lays the record on the green baize turntable. He gives the crank on the side of the cabinet a few turns, flips the switch, and sets the needle in the groove. He drops into the carved chair, raises the trumpet, and begins to play. Nathan gropes around to find the bass line, and soon the sad rock-a-bye sweetness of the tune takes hold, and he is as relaxed and happy rumbling away as Frank is embellishing the melody line way up above the staff. But there's no way of muting a tuba. It is so loud, every note makes the floor shake. And soon Alma comes up the stairs and makes them stop.

IT'S TERRIBLY LATE, HE'S VERY TIRED, he's way up in the foothills, but he can't stop walking in the rain, shivering, miserable, wishing he were dead. It came to a pretty sudden end, didn't it? *You are loved and cherished here. You are an important part of the Harlequin and always will be.* How? What's left for him to do? Write his play? It's not a thriller. Is it a comedy? He doesn't think so. That wasn't what he meant it to be. He meant it to be the truth. Some of the things that happen in it, some of the things said make him grin. But a comedy? Anyway, he's not a playwright. He's a nobody high school kid with a secondhand typewriter, a hundred sheets of blank dime-store paper, and voices in his head. A kid. He thinks what he's done so far is good. But is it, really? How can he tell? He has to stop worrying. He has to go home and sleep now.

He turns southward, head down, rain running off the crushed brim of Uncle Chester's old canvas fishing hat. And he collides with another walker. They are both startled, and they shout. Then they call up manners, and excuse themselves to each other. Then they recognize each other, and give crazy laughs.

"Littlejohn," Nathan says.

"Nathan," says Littlejohn Lemay, peering up under the brim of the hat. The rain has plastered Littlejohn's hair flat to his skull and childlike forehead. "What are you doing here? It's four o'clock in the morning."

"I walk a lot at night," Nathan says. "It helps me sleep." Off Littlejohn's shoulder hangs a bulging canvas sack. "What are you doing? Delivering papers?"

"Announcements for Beulah Land Church." He pulls out a mimeographed sheet. Nathan holds it close and in the poor light makes out the largest lettering. Good News—Jesus Is Coming Soon—Will You Be Ready? He hands it back. "Thousands," Littlejohn says mournfully.

"All by yourself?" Nathan says.

"Only when it rains," Littlejohn says. "When the weather's good, there's other kids."

"I hope they pay you," Nathan says.

"I do it so Jesus will save me."

"Littlejohn, they're exploiting you."

"Don't say that." It's not a simple protest, it's a cry of pain. "I have to do all I can, Nathan. Nothing's ever enough. Nothing ever will be. I'm such a sinner. I have to show the Lord I love him. I have to do all the good I can."

Nathan peers at the wet, tormented, boyish face. "What are you talking about? Such a sinner? What did you do—rob the cookie jar?"

"Don't laugh." Littlejohn tugs Nathan's sleeves. "The Devil's got me, Nathan. And he won't leave me alone. I pray and pray, but the minute I stop—." His face turns hopeless, he lets Nathan go and turns away. "You don't know what I'm talking about, do you?"

"Littlejohn—nobody believes in the Devil anymore."

"I fight him." Littlejohn turns back, frantic. "Sometimes I even win. Sometimes it's days before I—before I touch myself that way again. But then I'm naked in the shower or something, and I start all over. I can't help it. He's too strong for me."

"Will you stop?" Nathan's face grows hot. He sees in his head sleek shiny Littlejohn in the shower, whacking away. The picture makes him feel something he doesn't want to feel. "This is private stuff. You shouldn't talk about it to me."

"Who else is there to talk to?" Littlejohn cries. "My father? My minister? Don't you see? This is a miracle. Meeting you after all this time—alone, at four in the morning. Jesus must have sent you. Tell me what to do."

"I can't," Nathan says. "Look, it's not the Devil—it's nature, biology, physiology, chemistry. When human beings get old enough to breed, this urge happens. Why do I have to tell you this? You're the same age as me. Didn't you take sex education?"

Littlejohn shakes his head. "My folks wouldn't let me. It's against our beliefs. It starts kids thinking dirty. 'As a man thinketh in his heart, so is he.' "

"Quit making yourself miserable. If you don't believe me, ask Gene Woodhead." Gene went to Foothill Junior High with Littlejohn and Nathan. A fair-haired, blue-eyed child like an angel in a painting, Gene taught Nathan to jack off in his backyard tent, on a hot afternoon two summers ago. "He'll tell you. Every boy does it."

Littlejohn gapes at him. "No, no. That's not what you're supposed to say. Jesus didn't send you to say that."

Nathan spreads his hands. "It's the truth."

Littlejohn backs away, aghast. "The Devil sent you." He turns and runs, the heavy bag thumping his hip. His voice echoes back through the darkness and the rain. "You'll burn in hell, Nathan Reed. You'll burn in hell."

HE DIDN'T BURN IN HELL, but he got an awful cold. A week later, the sneezing, coughing, and aching are gone, but he still feels weak, and his voice won't come back. But Abou Bekker wants to see him, and here is the Bekker house, set far back on a narrow, weedy lot, and screened by roof-high shrubs. He follows a long, cracked strip of driveway to a side porch with a canvas swing, books lying on the striped seat. Potted plants stand around underfoot. He steps over them to rap a screen door. Abou comes to open it, smiling.

"Ah, I was afraid you might be too sick to come. Your grandfather was worried about you."

"He's my father," Nathan whispers. "What's up?"

"Come in." Abou pushes the screen open, and Nathan enters a tiny sitting room so crowded that the door opens only partway. Abou seats him in a threadbare armchair and himself sits at a desk between the armchair and tall bookshelves filled to overflowing. A butt-sprung couch stands along one wall, an upright piano opposite; a print of Van Gogh's blue-eyed self-portrait in a straw hat hangs

above the piano. At the far end of the couch, a small electric phonograph is stacked with record albums. Narrow doorways to farther
rooms are hung with faded cotton print curtains.

"You should take better care of your health," Abou says. "We
were all terribly worried about you."

"You don't need me. You've got Dr. Dick."

"There are things Dr. Dick can't do."

"Really?" Nathan is grumpy. "Such as?"

"He can't write," Abou says with a smile. "And the Harlequin
needs a publicist."

"Good morning," warbles a sweet voice, and Lucille Bekker
comes in, a short woman, as wide as she is high, her dark hair pulled
back and knotted in a bun, a nose like the prow of a ship, sensible
shoes on surprisingly large feet. She hands Nathan a glass of orange
juice, sets one on the desk for Abou, and gives his crinkly hair a
kiss. Her eyes flick over Nathan, and she says to her son, "My, he's
an Adonis, Bobby." She beams at Nathan and goes away. "Breakfast
will be ready soon. I hope you're hungry."

"Starving," Nathan calls. "It smells delicious." He drinks some
orange juice. It is fresh squeezed, and it makes his throat feel better.
He croaks to Abou, "How can I be a publicist? I don't even know
what a publicist is."

"A spreader of good tidings," Abou says. "People won't come
to the Harlequin if they don't know it's there. They won't buy
tickets if they don't know about the play, and who's in it, and so
on. You write it up. Fresh young talent adding new excitement to
the Fair Oaks cultural scene."

"Why not Peg Decatur?" Nathan says. "She's older, she's got
more experience—"

"She's not a genius. She can't string words together so they pop
like firecrackers. You can."

"She's funny, and charming, and beautiful—"

"Ah, as to beauty," Abou says, "you heard my mother just
now." He laughs. "You're blushing."

To hide his confusion, Nathan gulps the rest of his orange juice.

Too fast. Some of it runs down his chin. He wipes it off with his fingers, licks his fingers. "But Peg can talk the *Independent* and the *Times* and the *Daily News* into printing what she writes. I couldn't do that. I wouldn't know how to start. Anyway, I'm too young. They'd never listen to me."

"Someone else will take care of that part," Abou says. "You handle the writing—Travers or Peg or I will do the coaxing and cozzening."

"Not Moon?" Nathan says. "She'd be wonderful."

Abou guffaws. "The soul of tact."

And his mother's sweet voice calls them to breakfast.

ARMS LOADED WITH SACKS OF GROCERIES, Nathan bumps open Baumgartner's screen door and steps down onto the sidewalk. Tires squeal. Joe Ridpath's rusty water-tank truck stops in the street. The scraggy nurseryman leans out the window.

"Can you use a steady job?"

"Thanks, but I'm going to school now," Nathan says.

"You don't look like you're eating too good," Ridpath says. "Pale and thin. Same raggedy clothes. That crazy old man of yours don't look after you worth nothin'. I'll pay fifty cents an hour, and give you free room and all the grits and side meat you can eat. Cain't do better'n that noplace in town."

Nathan shifts the heavy sacks. The sun is in his eyes. He squints. "It's very gencrous, Mr. Ridpath, but not now. I'm sorry."

"Damn," Ridpath says. "You're a good worker. Left you on your own, you done everything I would have, and more." He yanks the noisy truck into gear. "You think it over, boy." Something clanks deep in the innards of the truck, and it rolls off. "When you need work, remember me."

ON THE BACK PORCH, THE MAYTAG, loaded with clothes and soapy water, steams and pounds like a heart, thump-*thump*, thump-

thump. He mops the kitchen linoleum, rinses it, and lays a covering of newspapers on it to soak up the water and the bleach smell. He puts away mop and bucket, then wrings the clean clothes into rinse water in a set tub, loads them into a bushel basket, and hangs them out to dry on limp lines strung under the massive backyard pines.

His mother is at Mrs. Gregory's house, where the Fair Oaks branch of the American Spiritualist Society holds its Sunday services. Frank left the house with her after breakfast, but Nathan doubts he went to Mrs. Gregory's. Like Nathan, Frank is a skeptic. Where is he? All Nathan knows is that he's away from the house a lot these days, and judging by the color of his face and hands and the back of his neck, he spends the time outdoors. Tramping around town looking for work as an organist? Nathan wonders.

He dusts and carpet-sweeps the gloomy living room, brooming down cobwebs from the spoolwork of the wide, high entryways and around the fireplace mirror. The mirror has grown foggy, and he washes it. He sweeps and dusts the staircase and the upstairs hall, puts fresh sheets on the beds, and changes the pillowcases. It's a big house, and by the time he's finished all the work, he is so tired he aches. This shouldn't be. He is used to these chores. But everything seems to tire him now. Ever since he had that cold. It's over. He even has his voice back. But no stamina. He has tried to walk at night, but going only a few blocks drains him, and he comes back home. For what? To lie awake until a little light shows in the sky. Then he falls into sleep as deep as drowning. But those few hours aren't enough, are they?

Now he drags his feet back up the stairs. A sheet of paper half-filled with words sticks out of the typewriter. He can't start ironing until the clothes dry. In that time, he could get some writing done. Not on the play. Writing sketches for Buddy and publicity about the Harlequin have been his alibis, but he really hasn't felt like trying anymore with the play. What if Travers read it and promised to do it, and then somebody came along with five hundred dollars and said, "Do *Hamlet?*" To hell with that. He turns away, sprawls facedown on the cot, and falls asleep.

WHEN HE AWAKENS, SOMEONE IS SITTING AT HIS DESK. "What the hell?" He scrambles up. "What are you doing here?"

"I've been here for hours." Donald Donald gives him a look of surprised innocence. "You almost caught me once. I had to duck behind the window curtains in the dining room."

Nathan stares. "Who let you in?"

"No one. I cranked that old doorbell two or three times, but no one came. So I walked around to try the back door. You were on the back porch. You hadn't heard the bell because that old washing machine is so noisy."

"Why didn't you speak?"

"Because people are more interesting to watch when they think they're alone." Donald leers. "They reveal more about themselves. You learn what they're really like, instead of what they pretend."

Nathan is disgusted. "You're a Peeping Tom."

Donald lifts his shoulders. "Every boy should have a hobby. Yours is walking. At night. All over town."

"I never saw you," Nathan says.

"But Kenneth Stone saw you. He can't sleep, either." Donald tilts his head. "He's hiding some secret, isn't he? What are you hiding?"

"I have to pee." Nathan goes down the hall to the bathroom. When he comes back, Donald is standing, swinging the saggy old screen in and out above the honeysuckle trellis. He turns and asks:

"Is this how you get out without your folks knowing?"

"If they knew, they wouldn't mind." Nathan takes the screen from him and hooks it shut. "So—you watched me for hours, awake and asleep. What did you learn about me that you didn't already know?"

"That you've got a slave mentality. Damn right, your parents wouldn't stop you going out at night, even if they knew. They don't look after you. You look after them."

"It's really none of your business," Nathan says.

Donald grins. "Do you tell them to pick up their room, get their hair cut, be home by eleven?"

"No, you were right—I'm their slave. If I don't do the laundry and mop the floors and scrub out the toilet, and dust and sweep and make the beds, they chain me up in the attic, strip me, beat me with thorn branches, and starve me on bread and water for a week."

Donald sits on the chair at the typewriter again. He smiles, shakes his head, and repeats, "They don't look after you—you look after them." He picks up the folder with the pages of Nathan's play. "Like Aunt Marie before you."

Nathan lunges at him and snatches the folder. "Keep your hands off that. You read it, didn't you? Damn you, Donald, what's wrong with you, anyway?" He jams the folder under the pillow on his cot. "Decent people don't do those things. Do you want everybody to loathe you, or what?"

Donald smirks. "What's wrong with you? It's not private. It's a play, Reed. A play is meant to be seen. Why else would you write a play?"

"It's not ready yet," Nathan says.

"It seems fine to me," Donald says. "Lots of laughs. Do I get to design the set?"

"What set? I don't even know if I can finish it."

"You'll finish it," Donald said. "You want it put on at the Harlequin—isn't that right?"

"They don't know anything about it," Nathan says sharply. "And don't you tell them."

Donald looks pained and reproachful. "What good is learning people's secrets if you can't tell them?"

"Just keep your mouth shut," Nathan says.

"And if I don't?"

"I'll beat you to a pulp," Nathan says. "Now, get the hell out of here."

"I can't do that. Not alone." Donald looks at his watch. "I was sent to fetch you. Emergency meeting of all hands at the Harlequin. We're hours late, but seeing how hard you worked, how tired you were, I couldn't bear to wake you up." Donald gets off the chair. "Don't look so worried. There's a rehearsal. They'll probably all still be there."

"You're a real shit-heel, aren't you?" Nathan says.

Donald leaves the room and heads for the stairs. His laughter drifts back. "Not yet, but I'm working on it."

NATHAN WANTS TO SULK, but the day is bright and breezy, and riding in the Model T cheers him up. The old car trembles in every joint, the engine clatters, and Donald drives it like Barney Oldfield, careening around corners on two rickety wheels, whipping along quiet Sunday streets, veering crazily from side to side. Nathan wants to shout, laugh, wave at the earthbound people on the sidewalks. He has never seen Donald so happy. He grins like a twelve-year-old. A Dodge sedan loaded with women in hats coming home from church rounds a corner. The Model T is on the wrong side of the street, headed straight at them.

Donald shouts, "Look out for flying glass!"

He wrenches the steering wheel. The thin old tires shriek. The Model T swerves, jumps a curb, misses a tree trunk, skids on a damp, freshly-watered lawn, barges through a hedge, cuts across a second lawn, sidewalk, curb, and hits the street again, running. Nathan looks back. The Dodge has stopped, two of its ladies have climbed out into the middle of the street and, holding on to their hats, mouths hanging open, stand staring after the Model T.

Donald is laughing so hard tears run down his face. Nathan laughs too. He's never felt so wildly happy.

"Let's go back and do it again," he shouts.

"See?" Donald says. "Shit-heels can be fun."

THE GLASS ON THE DOOR AT THE FOOT OF THE STAIRS has been washed, and a sign painter has been at work. THE HARLEQUIN THEATER is on the glass in big letters; beneath it has been painted a thin, willowy Harlequin in a black tricorn hat, a black domino mask, black slippers, and a diamond-patterned body stocking in pink and pale green.

"Your drawing," Nathan says. "It looks great."

"There are more." They climb the flights of stairs, and when they reach the last, which leads up to the loft, here, painted on the walls, are the fat Harlequin, the skinny one, and the one with a hump on his back—the same ones Nathan saw on paper in the office on that day of the rain and the pigeons.

"Did you paint them yourself?" Nathan asks.

"Do you set the type for your columns?"

Donald pushes open the doors into the loft, and voices echo around them, actor voices, sounding weirdly like natural speech but with that extra loudness that makes theater speech so mournful to listen to, like Alma's dear departed, lonely, calling from a place no one else can reach to give them human kindness. The loft is pitch black except for the stage, where lights glare down from Nathan's rack high above, and Dan Munroe, wearing a gray wig and seated in a rocking chair, rehearses a scene with Alex Morgan, who pantomimes handing him a cup of tea. Dan interrupts, peering out into the darkness. He asks:

"Abou, suppose she spills it."

"She doesn't spill it. It's not in the script."

Dan gets up from the rocker, walks out of the glaring light, and says, "There's been a long, long stretch of talk. Spilling the tea would make a nice break. Something happens, for God's sake."

"Ah, I see. You want Alex to ad-lib a few 'excuse me's' and 'oh, I am sorry's' and 'how clumsy of me's'—while she crouches to pick up the broken china."

"Right," Dan says.

"And you jump up and brush at your clothes muttering 'not

at all's' and 'no harm done's' and 'here, do let me help's.' Oh, good suggestion, Dan."

Dan is amazed. He cranes his neck and peers into the dark. "You mean it?" He pats his pockets. "Where's my memory book? I must write this down. Director gives actor credit for brains."

"I promise"—Abou comes at his springy-kneed walk into the penumbra from the stage, a fat-bellied silhouette—"it won't happen again. I don't know what came over me."

Nathan calls to him, "Abou, is Travers here?"

Abou staggers in exaggerated surprise. "Nathan, can it be you? Are you auditioning for ten o'clock scholar?"

"The meeting slipped Donald's mind for a while."

"Out of pure malice." Travers comes from the office, light pouring out when he opens the door. "I know you, Donald." The door falls shut. He is invisible. But Nathan hears his footsteps, smells gin. "I'm sorry, Nathan. There was no one else to send."

"It's all right," Nathan says. "We had a nice ride."

"Nearly killed four Methodist ladies," Donald says.

"Somebody will probably ask somebody to pay for that lawn and hedge we ruined."

"My brother Malcolm," Donald says. "You're my witness. Malcolm had the car. He's not supposed to drive, but my parents were at church, and I couldn't stop him, could I?"

"Nobody could stop him," Nathan says. "Crazy kid."

Travers's skinny arm comes across Nathan's shoulder. "Now that you're here, we have to talk." He leads him away. "It's urgent. You're my last hope." He pushes Nathan ahead of him past the dressing rooms to the office. "Nobody else has a single serious suggestion. Totally irresponsible."

The office looks more like an office today. There's a used typewriter, a dented filing cabinet, a telephone, and in a corner, a secondhand mimeograph machine. Travers drops into a swivel chair that twangs when he leans back in it. Behind and above him on the wall capers another Harlequin.

"Suggestion about what?" Nathan leans back against the window ledge. No pigeons roost outside. The day is fine. They're flying, aren't they, enjoying themselves? "What's the problem, Travers?"

"Don't be so distant." Travers stretches a long arm, drags a straight wooden chair up beside himself at the desk. "Come sit by Travers. He's lonely." Nathan pushes away from the window ledge and does as Travers asks. "That's nice." Travers makes the worst face Nathan has ever seen him make. It lasts only a moment. Travers clears his throat, shifts in his noisy chair, and turns grave. "We open Friday night. Sold out, naturally. We play Saturday afternoon and Saturday evening. Sold out again, both performances. Sunday evening? Sold out again."

"Great," Nathan says. "The ads pulled, then?"

"Bless you, yes. And Donald's posters in the store windows. And those masterly press releases you wrote." Travers makes another hideous face. "Lovely. Lovely."

Nathan laughs. "So, what's the matter?"

"Well, we're dark Monday, of course. The following Friday, Saturday, and Sunday are all right. What's the matter are"—he starts walking thin fingers up Nathan's arm—"Tuesday, Wednesday, and Thursday."

Nathan looks down at the fingers. "What are you doing?"

Travers crosses his eyes.

"Be serious." Nathan pulls his arm away. "What are you saying? Nobody's coming on those nights?"

"Nine devotees of the dramatic arts on Tuesday, thirteen on Wednesday, twenty-three on Thursday. That won't pay our bills, Nathan, and besides, it's hateful for the actors."

"Won't people tell their friends?" Nathan says.

"We can't depend on that. We have to do something." Almost weeping, Travers clutches Nathan's arms and shakes him. "Child, help me. You have to have an idea. Please."

And Nathan remembers Littlejohn. "It's simple," he says. "Mimeograph fliers and distribute them all over town."

APRON OVER HER SUNDAY-GO-TO-MEETING DRESS, hair beginning to lose its fresh marcel in the kitchen heat, Alma sets a bowl of peas and carrots on the table and, smelling of onions and lavender water, gives Nathan a hug.

"You're the best boy. The house looks lovely. And all that washing and ironing." She fetches plates of steak and onions to Frank and Nathan. "Dr. Fuller would be so proud of you." She gets her own plate and sits down at her place. "Where would we be without him, Frank?"

"Mmm." Frank nods, mouth full. He twinkles at Nathan. His eyes seem bluer, the more suntanned he gets. "Give him a raise in pay, or he'll be leaving us soon, to take a better offer from a rival firm."

Alma reaches across the table, a surprise move, awkward, sudden, bashful, and lays two twenty-dollar bills beside Nathan's glass of milk. "You get yourself some new clothes. Those corduroys of yours are simply awful. And those tennis shoes! It's a shame for you to go around looking like a ragamuffin, as if your mother didn't care."

THERE'S BEEN NO TIME TO SPEND THE MONEY. He's had to write those handbills for Travers, type the stencil, get Donald to transfer one of his Harlequin drawings to it, run out and buy two thousand sheets of pale green paper, get the inky old mimeograph to where it makes decent copies, crank the drum, crank the drum, and crank the drum for hours. Then he's had to supply the fliers to libraries and shops, tuck them into door handles in neighborhoods where people live that might go to a play, and trap them under the windshield wipers of cars parked along Sierra, Walnut, and Mission streets, and in the parking lots of stores.

This last errand has taken all morning and left him wildly hungry, and now, on the way to afternoon classes, cutting through

Cordova Street Park, he buys from a bowlegged little brown man in a straw hat who parks a catering truck there two fat tamales and a carton of chocolate milk, and sits on a teetery slatted bench under a peppertree, breathing the sun-warmed tangy smell of the tree, and eats, and drinks. The tamales—ten cents each—are wrapped in parchmenty white paper tied at each end with thick cotton string. There are raspy corn husks inside, and inside the corn husks is steaming hot yellow *masa* dough enfolding thick, brick red chili clotted around chunks of stringy, fatty, gristly beef, and one large black olive. They never sold anything like these in Minneapolis. Gobbling them, burning his fingers, burning his mouth, he closes his eyes in leaf-dappled sunlight and hums to himself, wishing he could eat nothing but tamales forever.

He drops the tamale wrappings, red-stained paper napkins, and chocolate milk carton into a wire trash basket and heads off across the park. Beyond sandboxes, swings, and teeter-totters, he comes on old men seated on orange crates and apple boxes, leaning over chessboards in the shade of big, shag-barked eucalyptus trees. The players are silent in concentration, only giving small grunts when one or another makes a move, takes an opponent's piece. Nathan moves from game to game, then halts. A gaunt old geezer in a cloth cap and sleeve garters is routing a paunchy man with a white goatee and a red nose. And the attack the gaunt man is using is the queen's rook's pawn opening Frank used the other night in the attic to demolish Nathan.

"Excuse me," he says. "Have you seen Frank Reed?"

They both look up. "Not today."

"Thank you." Nathan walks off.

At the corner, waiting to cross the street, he notices the discreet, rose-colored Spanish colonial front of Greiner and Tuttle. Right opposite the park. Just where Frank could keep it in view while he played chess. Traffic stops, and he crosses the street and heads for a neat walk that leads along the side of the building to the back. But before he reaches it, out of it comes a trim, red-haired, youngish man carrying a portfolio of sheet music. He notices Nathan, pauses, gives him a long, appraising look, followed by a slow, quizzical smile. Nathan looks away. The man slips into a glossy Buick at the curb and drives off. Nathan goes to find the mortuary's back door. It stands open. He leans into a dim hallway and calls, "Hello?"

A plump man in red rubber gloves and a black rubber wraparound apron peers from a doorway down the hall. He doesn't look happy at being interrupted, but he comes toward Nathan, peeling off the gloves, then seeming to wonder what to do with them. His rosy skin looks very clean. His rimless spectacles gleam in the daylight. "Can I help you?"

"Was that your organist who just left?"

"Desmond Foley, yes." He nods, with the faintest of smiles, and studies Nathan with the same intent interest Foley showed out on the sidewalk just now. It's a look Nathan doesn't understand, and it makes him uneasy. He feels his face redden. He shifts his feet. "Why do you ask?"

Nathan says, "I heard he was quitting."

The man cocks his head. "And you're interested in taking his position?"

"I'm not a musician."

"Pity," the undertaker says. "Such beautiful hands."

Nathan puts them behind his back. "No. Frank Reed told me he was next in line for the job. Is that right?"

"Frank Reed?" The mortician frowns, then laughs impatiently. "I'm afraid not. I'm Ethan Tuttle. I do all the hiring here, and I never heard of any Frank Reed."

ALMA IS OUT, AND FRANK IS PLAYING THE PIANO in the attic. Nathan climbs the staircase, leaves his schoolbooks on the sleeping porch, takes a deep, grim breath, and goes up to the attic. Frank is playing "Pennies from Heaven." When he looks over his shoulder and sees Nathan, he begins to sing the words in a bad, bub-bub-a-boo imitation of Bing Crosby.

" 'You'll find your fortune falling all over town. . . .' "

Nathan scowls. "You won't, Frank." He bangs the keyboard cover down. Frank barely saves his fingers. The strings of the piano hum. Nathan says, "Life is not a goddamned song. You want a fortune, you have to work for it."

Frank pales under his suntan. "What's the meaning of this?" He stands up, his hands fists. He is trembling. "I'm your father. You have no right to speak to me that way."

"Does being my father give you the right to lie to me?" Nathan is dangerously close to crying, and he is too old for that. So he shouts instead. "You never even applied to Greiner and Tuttle. Frank, if you weren't going to look for work, why didn't you just say so flat out?"

"I told you what you wanted to hear," Frank says. "That's what happens to people who try to run other people's lives. They get lied to. And when they go around checking up on people, they get shocked."

"I offered to work," Nathan says. "You said to leave it to you. So I left it to you. I trusted you. And what do you do? Sit under the trees in Cordova Street Park day after day, playing chess with old-age pensioners."

"I'm keeping an eye on Greiner and Tuttle, and the day Desmond Foley doesn't show up, I'm going over there, shabby old clothes or not."

"Here." Nathan holds out the two twenty-dollar bills. "Go buy yourself a new suit. Then go to the other undertakers. I assume you never applied to any of them, right?"

Frank wheels and stamps off to stare out a window. "Damn it, I wish your mother had never heard of Dr. Nathan Fuller. You're turning out just like him. All your sacrifices and sanctimony." He sighs grimly. "Put your money away. I pay for my own suits, thank you. I'll get a job. Nothing less will do—I can see that now. But you leave me alone about it, understand?"

Nathan turns and goes down the stairs.

Frank shouts after him, "You'll be old, someday. Then see how you like it."

MOON WEARS A GREEN DRESS. A slightly grimy slip shows at the back of her skirt. A green hat with a little net across the eyes perches cockily on the red hair she's had fixed at some beauty parlor. It's already frizzled, but not as much as when she pokes her head out of the kitchen at the diner. Gusting gin, cigarette at the corner of her raddled mouth, she staggers on her stick limbs up the stairs, clutching the rail, panting, wheezing to herself, "I pray, for all my sins, when the dead arise incorruptible, I won't be asked to work this hard to get into purgatory."

After her, Lucille Bekker climbs. Waddles. Her hair too has been newly set. It gleams, dark and glossy. She's dressed in black, with small cut-glass earrings and a necklace of cut glass. Strangers follow her; then a massive, gray-haired man and a brassy woman in a white fur stole—the Morgans, Alex's parents. He saw them first down on the street, getting out of a chauffeured Cadillac. More strangers climb the stairs, then a rabbity woman in brown fussily shepherds Dick Schwiller, Junior, and Larry Schwiller, in stiff-looking dark suits, their hair flattened with pomade.

Donald Donald wears a new tweed jacket and a bow tie. He smiles a lot, and in the weak, watery light of the old stairwell, there even appears to be some color in his face. He leads a limp looking man in old-fashioned steel-rimmed glasses and a plodding woman whose colorless hair is braided in thick ropes around her head. They must be his parents. Malcolm trails after them, a healthy, clear-skinned, younger version of his brother.

Someone has lent Charlie Vorak a suit for tonight. On his arm, Peg Decatur looks flushed and happy. Her dress is wine color, with a swatch draped across the breasts she's always worrying are too small, and another across the hips she's always worrying are too broad. Nathan thinks she looks wonderful, and gives her a big hug. Now comes Buddy Challis, carried like the small boy his body for-ever makes him in the arms of a clean-shaven, almost neatly dressed Wayne Hotchkiss, pale and winded by all the stairs, but determined to get up them somehow. Then come Dan Munroe's parents—he heavy and red-faced, she tiny, and dressed in flounces. She talks all the time, twitters like a bird. Nathan is startled to see Desmond Foley following them, elegant in a tuxedo, red hair gleaming. Foley sees him too, and gives him a nod and a smile. Why? They're not friends.

In the black painted loft, Sheila O'Hare, the girl from Moon's, blond hair piled on top of her head tonight, gives Nathan a wink and a comically harried smile. She's in charge of a card table by the door, with a reservation list and a tin fishing-tackle box of bills and change. Everyone appears to want to stand chatting. The lights from Nathan's rack shine down dimly on the set with its striped wall-paper, dull sofa, and chairs. Travers, ashen-faced, in a black suit too small for him, pulls Nathan aside and asks in a frantic whisper if everyone is here yet. Nathan counts heads and says not yet. Abou appears, looking rosy, talking with two men in plaid jackets rumor says are scouts from a movie studio.

At last, Nathan counts sixty heads, and goes to tell Travers, who by now looks green. He steps into a corner partitioned off by black-painted beaverboard panels, where Dr. Dick's bald head gleams faintly beside a handmade switchboard that trails a tangle of vari-colored wires. Travers gasps a word to him, and Dr. Dick works a switch that blinks the lights above the stage. There are small startled exclamations. Sheila O'Hare scurries around, peering at ticket stubs, waving a flashlight, showing stragglers to their places. Heels rattle and soles scuff. The rickety seats clatter and exhale their musty breath as patrons settle into them, clothes rustling. The lights go out. From the stage come faint noises of actors stumbling into place in the dark. The lights go up, there is a scattering of applause for Donald's London suburban parlor set, complete with umbrella stand and ferns—and far in the back rooms, audible, Nathan hopes, only to him, Travers throws up.

AFTER THE FIRST ACT, THE STAIRWELL IS CROWDED. Opening the loft windows would let in light and noise from the street below, so there's no ventilation. It's grown hot and stuffy. Everybody wants to get out. They need to breathe. As the act neared its close, Travers came like a ghost through the murk to bend over Sheila and whisper to her. And she slipped out into the hall and down the stairs to open the street door. So the stairwell is less stuffy than the loft. And most of the older members of the audience stay there. The younger ones, who don't mind the climb, go down and stand out on the sidewalk. They smoke and chatter and laugh. The night air is cool. Nathan breathes it in gratefully. There's a touch on his arm. A voice says:

"I believe you wanted to speak to me?"

The red-headed organist smiles. It's a warm smile, again. He has beautiful teeth. He's a nice-looking man. What's wrong with Frank? *He'll get into trouble. His kind always do. You keep away from him, understand?* He doesn't understand. He's taken Frank's warnings as gospel all his life. But all his life he's been a child. He's not a child anymore, and he doesn't really see the sense of this. What did Frank mean? What kind of trouble? Still, he's leery.

"I don't remember that," he says.

"I'm Desmond Foley." A hand is held out. Nathan takes it. There seems nothing else to do. Foley's hand is strong, the handshake firm. "I was told you asked for me at Greiner and Tuttle the other day."

Nathan shakes his head. "They got it mixed up."

"I'm disappointed," Foley says.

"Why?" Nathan says.

"I thought I'd found a new friend," Foley says.

ASKED WHY MOON DOESN'T OPEN THE DINER on Saturdays and Sundays, Travers has a stock answer—"She needs the weekends to catch up on her drinking." But this Sunday morning, Moon is in

the kitchen, singing, and the Harlequins and their friends are at the
tables, eating breakfast, drinking coffee among the strewn sheets of
the fat Sunday papers. News, sports, travel, business sections, the
color comics slither to the floor for Sheila O'Hare to kick through
like a child through autumn leaves as she brings the orders. All
anyone wants to see are the theatrical sections.

"Listen to the *Daily News!*" Wayne Hotchkiss shouts. " 'Here
is a lively performance of a thoughtful thriller. The suspense will
keep you on the edge of your seat. Hurry to the tiny upstairs Harlequin Theater before you miss it.' "

" 'Better than a movie,' " Buddy says. " 'Real, live actors so
close you could reach out and touch them. Los Angeles better take
these youngsters to its heart. If it doesn't, it doesn't have a heart.' "

"Catch me," Travers says, "I'm going to faint."

" 'As the mysterious police inspector of the title,' " Peg reads
ecstatically, " 'Dan Munroe displays a maturity and wisdom that
would be startling in an actor twice his age. He is also terrifically
good looking.' "

"I'll need dark glasses," Dan says. "It's hell being pestered for
autographs wherever you go."

Abou raises his voice. " 'Tall, striking Alex Morgan absolutely
convinces. A nuanced characterization by a very young actress with
a very bright future.' "

"You think mother will put away my bassinet now?"

" 'J. B. Priestley's suspense drama poses questions more facile
than profound,' " Charlie Vorak reads, " 'but young director Abou
Bekker has avoided the obvious, and brings out richly human
subtleties in his handling of the play and of his talented young
players.' "

Donald Donald stands up, waves the review he has found.
" 'Working with minimal materials on a skimpy stage, teenage designer Donald R. Donald has caught Priestly's atmosphere exactly in
his stuffy English sitting room set. One could almost smell the rising
damp.' " He looks around, puzzled. "What the hell is 'rising damp'?"

Travers staggers up out of his chair. " 'Here is a so-called amateur group,' " he reads in a trembling voice, " 'of very young people that outclasses in artistic sharpness and excitement many professional touring companies that visit L.A.' " Clutching the paper to his bony breast, he looks around at them, tears in his eyes. "Oh, my dear, dear friends, you've done it, you've made my dream come true. Bless you all." He collapses onto his chair, lays his head on Alex's shoulder, and has a good cry for himself.

NATHAN SHIVERS ON THE FRONT PORCH. Now and then a gust of wind brings rain into his face, and he steps back. The leathery leaves of the funereal old magnolia trees drip disconsolately. He keeps thinking he'll hear the telephone bell from indoors. This seems a bad day to go climbing in the canyons. He doesn't want to get another cold. But the phone doesn't ring. And soon a 1937 Pontiac coupe with a dented fender rolls to the curb beyond the broken picket fence. He runs down the walk, ducks into the car, slams the door. The windshield wipers slap and creak.

"Wet," he says.

Kenneth Stone says, "That's when the canyons are at their best." He wrestles with the gearshift level. "In mist and rain. Beautiful." He grips the steering wheel with leather-gloved hands and lets out the clutch. The car bucks ahead. Nathan's head jerks back. They whiz down Oleander Street. Is this the first time Stone has tried to drive? "You'll see a hundred Chinese paintings today."

"I never saw even one Chinese painting," Nathan says.

Stone looks at him. "Is that true?" Out of the corner of his eye, Nathan sees a red stop sign flash past. "That's a shame. Typical, though. The West thinks of itself as the only civilization. China was there well before us, thousands of years. There's a big portfolio. Fenollosa, Boston scholar. A hundred splendid sepia reproductions. I wish I could show it to you." He brakes the car at a signal.

"Why can't you?" Nathan says.

"It's—I don't have it anymore." The light changes. He shifts gears. "I left it behind." The car bucks across the intersection. "Left all my books behind."

"Behind where?" Nathan says.

Stone gives a short, sour laugh. "You expect me to say Keokuk, Iowa? Or have you been listening to the rumors?"

Nathan gulps and says feebly, "What rumors?"

"That I come from Germany."

"You don't sound German," Nathan says.

"I was born in Washington, D.C. My father was an undersecretary in the German embassy there. When Mr. Wilson declared war on Germany, my father was interned. My mother was American, and she took me back to her family's place in Iowa, and we lived there until the end of the war, when my father was released."

"Then you moved to Germany?" Nathan says. "So that's where your books are?"

"There was no way to bring them out," Stone says.

"Maybe, when the war is over—"

Stone stares at him. "You haven't heard about the bombings? My books'll be ashes, Nathan. So will everything else worth saving. It'll be the end of the world, this war."

HARROW CANYON IS ONLY A STEP FROM TOWN but it is true wilderness. They trudge upward beside a wash in which the force of muddy water, bristling with broken tree branches, tumbles boulders over one another as if they had no weight. They have great weight. The ground trembles when they clash against one another. The canyon narrows. Its rocky walls grow steeper. Chaparral brushes his new corduroys, and the cold moisture soaks through and makes them heavy, clammy, clinging.

Tramping ahead of him in knickerbockers, knapsack on his back, small pickax hooked in his belt, coil of rope over his shoulder, the stocky Stone looks a little comical, but he is strong and tireless and seemingly waterproof. He ignores the rain. No crevasse or outcrop stops him. He stumps on upward or, if need be, scrambles upward on all fours. Nathan follows, but his night walks on the flat paved streets of town have not prepared him for this. His hands are scraped and raw from grabbing rocks and branches to haul himself after Stone. Tennis shoes, even new ones, were the wrong footwear to choose for this. His feet are bruised.

He pauses, panting, and peers ahead through the rain. Mist swirls up there, in rags and tatters, among towering thrusts of savage rock and ancient scraggy pines that grip the slopes with desperate roots. He is already tired, and the climb ahead looks too rough, too steep for him. He opens his mouth and draws damp air into his lungs to shout he's had enough, and Stone turns back to look for him. He's got many yards ahead. He lifts an arm, beckoning.

"Come along. The worst is over."

"Looks to me like it's only beginning."

Stone laughs. "Come. I'll show you a miracle."

Nathan sighs, puts his head down, and clutching brush to pull himself up, and kicking around blindly for rock footholds, he finally gets to where Stone is standing. Stone points. Breathless, Nathan blinks, wipes rain out of his eyes, squints in disbelief. A narrow staircase of weathered planks and two-by-fours bends its way up and up the cliff face until, high above, it disappears in the mist. Stone laughs, claps Nathan on the back, and begins to climb.

AT THE TOP OF THE STAIRCASE LIES A PATH that takes them at an easy upward slope along the edge of the ravine out of which they've climbed. Below them, rags and tatters of cloud swirl, form trailing shapes, break up, form shapes again. Scarps and screes show up for an instant and are swallowed again by the eddies of cloud; trees are there one instant, gone the next. Stone halts, bends, picks up a rock, tosses it over the edge. The two of them listen in a silence only deepened by the whisper of the rain. Nothing. Then, far, far below, Nathan hears the rock land. Stone smiles at him.

"You see how far we've climbed out of the world?"

"I hear," Nathan says.

They cross the ravine on a shaky little wooden footbridge, and follow a path along the other side for a while. They reach a second bridge. Stone starts across, but Nathan hangs back. Boards are missing from this bridge, and he sees it sway under Stone's weight, and hears it creak. Stone turns, hand on the rail.

"It's not much farther," he says.

"It's a long way down," Nathan says.

Stone laughs and playfully stamps on the bridge. "It's not going to collapse. See? You're safe with me, Nathan. I lead a charmed life." The phrase seems to have unspoken meaning for him. His grin vanishes. For a moment there's terrible sadness in his homely face, and then he turns and crosses to the other side.

Nathan sighs, "If you say so," and steps after him.

THEY HAVE EATEN DRY ROAST BEEF SANDWICHES, pickles, and Hershey bars from Stone's knapsack. They drink strong coffee. They sit under a rock ledge surrounded by towering pines on three sides, a waterfall on the fourth. Swollen by the rain, it crashes and foams. They watch it and talk.

"We had it planned down to the last detail," Stone says. "The Gestapo is thorough. You've heard that, I expect. We didn't dare slip up." He pours coffee from the thermos into Nathan's cup, his cup. "But above all, we had to be sure no word of what we were up to leaked out."

"Where were you going?" Nathan says.

"Portugal. Then Brazil. And finally the United States. Documents, passports, visas were ready. All from underground sources, false names, false backgrounds, all very expensive. Cash had been smuggled out through friends. It all took a lot of time. Seemed like forever. The Gestapo kept knocking on doors at midnight. Colleagues kept disappearing. Then, only two days before we were slated to make our move, I was on my way to lecture when a friend caught my arm and whispered to me in the hall." The hand holding the mug of coffee shakes. Stone sets the mug on the ground. "I rushed to my office and rang my wife to warn her." He stops speaking.

Nathan says, "She wasn't there?"

"The Gestapo was there," Stone says tonelessly. "A Captain Matthiesson answered. He didn't give his name. He didn't have to. I knew his voice. He'd interviewed me about a colleague only the week before. I didn't speak. I hung up. I knew I was too late."

"What happened to your wife?"

"My wife and daughter." Stone is pale. He blows out air and gazes across at the waterfall for a long moment before answering. "It took me nearly a year to learn for sure. Then someone coming through Rio told me. The Gestapo took them away that day. They never came back. I hope they're alive somewhere, but nobody knows."

"I'm sorry," Nathan says. "What did you do?"

"Hid for thirty-six hours in a smelly cellar, shaved my hair off, borrowed a pair of glasses, and dressed in someone else's hat and coat. I followed the plan, and escaped." Stone smiles grimly. "Only me, and there'd been six of us."

"Who betrayed you?" Nathan asks.

Stone gives his head a shake, pushes to his feet, walks across to stand, hands in hip pockets, watching the tumbling, foaming waterfall. Over its roar, he calls, "Donald says you're writing a play."

"Damn him," Nathan says. "I told him not to tell."

"All about your family. Your father's a musician?"

Nathan nods. "First he was a child prodigy, then a symphony player, then an orchestra player in silent movie theaters, then a dance band player, then a church organist."

Stone turns. "And now—?"

"Now?" Nathan smiles ruefully. "Now he's a player in his own attic, hoping nobody will hear him."

"Did you inherit his talent?"

"Yes, but when I saw what it did to him, I decided I'd rather be a carpenter, like my uncle Chester. It's steady work, and you never have to travel."

Stone frowns. "What was it music did to your father?"

"Kept him away from home all the time. I hated that. He hated it too, but he couldn't seem to stay anyplace long enough to settle down." Nathan drinks some of his coffee. It steams in the chill air, but it's not hot enough to warm him. He shudders. He doesn't think he'll ever be warm again. "If he'd stuck with any one thing—brass, reeds, strings, keyboard—maybe it would have been different, but it's not in him. He gets bored."

Stone comes back and sits down by the knapsack. "It sounds as if he should have been a conductor."

"You have to be able to charm people. That's what he says. He can't be bothered." Nathan's nose runs. He wipes it with the back of his hand. "Till I was four, my mother and I traveled with him. City to city. As the jobs came and went. But my aunt Marie said it wasn't good for me, all those hotel rooms, all those greasy eateries —and my mother and I settled down with her in Minneapolis after that." He sneezes. "So we hardly ever saw him. It was a hell of a life, but it was music, and music was everything to him." He snuffles, and wipes his nose on his hand again. "And now, look at him. Sixty years old, and not a dime to his name." Nathan laughs to himself. "I never thought of it before, but maybe I got a vision of where he was heading, where music was taking him, and that's why I slammed down the keyboard cover at age eleven and never opened it again. Maybe I inherited my mother's gift too—for seeing into the future."

"That's quite a gift," Stone says. "What it amounts to is the ability to understand the past."

"She reads cards and horoscopes and tea leaves, and there's nothing in that. No, Frank was the person I loved best in the world. He still is. I was sore at music for keeping us apart, and I didn't want any more to do with it."

"But you didn't become a carpenter." Stone closes the knapsack, buckles its straps. "You became a writer."

"It happened," Nathan says. "I don't know why. Books. Mark Twain, Jack London, Edgar Lee Masters." He gets to his feet,

crouches so as not to bang his head on the rock outcrop, and steps
into the rain. "Do you really think the war is going to be the end
of the world?"

"Of one world, anyway." Stone shrugs into the knapsack straps.
"The world I chose. The Old World. Cathedrals, museums, orchestra
halls, the Parthenon, the Prado, the Pitti Palace, two thousand years
of civilization, from Sophocles to Eliot, from Dickens to Thomas
Mann, from Giotto to Picasso, from Monteverdi to Bartók"—he
picks up the alpenstock and the coil of rope, and steps out from
under the rock shelf—"all of it will be bombed and burned out of
existence." He sighs, summons a smile, and claps Nathan's back.
"Now—have you had your fill of Chinese landscapes?"

Nathan shivers. "I hope the artists had umbrellas."

"The Chinese invented the umbrella," Stone says, not thinking
about it, thinking about the place, studying it. "I like coming here.
Completely away from the world. If only—." He doesn't finish the
thought. He reads his watch instead, and says, "We've got to get
moving. Don't want to be overtaken by darkness. Not up here."

They trudge on down the muddy paths and cross again the
rickety bridges. After long silence, Stone says over his shoulder,
"Don't let yourself be drawn into it, Nathan. They'll tell you it's
your duty to shoulder a gun and march off to kill other kids like
yourself—my boy Kurt, for example. It isn't. Any more than it's his
duty to kill you."

Nathan sneezes. "Maybe America won't get into it."

With a glance at the darkening sky, Stone strides on down the
path. "America got into it in 1917," he says. "It's the same war,
Nathan."

THIS BEDROOM, WITH ITS WALLPAPER of tiny faded pink
roses, has been shut up too long and smells of mildew. The mattress
and springs were wrapped in newspapers, but they smell of mildew
too, right through the clean sheets. For a long time—he doesn't
know how long—he was too sick to care. He ran high fevers and

was out of his mind half the time. He didn't know where he was.

Now that the sopping sweats and shuddering chills are past, the struggles to breathe, to cry for help when he couldn't make a sound—he wants to get out of this room. He hates its bare window-frames, the dark rectangles on the wallpaper where pictures used to hang, the spidery gaslight fixture in the middle of the rain-stained ceiling. His voice is as weak as the rest of him. He whispers to Frank:

"I want to go back to the sleeping porch."

Frank stands holding the tray on which Alma brought a big plate of pot roast, potatoes, and green beans to Nathan half an hour ago. "It's too damp and cold out there."

"At least I could breathe," Nathan says.

"You're breathing all right now," Frank says. His expression is grim. "But it was touch and go there for a while. You damn near left us—do you know that?"

He tries for a reassuring smile. "I'm still here."

"You're still not out of the woods." Frank nods at the supper. "Doctor says you've got to eat."

Nathan has a shadowy image of a man bending over him, a thin, gray-haired man in spectacles, with a quiet, firm voice, cool, thin fingers on his forehead, a worry-wrinkled face in lamplight. "I hope he didn't charge too much."

"He did, but your friend Stone paid for it. Insisted. Argued it was his fault, taking you hiking in the rain."

"I could have said no," Nathan says.

Alma comes in, takes the tray from Frank, and exclaims in pain to Nathan, "Oh, child—you'll never get your strength back. You hardly ate a bite."

"Tomorrow," Nathan says. "All I want to do is sleep." No strength to his arms, he pushes to the floor the extra pillows that have propped him up to eat. He starts to turn on his side, then notices Frank's starched white jacket. A dentist's? A waiter's? "What's that you're wearing?"

"Stone got me a job," Frank says.

"You got the job yourself," Alma says crossly.

"Well, all right," Frank says. "Stone told me there was an opening, and I went over, and they hired me."

"What kind of a job?" Nathan says. "Not music."

"Sierra Tech," Frank says. "That guesthouse they've got—the Atheneum?"

"The one designed like a Greek temple?" Nathan says.

Frank nods. "For visiting professors, scholars, scientists. Come from all over the world. I pick them up at the station. I carry their bags up to their rooms."

HE OPENS HIS EYES. Donald Donald stands in the doorway, something under his arm. The cracked green roller shades are down, so only a little daylight leans in around their edges, and Nathan can't make out what he's brought. Evidently Donald can't see well either. He raps the open door with a knuckle. Hesitantly. Softly. He speaks in a whisper:

"Nathan?"

"What are you doing here?"

"Ah, you're awake." Donald comes in and stands at the foot of the bed. "I brought you a radio. I came last week, but your mother said you were too sick to have visitors."

"A radio?" Nathan pushes himself to a sitting position, something he hasn't been able to manage without Frank's help till today. He's getting better. He peers. "A radio?"

"I didn't see one in your room." Donald looks around for an electric outlet. "I've been in hospitals a lot, and I know how lonesome it gets." He crouches, plugs the cord in, pushes aside water glass, alarm lock, medicine bottles on the bedside table, and sets the radio there. "People come, but they don't stay. They go on about the business of being healthy and alive." He switches the radio on. Dance music plays. Ray Noble—"Cherokee." "A radio's company."

Nathan says, "I must be hallucinating again."

Donald grins. "Nobody's all bad."

"I'd have bet on you," Nathan says. "But thanks."

Donald pretends to look carefully around the room. "What—no flowers from your new friend, Desmond Foley?"

"I hardly know him," Nathan says.

"You were awfully cozy the other night at the Harlequin. Everybody noticed. Everybody's talking about it."

"We weren't cozy," Nathan says, and coughs. It takes time to recover from coughing. Finally he gasps, "We said about six words to each other."

Donald clucks. "Isn't it awful how people exaggerate."

"It's awful how you do," Nathan says.

"Did he invite you to his house?" Donald says.

Nathan squints. "What the hell are you talking about?"

"I wouldn't know, myself," Donald says, "but I hear he likes filling his house with good-looking high school boys on weekends. It's up in the hills. Isolated. They say he's got a rule about the swimming pool. No suits. If you don't swim naked, you don't swim."

"Go away, Donald. I have to sleep." From the radio, a chirpy voice sings, "'Rinso *white*, Rinso *white*—happy little washday tune.'"

Donald raises his pale brows. "Your theme song?"

"Son of a bitch," Nathan says. "Take your damn radio."

"No, no." Donald holds up both hands in protest. "You really will enjoy it." He retreats to the door. "Anything else I can bring you? No one's home. Can I heat you some soup or something?"

"I'm not hungry."

"Okay, then—enjoy the radio." And Donald is gone.

"Moonlight Cocktail" plays. Nathan drifts to sleep.

WITH ALMA BUSY WITH CLIENTS DOWNSTAIRS and Frank away at the Atheneum, sweeping floors, mopping washrooms, unstopping toilets, and maybe, just maybe, now and then, carrying the bags of distinguished scholars up to their rooms—there was no one to prevent Nathan moving back out to his sleeping porch, once he was able to walk without help. He lies under blankets and two moth-eaten overcoats on his cot. It's cold, raining again, and he is bundled in old sweaters and a stocking cap, but he's happy.

Donald's radio plays, and Nathan reads "Self-Reliance" by Ralph Waldo Emerson. He's finished with "Civil Disobedience" by Thoreau. It still lies beside him. His mind swims with the daring of these essays. Their outrageous phrases shunt his spirits dizzily between courage and cowardice. Stone brought him the books.

"You have to protect yourself," he said.

How many days ago was this? Not out here. In the rosebud-papered room. It seems like a dream. The books are all that prove to him it wasn't. Stone squatted, broad and solid, on a little carved walnut chair beside the poster bed. His raincoat was damp, a tweed cap rode low on his forehead.

"Plan how you're going to survive. It's up to you, Nathan. The men in power don't give a damn for your intelligence, your sensitivity, your talent. What's the loss of a few plays to them—plays not even written yet? You know what you are to them—a means to an end, that's all."

Nathan nodded sleepily. "Yes, I know."

"Well, don't forget it. They'll try to manipulate you with speeches and slogans to make you feel you owe your life to presidents and generals, to the Constitution, the flag, the Declaration of Independence, home and Mom and apple pie. Don't fall for it, Nathan." Agitated, he got up off the little chair and paced. "That's the really lethal thing about monsters like Hitler. They turn their enemies into monsters too."

"I'm very tired," Nathan mumbled.

"Yes. I'll go." Stone pats the rain-spotted books beside Nathan on the bed. "But when you're well again, you read these. Emerson and Thoreau understood this country better than any FDR ever did or ever will." Stone moved away, voice fading. "To Emerson and Thoreau, 'liberty' and 'justice' are more than mere words. In their democracy, each man controls his own destiny." Standing in the bedroom doorway, buckling the belt of the trenchcoat, he said, "Control yours, Nathan. Use your wits. Use your legs, if you have to. Run away, hide. 'Exile and cunning,' as James Joyce said." Nathan couldn't see well, but he thought Stone had tears in his eyes. "They took my son. Don't let them take you too." The door closed, and he was gone.

ABOU BEKKER STANDS LOOKING DOWN AT NATHAN. His plump cheeks are ruddy, his crisp curly black hair is beaded with raindrops, and he holds a tall stack of magazines. He breathes heavily. "These weigh a ton," he says, looking around. "Where shall I put them?"

"Just on the floor." Nathan closes Emerson, lays the book aside. "What are they?"

"*Theatre Arts.*" Abou hesitates, then walks to the other side of the cot, squats, and sets the magazines down among stacks of books. He stands. "There's a new Broadway play in every issue. Donald says you're writing a—"

"Donald's a liar, Abou," Nathan says.

Abou blinks, takes a breath, starts again. "Donald says you're writing a play, all about a traveling musician called Frank, his wife Alma who tells fortunes, and a little boy called Nathan."

"I told Donald not to tell anybody," Nathan says.

"I'm anxious to read it." Abou sits at the table that holds Nathan's typewriter, and fits a cigarette into an ivory holder. "You do so well with dialogue in your *Monitor* pieces."

Nathan sulks. "I don't even know if I can finish it."

Abou lights the cigarette, drops the match into the peanut butter jar that holds Nathan's pens and pencils. "Of course you'll finish it." He smiles. "Any work seems daunting when you've been as sick as you've been. You don't look after yourself, and according to Donald, no one looks after you. He says you go out walking half the night, and your parents don't even care." He rises and peers out into the hallway and stairwell. "It doesn't take an expert to see you're still a long way from well, yet there's no one here. You shouldn't be left on your own like this."

"There's someone here," Nathan says. "You."

"I came before, but you weren't allowed visitors."

"I wasn't even conscious."

"Poor Nathan." Abou looks down on him, forehead wrinkled. "My mother wants you to eat with us more often. She thinks you're too thin. And don't eat at Moon's so much. All that cheap grease. It's poison, Nathan."

"Thank your mother," Nathan says. He picks up Emerson again and opens it. "And thank you for the magazines."

"You'd like me to go, and I will. In a minute." Abou puts his broad butt down on the chair again and leans toward Nathan, frowning, troubled. "First, allow me a word of caution. You were seen talking to Desmond Foley at the Harlequin opening night. I wouldn't, Nathan."

"It was a case of mistaken identity," Nathan says.

"Ah?" Abou hesitates, doubtful, then smiles and rises. "All right, if you say so. Get well soon." He goes out, calling back from the staircase, "Everyone misses you."

ALMA COMES IN, DRESSED IN HER BEST. She's brought a small plate with a humpy-crusted wedge of apple pie on it. He has eaten a large helping of ham and scalloped potatoes topped with melted cheese. He has drunk two glasses of milk. She smiles, kisses the top of his head, takes the plate and glass, and hands him the pie. "Good boy. You'll be well again in no time."

"Where you going?" He fills his mouth with pie.

"A séance at Mrs. Gregory's." Alma drifts out into the hallway as lightly as ectoplasm, but a lot more cheerful than any ectoplasm he's ever read about in her weird books. "How pleased she'll be to know you're getting better. She was worried about you. Telephoned me every day."

Nathan starts to ask whether the medium was worried that he might become a ghost, or that he might not—but Alma wouldn't see the humor. "That was nice of her."

"She's a wonderful woman." Alma's heels clunk on the stairs. The old doorbell jangles. "Oh, my goodness, my ride's come early." She hastens down, the door opens, but it's not women's voices Nathan hears. He stops chewing, flings off the heavy bedclothes, sets the pie plate on the desk, and totters to the door to listen. It's not police. It's Wayne Hotchkiss. He sighs with relief. But his heart pounds and his legs feel weak. He crawls back into bed.

And Charlie Vorak comes in with Peg Decatur, both of them wearing worried looks. Peg hugs a damp grocery sack. A scarf hides her wonderful hair. On Charlie's head is a faded baseball cap. Their faces are rosy from the cold. "Your mother says you're okay for a little company at last."

Nathan nods, smiles. "Thanks for coming. Sit down."

Peg sits at the foot of the cot, Charlie at the desk. Peg pats Nathan's ankles under the covers. "You had us frightened to death."

"Me too," Nathan whispers, "only not quite to death."

Charlie pushes back his cap and frowns thoughtfully at the typewriter and the papers lying beside it. "We came with a proposition."

"As soon as you're up and around again," Peg says.

"It's been a long time," Nathan says. "How long?"

"Too long," Peg says. "The *Monitor*'s like a mortuary."

Nathan smiles wanly. "I'd fit right in. How's Buddy?"

"He's got the flu or he'd be here. He misses you worst of all. Without the Listener, his feature page is nothing."

Nathan peers over his shoulder. "I thought I heard Mr. Hotchkiss. Where is he?"

"Your mother's reading his cards for him."

Nathan stares. "You're not serious."

"The kids are sick again," Charlie says. "Joanie's nagging him to find a place to move to, get out of that damp house before they die of pneu—." Charlie chokes and gets red in the face.

Nathan laughs. "It's okay. I'm not dying anymore."

"And he wants to know if things are going to get better," Peg says. "Or worse. They had a hired girl for a while but she kept getting drunk on Wayne's scotch and they had to fire her, so now Joanie's stuck with the kids twenty-four hours a day. Wayne's got student papers to correct, lectures to prepare. If he's to spell Joanie so she can get a little rest, there isn't time for him to even think about his novel, let alone sit out in the garage and write it. He's at the end of his rope."

"I hope my mother turns up nothing but diamonds for him," Nathan says hoarsely. But he is disappointed in Hotchkiss. He thought the man had better sense. Nathan nods at the sack Peg has brought. "What's that?"

"Oh." She pulls a large can with a sunshiny label out of the sack and holds it up. Ruefully. "Orange juice. Charlie recommended champagne—to celebrate your being back from the dead. Lovely idea. But"—her smile goes, she sighs—"then we remembered you're only seventeen, *and* you live with your parents, and they might not approve."

"I tasted champagne at Dan's party after the play," Nathan says. "I think I like orange juice better." He reaches for the can, she puts it into his hands, and he nearly drops it, he's so weak. When he gets control of it, he hugs it to himself, rocks it like a baby, grinning. "Thank you."

"What's this?" Charlie has picked up a notepad from the desk. He reads, " 'Society everywhere is in conspiracy against the manhood of every one of its members. The virtue most in request is conformity. Self-reliance is its aversion. Whoso would be a man must be a nonconformist.' " His pale red brows go as high as they can go, and he blinks at Nathan. "Hey. That's pretty radical stuff. What have you been reading?" He flips a page. " 'A common and natural result of an undue respect for law is, that you may see a file of soldiers marching in admirable order over hill and dale to the wars, against their wills, ay, against their common sense and consciences, which makes it very steep marching indeed, and produces a palpitation of the heart. They have no doubt that it is a damnable business in which they are concerned; they are all peaceably inclined. Now what are they? Men at all?' "

Nathan smiles at Charlie's appalled expression. "Emerson," he croaks, "Thoreau." He paws around for the books on the bed and holds them up. "Mr. Stone lent them to me."

"Stone. Jesus, no wonder they're saying he's a Nazi." Charlie lays the pad down and looks very seriously at the thin, pale boy in the bed. "Talking against the Allied war effort. Isolationism? Nathan, Hitler is winning. The U.S. has got to step in and stop him, or he'll wipe out democracy and send the world back to the Middle Ages." Charlie points at the books, scowling. "Those ideas are poison. Stone's asking for trouble."

Nathan can't believe this. "Will you be serious?"

"Nathan," Charlie says strictly, "whatever Stone says, or Emerson or Thoreau or anybody, this is a country of laws. And last year, Congress passed a law called the Selective Service Act. Have you heard about that? The draft, Nathan. I'm already signed up. And this coming June, every boy your age is going over to city hall and sign up too. I didn't have any choice, you don't have any choice."

"It's stupid," Peg says. "Hitler's not bombing us. Why should we get into the war? Why should you? Why should Nathan? Men! Honestly, Charlie—what's wrong with you? You have to prove your manhood every generation by running out and slaughtering people? Isn't that a little primitive?"

"Don't talk Psychology 101 to me, Peg. Congress passed that law for a reason. They know something the rest of us don't know. That there's no way this country can keep out of that war, and that we've got to be ready."

"Mr. Stone is not a Nazi," Nathan says. "He hates them. But adding our bombs to their bombs is only going to make things worse. It's going to destroy everything fine that man's built up over the centuries. That's what he says. And what's the sense of you and me dying for that?"

"Double-talk," Charlie grunts. "Don't listen to him." Rain has begun to fall again. He looks at it through the old black window screens and shivers. "Should you be out here on this porch, sick as you've been?"

"I bundle up," Nathan says. "I like the fresh air. I hate being boxed up in a room." Footfalls sound on the staircase. He turns his head. Wayne Hotchkiss appears gray-faced, rain-damp in the doorway.

"What did she tell you?" Peg asks eagerly.

"That a friend is going to die." Hotchkiss gazes bleakly down at Nathan. "She's a nice woman, your mother. Guess I should have known that, knowing you." He lights a bent cigarette with a paper match from a book imprinted Laughing Jack's. He coughs smoke and looks at Peg. "In brief, the kids will get over the croup in due course, we'll get another hired girl, but no way are we going to find a house to move to."

"Maybe you better not tell Joanie," Charlie says.

With a wry smile, Hotchkiss sits on the bed next to Peg. "Maybe I better not." He gives Nathan a tobacco-stained grin. "Good to see you, kid. I stopped by a couple times, and things were looking bad. You made a nervous wreck out of your grandfather."

"He's my father." Hotchkiss chokes on smoke, and Nathan tells him, "No, it's okay. I was a late arrival."

"Late babies are the brightest," Peg says.

"Have they told you our idea?" Hotchkiss asks.

"We got sidetracked," Charlie says. "You tell him."

"I've fixed up my garage to write in. Far from the madding family. I thought when you're better, we'd arrange a night—Friday would probably be best—and we can all get together there, and you can read us your play."

Nathan stares. "What play?"

"Donald says you've written a marvelous play."

" 'All talking,' " Peg says, " 'all singing. You'll laugh, you'll cry.' "

"Stop," Nathan wheezes. "It's a lie. Donald's just making trouble. There is no play."

Charlie looks bewildered. "He described it in detail, Nathan. Cast of characters—"

"—sounded like you and your parents," Peg says.

Nathan turns on his side, away from them. "I'm working on something," he mumbles. "But it's nowhere near ready."

"Okay." Hotchkiss slaps his knees and stands up. "Then we'll have our evening when it is, how about that?"

"No one was supposed to know about it," Nathan says. "What if it turns out to be no good?"

Peg's cool hand lies on his cheek for a moment. "It will be good, Nathan. You have a lovely talent. How could it not be good?"

"Yeah, well, you're my friends." He turns, sits up, looks at them. "And, excuse me, but you're not experts on the theater, are you? I mean, Abou's heard about it. He told me so. And ten to one Travers has too. Of course. You know Donald. He doesn't do things by halves, and he doesn't do things to be kind. He's built it up as wonderful because he thinks it's lousy. You can bet he won't want to miss that reading. To see my face when they sneer at me."

Charlie says, "Why should they do that?"

"They know all about plays," Nathan says. "I never wrote a play before. I'm just a kid. What do I know?"

"You're tired," Charlie says, and takes Peg's arm. "We'll get out of here and let you sleep."

"When you're well again," Peg says, "you'll get back your faith in yourself."

They leave the room together, and Nathan hears them hurrying downstairs. Eyes dropping shut, he pulls up the heavy covers. Then he's aware Hotchkiss hasn't gone. He peers up at him. Hotchkiss puts a finger to his lips, slides a flat bottle from his pocket, and pushes it under the pillow. "Brandy," he whispers. "Nothing better for keeping out the cold." He squeezes Nathan's shoulder and leaves.

NATHAN HAS BORROWED CHARLIE'S 1932 CHEVY. He swings it in at the long, weedy driveway of the Bekker house. Standing on the flowerpot-crowded porch, with the stack of *Theatre Arts* in his arms, he rattles the screen door gently with his foot. The day is warm and pleasant, and the inner door stands open. Lucille Bekker's musical voice warbles a question from inside. He calls out his name. She comes to the door and blinks at him against the daylight, shielding her eyes with a plump hand.

"Ah, it's Adonis." She smiles and pushes the door open. "Here. Look how pale and thin you are. You've been sick. Bobby said you almost died. You shouldn't be carrying those. They're too heavy. Here." She takes half the stack and turns back, saying to him, "Come in, come in. Bobby's not home yet. I expect he stopped off at the Harlequin. Everyone's had the flu. It's upset their plans." She sets her stack of magazines on Abou's desk, and steps aside so he can put the rest down. "They've fallen terribly behind."

"*Giants in the Earth*," Nathan says. "Right?"

"Such a gloomy play," she says. "I don't know if it was a good choice. I think people would rather laugh."

"I read the novel once," Nathan says. "It's gloomy, all right. But sometimes that's how life is."

She laughs up at him, this dark, roly-poly little woman, and pats his cheek. "Such a solemn child you are." She spins away, surprisingly light on her big feet. "Look here."

What he sees is a wooden rack as tall as she is. From it hang on intricate strings four marionettes, each about two feet high, beautifully painted and costumed. He touches them cautiously, awed. "Did you make these?"

"It's what the Department of Parks and Recreation pays me for," she says. "Yes, I make them, and I put on little plays for the children in the schools. Fairy tales, mostly."

"There's Simple Simon," Nathan says, "and the Pieman. Mary and her Little Lamb." In those lonely hotel rooms, Alma read him Mother Goose when he was small, holding him on her lap. The warmth of it comes back to him now. He feels a rush of love for Lucille Bekker. "Who's this?"

"Tom, Tom, the Piper's Son." She laughs, and takes the clickety figure down from the rack and, fat fingers playing virtuoso tricks with the two flat pieces of wood from which the strings depend, runs him across the worn rug, looking back in panic over his shoulder. "Don't you see the pig under his arm?" She hangs the marionette up again, where it swings jiggling on its strings, stupid and blank-eyed, all its life gone in an instant. "Sit down," she says. "Let's have some lemonade while we wait for Bobby."

"I can't, I'm sorry." Nathan steps to the door. "I have to return the car I borrowed—and I still have another errand to run." She looks disappointed, and he gives her his best smile and says, "If I come again, will there still be lemonade?"

"For you?" She stands on tiptoe and puts a little dry kiss on his cheek. She squeezes his arm. "Any time." She pulls the door as far open as the furniture will let it go, so he can reach the screen door. "Bobby says you're writing a play. He's dying to read it."

The screen door spring twangs. Nathan steps out onto the porch. "It's not finished yet."

"He hoped the plays in those magazines would inspire you to finish it." She waddles out after him and pokes at the dirt in the flowerpots with a finger, to see if the plants need watering. "Donald says it's a cheerful play."

"So you'll like it, anyway." Nathan goes down the short porch steps into the sunshine. "I missed classes for three weeks. I have a lot of schoolwork to make up. But you tell him they did inspire me. I can't wait to get back to writing the play." He pulls open the door of Charlie's car. "Oh, and thank him for coming to see me when I was sick."

"He thinks the world of you," she calls.

MALCOLM COMES TO ANSWER THE BELL at the sprawling, white, shingle-sided Donald house. A low-roofed porch with heavy beams goes across the front of the house and around one side. In a torn sweatshirt and dirty work pants, Malcolm wipes greasy hands on a greasy rag and squints at Nathan through the screen door. Nathan holds out the radio. Malcolm says, "Donald's at the hospital."

"He looked all right when I saw him," Nathan says.

"He has to go for checkups all the time." Malcolm frowns, stuffs the rag into a hip pocket, and pushes open the screen door. "Hey, that's my radio. Where did you get it?"

"He lent it to me when I was sick," Nathan says.

"The son of a bitch." Malcolm takes the radio. "Claimed he didn't know anything about it. Said one of my friends must have swiped it."

"I didn't know," Nathan says.

"You should have suspected." Malcolm strokes the radio, turns it over in his hands, looking for damage. "When did Donald ever do anything nice for anybody?"

"It did seem a little funny," Nathan says.

"Ha-ha," Malcolm says, and slams the door.

THE TYPEWRITER KEYS RATTLE. It's late; how late he doesn't know and doesn't care. Now that he's made up all that schoolwork and the play is under way once more, he lives in panic fear that if he doesn't keep at it, the voices will go silent in his head, the words will dry up. Before he got sick, he didn't often worry about time. But then he damn near died, didn't he? And now it seems to him he could die at any minute. So he'd better get on with the play and finish it. A hand comes into the circle of lamplight and sets down a mug of steaming milk. He is so startled he nearly falls off the chair.

"Jesus, Frank, you scared me."

"Drink that," Frank says, "and go to bed." Then picks up the loudly ticking clock. "Look at that. Three in the morning. And it's not the first night, is it? It's every night, and you can't keep that up. You'll get sick again."

"If you don't want to lie awake listening to me," Nathan says, "why don't you drink that yourself?"

"Don't use that tone to me," Frank says.

"I'm sorry," Nathan says, "but I have to finish the play. *Giants in the Earth* has already opened. The Harlequin will have to start rehearsing a new play soon."

"And you want it to be yours?" Frank sits on the side of the cot. He nods at the mug. "Drink that."

"I want it to be mine." Nathan takes up the mug and blows at the steam. "Before I got sick, I had so many doubts about it, I couldn't make myself finish it."

"Well, I'm glad you got over that." Frank gives him a dry smile. "But three in the morning?"

"Schoolwork, work on the paper—I don't have a lot of free time."

"Yeah, well"—Frank gets to his feet—"what was it you told me George Kaufman said to the movie producer—'Do you want it good, or do you want it Wednesday?' "

Nathan drinks some of the hot milk and doesn't really hear Frank. He's reading lines on the page in the typewriter. They make him smile. Then that chill forms in his belly. What if the pneumonia had killed him? The words wouldn't have been here to smile at. He says, "Did you ever almost die, Frank? Like in the war?"

"In the war, I never got overseas. Stateside. Bands. Dusty parade grounds. For a while, I even had to play trombone riding a horse. But now you remind me, I did get shot once. I was playing E-flat alto sax with the Rollo Mills outfit in a speakeasy when the police raided it." Frank studies the shadowy ceiling. "Kansas City. When? Nineteen thirty? I dived for cover, and the bullet only hit me in the butt, so by dumb luck, I didn't even come close to dying. But it would have scared me out of the dance band business, except the talkies had finished off all the movie theater orchestras, and the Reed family had to eat."

"Didn't you think about dying a lot after that?"

"It wore off," Frank says. "Nathan—drink that milk and go to bed."

HE LAYS HIS SCHOOLBOOKS ON THE KITCHEN TABLE and opens the refrigerator. He is still thin, and always hungry. Half a meat loaf lies wrapped in wax paper on a plate. He makes himself a sandwich, drinks a glass of milk, washes up and puts things away, picks up his books, and goes quietly along the hall to the foot of the stairs. When he got home, he noticed a car in the driveway. This means Alma is with a client. But she's been listening for him, and now she calls in her merry professional voice:

"Nathan, guess who's here?"

Nathan steps to the wide, jigsaw-lacy opening of the living room. It's a bright day, but the room is gloomy, and he's not sure, for a second, who the woman is at the card-strewn table with Alma. Then she turns to smile at him, and wiggle her fingers in a little wave, and a sunbeam strikes her very fair hair, and he knows her.

"Mrs. Woodhead," he says. "How are you?"

"Fine, Nathan. My, how you've grown."

The Woodheads moved away some time ago. They used to live around the corner. Back then, because Gene Woodhead, like Nathan, was extra bright, the staff at the nearby junior high school got both boys transferred to Foothill Junior High, where the studies were tougher. And since the Reeds didn't own a car, it came about that on days too rainy for Nathan to ride his bike, Mrs. Woodhead drove him to and from school with Gene. New to California, Nathan had no friends then, so Gene became his friend. But that had ended months before they moved away. To avoid Gene, Nathan had found excuses not to go with Frank and Alma to supper at the Woodheads, or on picnics or excursions with them. Gene doesn't go to FOJC. His father wants him to have a jump on other boys when the U.S. gets into the war, so Gene is in Dodd Military Academy at the beach. Nathan doesn't care, but it's the polite thing to ask, so he asks:

"How's Gene doing?"

"See for yourself," Alma trills. "He's waiting for you in your room."

THE DOOR TO THE SLEEPING PORCH IS CLOSED. What for? Books angled at his hip, Nathan approaches it slowly, frowning. He lifts a fist to knock, then doesn't knock. It's his room, damn it. Alma shouldn't have put Gene into it in the first place. He will have to ask her not to do that again. He turns the knob, walks in. And stops dead.

Gene lies face up on the cot, naked except for socks and a blue officer's uniform cap. He has moved the pillows from the head of the cot to the foot so he faces Nathan. He grins and says, "Come in, and close the door." His long legs are spread apart. He lazily pumps his cock with one hand, runs the other hand on his chest and belly. Nathan shuts the door and drops his books.

"Stop that." He stands over Gene. "Are you crazy? What the hell do you think you're doing?" He looks around. Gene's clothes are on the chair, uniform trousers neatly folded, tunic hung over the chair back. Undershorts and undershirt lie on the trousers. Nathan snatches these up and flings them at him. "Get dressed. Get off my bed."

Gene pauses in his slow masturbating, but only for an instant, to flip the white knit garments off the cot. He doesn't stop grinning, but his eyebrows go up. "What's the matter with you? Get naked, Nathan. Lie down. You used to like to do it with me. Summer before last? In the tent in my backyard? Don't tell me you've forgotten. I sure as hell haven't."

"Come on, Gene. That was little kid stuff."

Gene laughs, looks down at his cock, proudly waves it. "Yeah, well, it's not so little anymore, is it?" He sits up suddenly, reaches out, catches Nathan's belt. "And I'll bet yours isn't, either. Let's see."

Nathan knocks his hand away. "Get dressed."

"Come on, Nathan." Gene lunges again, grabs where he has no right to grab, and squeezes. Sitting on the side of the bed, hand moving fast on his cock now, making the old springs squeak, he laughs up into Nathan's face. "Hey, you're already half hard. Come on. You want to do it. You know—you—do." He tries to run down Nathan's fly.

"No." Nathan gives him a shove, so he falls back across the cot, but he doesn't let it break his rhythm. Nathan bends over him to grab him and wrestle him to his feet. Gene yelps, and semen splashes Nathan's face. He jerks upright, wiping at his face with a hand. Gene lies back with his eyes shut, laughing between gasps for breath. "Baby Jesus," he pants, and opens his eyes. "Now, don't tell me that wasn't fun."

Nathan is shaking. He stoops, picks up Gene's shorts and undershirt, mops his face with them, pushes them into Gene's face, and scrubs them around, while Gene laughs. Nathan says, "Now, put those on and get out of my room."

"But you haven't come yet." Gene sits up, pulls on the undershorts, reaches out again and squeezes Nathan's crotch. "It's still hard."

"It doesn't have any sense," Nathan says. "I do."

Gene pulls on his undershirt. "You were nicer when it was little kid stuff." He stands, picks up his trousers, kicks into them. They have very sharp creases. "When you didn't think about it, when I just pried it out of your pants and jerked it a couple times and you squirted like a shook-up bottle of pop." He giggles to himself. "It surprised hell out of you the first time. I still remember the look on your face."

"I didn't know what it was all about," Nathan says.

"You still don't." Gene zips up his fly, buckles his belt, puts on his shiny shoes. "You look grown-up, but you're not." He lifts his tunic off the chair back, shrugs into it, briskly buttons it up to his chin. "What are you going to do with that hard-on when I'm gone?"

Nathan picks up his books. "Take a cold shower."

"Just like coach tells us to." Gene finds his cap on the floor, flicks dust off it, puts it on. "Sure you are." Hand on the doorknob, he says, "Let me know when you're ready to quit lying to yourself." He goes out and shuts the door.

WAYNE HOTCHKISS'S HOUSE SQUATS on a downhill lot below street level, a dark gray, one-story, stucco place with shaggy trees bending over its faded red tile roof. Beside it, the driveway is almost as overgrown as the Reeds'. Charlie Vorak and Kenneth Stone have lined their cars up behind Hotchkiss's tonight. And now Donald Donald parks Malcolm's Model T at the end of the line. It sticks out over the sidewalk, but when Nathan points this out, Donald only shrugs and strolls off into the twilit shadow of the house, making for the garage, where yellow light falls from a side door into flower beds choked with weeds. Donald stands in the light and announces loudly:

"The playwright approacheth."

Ragged cheers and clapping come from inside. Donald goes in, Nathan following. A naked lightbulb from a cobwebby rafter shines down on a worn-out carpet, a pair of saggy old sofas, a hard-used desk that holds Hotchkiss's typewriter, a small hooded lamp, bottles of White Horse scotch, glasses, and a bucket of ice cubes. Drinks in hand, Charlie and Peg, Buddy and Kenneth Stone sit on the sofas, Hotchkiss on a straight chair at the desk. He squints through cigarette smoke at his watch.

"What kept you?"

"When I didn't show up with a corsage," Donald says, "Nathan didn't want to ride with me."

Nathan scowls. "He was late."

"Have a drink." Hotchkiss gropes for a glass, knocks it to the rug, ignores it, takes another, and plinks into it those ice cubes that don't also fall to the rug. He seems awfully unsteady to Nathan, but it doesn't appear to trouble him. He acts happy. "Nothing like a tot of highland dew to make us forget our little differences."

Nathan holds out to him the pint of brandy.

Hotchkiss blinks. "Isn't this the cure-all I brought you when you were sick?"

"Charlie asked would there be free booze, and you said, 'Bring your own bottle.' It's the only bottle I had."

Hotchkiss shakes his head sadly. "Here I thought this was what snatched you from the jaws of death, and you haven't even pulled the cork."

"That was probably what saved him," Buddy says.

"Read us your play," Stone calls.

"Where shall I sit?" Nathan says.

"Sit here." Hotchkiss wavers to his feet. "The lamp will help you see. But first"—he reaches for and knocks over the whiskey bottle, and just catches it before it can roll off the desk—"let's freshen everybody's drink." He stumbles around cheerfully tilting the bottle over glasses, till he can set it down empty and, clutching his own glass, slump down beside Stone with a satisfied sigh.

"Ret the levels begin," he says.

"Hold it." Donald Donald goes to the door. "Permit the stage designer to create a little atmosphere here, a little theatrical nuance." He clicks off the overhead light. Now they are all in deep shadow except Nathan at the desk, the hooded lamp bending light onto the white pages of the play that rattle in his trembling fingers.

"Take some scotch to calm you down," Charlie says.

Nathan obeys, gasps, makes a face at the glass, and sets it far away from him, back out of the light, out of reach, unless he stretches for it. "It tastes like medicine."

"That's the peat smoke," Hotchkiss says.

"It's the mildew from old bagpipes," says Charlie.

"Nathan's waiting to read his play," Peg says.

"And I'm waiting to hear it." Stone smiles and gestures with an open hand to Nathan. "Nathan, please?"

Nathan finds the scotch glass, gulps from it, clears his throat, and reads, " 'Act One. It's—' "

"Does your play have a title?" Peg asks gently.

"What? Oh, God, I forgot." Nathan feels stupid. He wishes he hadn't come. *The Shotgun Flat,*" he mumbles.

"How do you tune a shotgun?" Buddy asks.

"No, no," Hotchkiss says. "A shotgun flat is an apartment built with all the rooms in a row. You could stand at the front door and fire a shotgun and the blast would go straight out the back door."

Nathan gives him a wan smile. " 'It's morning,' " he reads, " 'and Frank Barber, Alma Barber, and Aunt Marie, her older sister, are in the kitchen. It's not an ordinary kitchen. It has a lot of books in its cupboards, along with the canned goods and chinaware, and a lot of musical instruments lying around, the kind you usually see hanging in the windows of pawnshops. Frank and Alma are at the table, Aunt Marie is at the stove dishing up food, and Nathan sits on the floor, playing with a dented trumpet. He is four years old—' "

"Gee, this play couldn't be autobiographical, by any chance, could it?"

"Shut up, Charlie," Peg says. "Go on, Nathan."

"Yeah, go on," Buddy says. "I like it already—it's got a trumpet in it. Any jazz?"

"In the second act." Nathan shuffles the pages of the play. "Maybe I should just read that part. It's a good scene." He can't seem to find it. "I don't think you really want to hear the whole play." He gulps some more whiskey, licks his thumb, pages through the script again. "I mean, it's awfully long." The pages fall off his lap and slither across the rug. With a silent moan, he drops to his knees to gather them up. "It'll put you to sleep."

"Nathan," Stone says sternly, "read us your play."

"Yes sir," Nathan whispers, straightens the pages, reads.

AT FIRST, HE IS AWARE OF THEIR SHADOWY SHAPES beyond his circle of lamplight, of their breathing, the tinkle of ice in their glasses as they drink. But soon the sound of his own voice going on and on in this odd unfinished place is all he hears. He's as absorbed in what he's reading as if he were alone in the night on his sleeping porch at home. Then there is a new sound. He squints into the dark. Hotchkiss's chin rests on his chest and he snores. Stone nudges him, and he jerks awake, startled. "What's going on?"

"Shush," Peg says. "Nathan's reading."

"And I'm listening." Hotchkiss struggles to get up, waving broomstick legs. "Time to freshen drinks again."

"Wait'll the end of the act." Stone sounds drowsy too.

Hotchkiss lurches to his feet, stumbles to the desk and bends over it, leaning heavily on Nathan's shoulder. "S'wonderful stuff, Nathan. Totally original. I'm so glad"—he finds a full scotch bottle, waves it in triumph—"we're doing this. Go down in the annals of American literature as a night when—"

From somewhere not far off comes a woman's scream. Muffled. In the house? "That's Joanie," Charlie Vorak says, and scrambles up off the couch.

Hotchkiss nods slow agreement. "That's Joanie, all right. I'd know that shriek anywhere." He fills his glass. "Don't be alarmed. It's probably ants in the kitchen. She dramatizes life a lot." He turns, tottering, steadying himself again on Nathan's shoulder, blinking at the darkness outside the open door.

Charlie starts off. "I'd better go see."

But there's no time. A woman appears in the doorway. The overhead light glares on. She is thin, small, very like a college girl at first glance, until Nathan sees how tired her face looks, lined with vexation. Vexation is in the way she snaps her eyes now, sizing up the scene, its characters: Nathan still seated, clutching his script, staring; Charlie and Peg standing; Buddy looking pale, searching with his eyes for his wheelchair that has been pushed into a far corner; Stone asleep, head thrown back, mouth open, his glass tilted, ready to spill.

"Didn't you hear me scream?" his wife asks Hotchkiss.

"I'd have heard it on campus." He is shakily lighting a bent cigarette. "What's supposed to be the matter?"

"Supposed to be!" she yelps. She waves an arm behind her. "There's some rotten pervert looking in the windows. I just got the kids to bed, I was going to have a quiet bath, I was undoing my blouse, when I happened to look up, and here's this horrible, leering face—"

Nathan stands up. "Where's Donald?"

Everyone gapes around. Even Stone, glassily. Donald is missing. Nathan tells Joanie, "Don't worry. He's just a prankster. He thinks he's being funny."

She glares at Nathan. "Someone you know?" She glares at Hotchkiss. "Someone you invited, is he? Another of your baby geniuses? God, what a filthy, wretched place. And you're drunk. You're all of you disgusting drunk."

Out front, the Model T starts. Its motor clatters like it's going to fly to pieces. Nathan bolts out the door. "Donald?" He stumbles up the driveway, legs wobbly, head reeling. And he's too late. The Model T lurches into the street. Nathan shouts, "How am I supposed to get home?" But Donald keeps on going in reverse until he reaches the corner, when he changes gears and speeds away, looking back over his shoulder, jeering.

Nathan staggers back toward the garage. He sweats. His stomach churns. Charlie and Peg meet him. Charlie hands him his manuscript. "You can ride with us."

"Thank you," Nathan says feebly. "Excuse me." He lunges to the flower bed and throws up, hangs over the flower bed, drooling strings of vomit, ready to die of shame. Peg comes, takes the script from him, lays a cool hand on his forehead. "Poor boy," she says.

"I'm disgusting," he moans. "Don't watch me."

"You sure you'll be all right?" He nods, and she says, "Okay, then. We'll wait in the car."

Inside the garage, Joanie screams that all Hotchkiss does out here is drink. A glass smashes to punctuate the sentence. "You're supposed to be writing a novel." Another glass underscores that word. "Where is it? Show it to me, Wayne. You can't, can you?"

"Can't find it, Joanie," Hotchkiss says. "Too drunk."

"Too drunk, hell." This warrants another smashed glass.

Nathan's stomach heaves again, and up comes still more White Horse whiskey mixed with Alma's roast lamb and mint jelly and chocolate pudding, all turned sour. Out his mouth, up his nose. God, is he ever sick.

Joanie shrills, "You can't find it because there isn't any novel. And there never will be. Never."

Wiping miserably at his mouth, Nathan hears a familiar rattling sound. It's Buddy's wheelchair. He squats down behind Hotchkiss's car. He doesn't want Stone to see him like this. Or Buddy, either. Stone wheels Buddy past. The door of Stone's car opens.

Joanie rants on, "You piss your novel away down Laughing Jack's latrine, with that creepy Communist nobody else on the faculty even speaks to—your best pal, of course."

The door of Stone's car closes. The trunk opens, and the wheelchair clatters as Stone lays it inside. The trunk closes down. Stone gets into his car and starts it.

Joanie jeers, "Why should you bother to write? Any time you want to feel like a big shot, you can fill this crummy garage with misfits and cripples, children to goggle at your erudition, how clever you are, how worldly-wise. . . ."

Nathan's stomach muscles grab and double him over. On his knees, he heaves noisily, but nothing comes up. He climbs weakly to his feet. Sweat has soaked his shirt. He shivers. Stone and Buddy back out the driveway.

Hotchkiss says, "Oh, give your mouth a rest," and the garage door slams. It's pitch dark, but Nathan hears him wobble past. The door jerks open, the light pouring out again. Joanie yells, "Do me a favor! Don't come back!"

"Never fear." Hotchkiss's voice comes from afar.

Sharp fingers grab Nathan's arm. He is jerked around to face Joanie. "What the hell are you doing? Dear God—wipe the vomit off yourself and get away from here." She lets go his arm as if she were throwing it away. "Disgusting." She stalks off. "The hallowed halls of academe. Peace, order, learning, the gentle life of scholars.

Shit." The house door opens, children's voices pipe anxiously from inside. She calls wearily, "It's all right. Mommy's coming." The house door slams.

TRAVERS JONES STANDS AT MOON'S KITCHEN screen door, in his apron, sweating from the stove heat, a pan of sausages in his hand. For a second he is blank with surprise. Then he makes a hideous face. "What are you doing at the back door? Applying for work? You want to be a scullery boy?"

"I want to be a playwright." Nathan holds out *The Shotgun Flat*. It is in a new folder. The old one got vomit on it. "Will you read this, Travers, please. I'd like the Harlequin to put it on."

"You're pale, you're trembling." Travers unhooks the screen door and pushes it open. "Why? You surely can't be afraid of me. We're friends. Come in."

"You know all about plays." Nathan comes in. The heat is breathtaking. "I'm afraid you'll think it's no good."

"Not if what Wayne Hotchkiss says is true."

Nathan grimaces. "He was drunk when he heard it."

Travers takes the script. He smiles thinly, cocks a knowing eyebrow. "And so were you, I'm told."

Moon squawks, "Travers, the ragged, starving multitudes are about to snatch the food off the stove."

Nathan says, "That's why I came to the back door."

Travers laughs. "Oh, come now, Nathan. Everybody sicks up the first time. It's a rite of passage."

"They're laughing about it," Nathan grumbles.

"And the way to handle that is to go in to breakfast with them and laugh about it yourself." Travers waves the folder toward the swing door. "Go on, they've been missing you. We all have."

Nathan sulks. "They asked to hear my play, then all they did was get drunk."

Moon wails, "Saint Michael and all angels, Travers."

Travers tells Nathan, "Stop acting like a child." He slaps the script on top of the refrigerator, bangs the pan of sausages on the stove, gathers up plates from the service window, and sails out with them through the swinging door. Nathan follows, and collides with Sheila O'Hare. The blond girl is carrying a bin of dirty dishes. She sits down on the floor. The dishes go sliding every which way. Nathan tells her how sorry he is, gathers them up, takes the heavy bin off her, and pushes into the kitchen with it. "No, no." She scrambles up and follows. Moon gives the two of them a glare from her place at the looming black stove.

"Keep your courting out of my kitchen," she says.

"He just took it away from me," Sheila says helplessly.

"My fault," Nathan says, and sets the bin by the sinks.

Sheila tugs at her rumpled uniform, brushes a strand of hair off her forehead, and hastily gathers up three more breakfasts from the service window. She hurries past him, with a pretty smile and a whispered "Thank you," and this time it's Travers she almost collides with. Stonily, he holds the door open for her to go out, then marches straight to the stove, pointedly not making a face at Nathan.

HOTCHKISS, CHARLIE, AND BUDDY ALL GRIN stupid grins at Nathan when he pulls out a chair and sits down at the table under the Acme beer sign. "Three days," Hotchkiss says. "That's some kind of record for a hangover."

"What took three days," Nathan says, "was getting over being sore at you. Three days, and three all-night walks." He holds up a foot so Hotchkiss can see the sole of his shoe. "You want to buy me a new pair?"

Charlie and Buddy look alarmed. This is not how they talk to Hotchkiss. They have certainly never heard Nathan talk to him this way.

Hotchkiss turns pale. "You were late," he says.

"That was Donald's fault. I'll take the bus next time. I'd have been a hell of a lot better off without him. He wrecked the whole thing."

Hotchkiss shakes his head. "Only the last part. No, I started it," he says humbly. "Forgive me, Nathan. No excuse for my getting so smashed."

"You didn't take it seriously," Nathan says. "None of you. Why would you? I'm nothing but a high school kid. I proved that, didn't I, by the way I held my liquor?"

"Forget that," Buddy says. "It's a good play, Nathan. We all thought so. Terrific. Funny and sad, like all your stuff. And honest. No fakery."

Travers bangs coffee down for Nathan. It slops in the saucer. "Will there be anything else?" he asks frostily.

"Don't be sore," Nathan says. "Next time, I'll carry the dirty dishes for you, okay?" He smiles hard. He's done another stupid thing, hasn't he? After giving Travers the play to read, he's gone and made him jealous. Of Sheila, of all people. A girl. What are girls to Nathan? He's not interested in girls. "I'll even wash the whole load for you, how about that? I'll be your scullery boy."

After a grudging pause, Travers trots fingertips through Nathan's hair, makes a silly face at him, and swishes off to fetch him something to eat.

Charlie looks after him in disgust. "I'm glad I'm fat and homely. I'd hate having them after me all the time."

"He's only kidding," Nathan says. "Wish me luck. I've given him the play to read."

"We've touted it to him," Hotchkiss says.

Nathan nods, burns his mouth on the coffee. "He told me and I appreciate it." But he has had a startling idea. He watches Sheila set plates on a nearby table, then hurry to take money at the cash register. She smiles while she counts out change. Her mouth is a nice shape, teeth very white and only a little crooked. He looks at Charlie. "If I fill the gas tank," he says, "can I borrow your car again?"

THE ADDRESS IS A BUNGALOW COURT ON MAPLE WAY.
He switches off the engine and the lights, and sits in the car. His
mouth is dry. His heart beats fast. Sweat leaks down his ribs. He
wishes it wouldn't. He's wearing all new clothes. That ought to make
him feel good by itself. It doesn't. He is anxious and depressed. He
doesn't want to be here. But he has to be, doesn't he? He has to.

Most of the time, as Charlie and Peg drove him home from
Hotchkiss's the other night, he slept, slumped in a corner of the
backseat. But he woke up now and then. And there they were, side
by side in the front, Charlie's hand resting lightly, affectionately on
the nape of Peg's neck, beneath the rich, dark fall of her hair. Once,
halted at a stop sign, they kissed. Their voices were low, and sometimes they laughed quietly, privately. They were in love, and happy
with each other. They slept together—everyone said so.

He tried to picture it, the two of them lying naked in each
other's arms in that rumpled bed that pulls down from a closet in
Charlie's shabby, paper-strewn apartment. Plump Charlie—freckled
all over? Peg, with her creamy skin, long legs, small breasts, moth-
erly hips. The picture wouldn't hold. It fell apart like a jigsaw puzzle
sliding off a tilted table.

In his cot on the sleeping porch, the wind sighing in the pines
outside, he's tried over and over to put the picture back together—
only with himself instead of Charlie, and instead of Peg, some girl,
any girl. But this picture won't hold either. As he drifts into sleep,
the vague girl shape he hugs against his nakedness becomes Gene
Woodhead's. And Nathan is doing with him what Gene wanted him
to do that crazy afternoon weeks ago. Willingly, happily, frantically.
And he wakes, heart pounding, belly wet with semen. It angers him
and scares him.

He has to change it. There has to be a girl, a real girl. Sheila
O'Hare is sunny, good-tempered, almost pretty, has always smiled
at him. And he doesn't know any other girls. So he climbs out of
Charlie's car and trudges up the dim strip of walk between the
bungalows. A chunky little woman in a gas station uniform with a

red Texaco star stitched to the pocket opens the door. Cats swarm around her feet, bumping her legs, looking up at her and squalling.

"You're here for Sheila, are you? Get away."

"Roz!" Sheila protests from someplace out of sight. "Don't tell Nathan to get away."

Roz grins at Nathan through the screen. "I didn't mean you— I meant the cats." She turns and calls into the back of the house, "Ruby, are you feeding the cats or not?"

Nathan glimpses another Roz, who appears in a far, lighted doorway for a minute: same chunky shape, same gas station uniform. It's like seeing double. "I can't do it alone!" she shouts. "What's keeping you?"

"Best-looking boy I ever saw in my life." Roz wiggles her eyebrows at Nathan. "Sheila, if you don't hurry, I'll go off with him myself."

"I'm here, I'm here." Breathless, laughing, coat over her arm, Sheila comes to the door. "Hello," she says.

"Ready?" Nathan asks. But he's really asking himself.

"THEY'RE TWINS," SHEILA SAYS IN THE CAR as they head toward Sierra Street. She's pretty tonight, lively, smiling, and he likes the blouse she's chosen, and the pink cardigan she's hung around her shoulders, and the little single pearl on a thin gold chain. "They own a filling station, they're happy all the time, and they collect cats."

"And girls named Sheila?" Nathan says. "How come?"

Her glow dims. "That's a long story."

"Are they your aunts or something?"

"Not really. Old friends of my mother. See, when I was very small, my father fell under a train and lost both legs. He's bedridden. Nerve damage or something. He was young, and he hated it. He resented any time my mother gave to me. Roz and Ruby sized up the situation and thought I needed love, a warmer place. They didn't say so, not for a long time, but when they did, they didn't get any argument. I wanted to go with them, and my father wanted me gone."

"What about your mother?"

"I was a sore point between him and her," Sheila says, "always causing fights. I guess she thought she'd have some peace, at last. She packed my things, kissed me good-bye, shut the door, and never shed a tear."

"How old were you?"

"Seven and a half."

"And you never went back?"

"Roz and Ruby make me go sometimes." Sheila gives a little shrug. "I know my father's in pain all the time. And I always go say hello to him. He doesn't speak. Mostly he won't even look at me. So I sit with my mother in the front room, but she can't think of anything to say to me. I try to keep talking, but she doesn't listen—she's listening for my father to call out. I don't stay long."

"That's terrible," Nathan says. "I'm lucky. My parents love me."

She throws him a quick smile. "That would be easy."

This alarms him, and a wheel hits the curb as he swings Charlie's car in at the theater parking lot. They walk toward the bright box office, and her hand brushes his. He wants to step away so it doesn't happen again. But this is not what he should want, so he squelches what he feels, and after he buys the tickets, he takes her hand. It is small, soft, and damp, and it doesn't give him joy.

While cartoons squawk and jitter on the screen, Sheila leads him along an empty row to seats away from others in the dark. Music booms, and the title of the main movie comes on in massive black and white. He scarcely notices. He's not alone. He has brought a girl. In a panic, he calls to mind the hours of talk he has heard from boys on the subject of girls. Not because he was interested—he wasn't, and he couldn't understand why they were—but because he has the kind of memory he has, so sticky he can write out whatever he hears in reams if he chooses. This is why Charlie and Buddy titled his column "the Listener."

So he knows that now, or very soon, he must put his arm across the back of Sheila's seat. Later, when the mood of the movie is right, he can move his arm slightly, so it is across her shoulders. If there's a love scene, he must lean close and smell the perfume of her hair. If there's a passionate kiss in the moonlight or something, maybe he can turn her head to him and kiss her mouth. It chills him to rehearse this stuff in his mind. But he is soon easy. This picture doesn't look like it's going to have many scenes of that kind in it.

He does lay his arm across her seat back, and she turns him a smile. Later, she gives a little impatient sigh, and wiggles her shoulders, and he guesses it's time to move his arm so he's touching her. Through the thin fabric of the blouse, her skin is warm and smooth. Soft. Alien. She gives him another smile. Watching the picture, he almost forgets her. Then, suddenly, she makes a low humming sound and lays her head on his chest. Oh, Jesus. He gives her hair a quick, nuzzling kiss. That's how he's heard it's done. Nuzzling. Her hair smells faintly of tar soap.

With a soft laugh she lifts her face to him. He shuts his eyes and kisses her mouth. She opens her mouth. Dear God. French-kissing. Do they really? Despairing, he opens his mouth and puts his tongue into her mouth. She moans quietly, shivers, her tongue meets his. She grabs the back of his neck with one hand. The other hand slides on his thigh. Through the strugglings of their tongues she makes urgent mumblings. Finally, impatient, she grabs his hand and lays it on her thigh, under her skirt.

Then her hand gets busy at his fly, digs inside, gets hold and pries his stiff cock out of his shorts. He slides his hand under the elastic of her panties and touches the downy place between her legs, soft and slippery damp. She gives a little cry of delight as his finger slides inside her. She pumps away at his cock. He does for her what he's heard a hundred boys brag they've done with girls at the movies. He never thought he would. He is stunned. She moans. He gasps. She shudders. He shoots.

She falls back panting in her seat, tugging down her skirt. He stuffs his cock away, grabs his handkerchief, and tries to mop the semen from his new pants. She sits up, arranging the pink sweater around her shoulders. She gives him a secret grin, bends across to kiss him briskly, and to whisper, "Ooh, wasn't it nice?" He gulps, kisses her in return. "Wonderful," he lies, and worries what the dry cleaners will think of his pants.

Outside, walking to the car, she says, "What a weird movie. The way everybody talked so fast. All those jokes. I couldn't understand half what they were saying."

FRANK SWALLOWS HIS LAST FORKFUL of scrambled eggs, pulls off his napkin, and lays it by his plate. He pushes back his chair, stands, ruffles Nathan's hair. "It's nice having you here for breakfast every day." He picks up the plate and carries it to the sink. "I'd begun to think you only materialized at sunset."

"About three thirty"—Nathan slurps coffee—"when I get home from school."

"That reminds me," Alma says, frowning at the cards she has laid out, "that girl called for you again."

Nathan spears chunks of fried potato on his fork and with them mops ketchup off his plate. "I saw your note. Thank you."

"She's rung three times this week." Alma gathers up the cards. "Aren't you ever going to call her back?"

Nathan fills his mouth and shrugs.

"She sounds like a nice girl. Polite. Well-spoken. And cheerful. I like that in young people." She waits for him to look at her, and when he does, her expression is displeased. "You're a regular Gloomy Gus lately."

Frank laughs. "That's how you get when the girls won't leave you alone." He shrugs into his white Atheneum jacket and gives Nathan's shoulder a jokey nudge with his fist. "That's why you don't take breakfast at that Moon place anymore, right? Keeping out of her way?"

Nathan feels himself turn red. "That's about it."

"Well, I've got some advice for you about that." Frank looks at the fancy wristwatch he's buying on time with his new paychecks, then arches an eyebrow at Alma. "If your mother will excuse us?"

"I'll go take my bath." She lays the deck of cards in a cupboard. "You go ahead and have your man talk." She breezes off, chin in air. "I guess if I stayed, I wouldn't learn very much." The swing door flaps behind her.

Nathan finishes off the last piece of toast, which he has swamped in grape jelly. "What advice?"

"Tell every boy you know what a great lay she is, how easy, what a pushover. If it's a lie, she'll be so busy fighting them off, she won't have time for you, and if it's the truth, she'll soon forget you."

Nathan chokes, gulps coffee, stares at him. "Frank. You shock hell out of me. That's repulsive."

Frank holds up his hands, palms out. "Sorry. I forgot for a minute you're made of finer stuff than your old man." He looks at the watch again. "Whoa. Gotta run." He rubs the back of Nathan's neck. "Just tell her you're not interested. She'll burst into tears, or slap your face, but stand your ground." His heels thump the back porch. "You might as well practice. With your looks, it's going to keep happening." The screen door bangs. He's gone.

Nathan walks hunchy side street sidewalks through sunlight and tree shade, to the bungalow court on Maple Way. It's Saturday. There's no school. Moon's is closed. So Sheila will be home, won't she? Home alone. Roz and Ruby will be at the gas station. He has to try again. When he kissed Sheila good night after the movie, he returned Charlie's car, then walked until 4:00 A.M., trying to figure out why he was so miserable. Any other boy his age would have been out of his mind with joy. He didn't figure it out.

And when he climbed the honeysuckle vine, stripped his new clothes, fell exhausted into bed, and shut his sorry eyes, nothing had changed. He dreamed as he'd dreamed before, and woke twice in the lonely darkness smeared with his own jism, as if he'd never spurted in her happy fist at all. It's happened night after night this week— not with Gene, now, with boys he's seen in the showers after gym, boys whose names he doesn't even know.

But never once with a girl, never once with Sheila. Why? He's driven himself half crazy asking that. Gloomy Gus, Alma calls him. She doesn't know the half of it. If he could only talk to Frank. Frank's always straightened him out. But Frank wouldn't listen to this, would he? He would scoff at the idea Nathan was turning out to be a sissy boy. So he's got to try again with Sheila, doesn't he? He's got to. Maybe what's wrong is that what they did at the movie was no different, really, from what he and Gene used to do in that sun-baked summer tent.

Maybe today they can do the real thing. In Sheila's bed. Naked, clasping each other as it's supposed to happen. He doesn't want to do it. The idea sickens him. But he's reached the bungalow court now. Going up the walk, dry-mouthed, heart thumping, he wants to run away. The idea of her bed panics him. He'd rather it happened in his bed. To banish those dreams. When? Tomorrow, Sunday, when Alma's at the Spiritualist church, and Frank is playing chess and swapping stories with the old men in the park. Tomorrow? He snorts derision at himself. He's trying to put it off.

He takes a deep breath and pushes the doorbell. No one answers. He leans to peer through a window. On a table inside, a gray striped cat sleeps in a spot of sunshine. He taps on the glass. "Sheila?" The cat opens an eye, looks at him, stretches its legs, quivering, then curls up tighter than before and goes back to sleep. He pushes the bell button again. In the Saturday morning quiet, he can hear the buzz from back in the kitchen. But nobody comes. Maybe she's taking a bath. He sits on the step for ten minutes, then gets up and tries once more. No Sheila. Damn. She's the only one who can save him. And where is she? If he doesn't find her, now, today, he's lost.

FROM HIS WALKS, he knows every filling station in Fair Oaks. And the Texaco station that belongs to Roz and Ruby surely has to be the one where cats hang around all night, playing, sleeping, stalking mice and crickets in the tall weeds of the vacant lot next door.

Doesn't it? It does. Roz is cleaning the windshield of a car. Ruby is inside the tin-and-glass office, seated at a desk, working on accounts or something. Cats sleep on a pyramid of motor oil cans. Cats play on the desk. A young, skinny one pats Ruby's moving pencil, tries to bite the eraser.

"Excuse me," Nathan says. "Where's Sheila?"

Ruby looks up, startled. "Oh, it's you."

"She tried to phone me. I want to talk to her."

Roz comes up, smelling of gasoline, wiping stubby hands on a greasy rag. "She's gone home to mother. Got tired of our company." Roz's small, square face is grim and hurt.

"Oh, now, Roz," Ruby says, and smiles at Nathan, though there isn't a lot to the smile. "They fired her at Moon's Café, she looked for another job all week and couldn't find anything, and she's moved to the beach with her mother—"

"And that self-pitying son of a bitch, Michael." Roz opens the lid of a red chest and pulls from a bed of chipped ice three bottles of Coca-Cola. She pries off the caps and hands a bottle to Nathan and a bottle to Ruby, and keeps one for herself. "He'll torment her, same as when she was little."

Nathan drinks some of the icy Coke. "She told me he hates her. And her mother hardly speaks to her."

Roz nods grimly. "But when a female her age gets an idea in her head, there's no reasoning with 'em." Roz tilts up her Coke and drinks off half of it. "And Sheila all of a sudden decided Fair Oaks is hell on earth, and to get shut of it, she'll even put up with her father."

"Keep your temper," Ruby says. "She'll come back."

"Why did she lose her job?" Nathan asks.

Roz shrugs. "It wasn't fair. That's all she said." A car swings in and stops by the pumps. She sets her Coke down and heads for it, calling out, "Yes sir, good morning."

Nathan leans in the office door and asks Ruby, "Where at the beach? Which town? Can you write down her address for me? The telephone number?"

Ruby looks pained, apologetic, shakes her head. "I'm sorry, Nathan. She made us swear not to. She said everybody hates her here, and some of them might make trouble for her, and not to tell anybody where she's gone."

THE HOUSE STANDS UP ISOLATED, white-walled with red tile roofs, round turrets, and deep windows, at the top of a long, winding road that climbs into the foothills above Fair Oaks. He has passed it once or twice on his night walks. Then it was always asleep. Now, in the sunny noontime stillness, it seems still asleep. Young, slender eucalyptus trees stand in spaced clumps beside the road. The empty slopes he has passed have taken on the tender young green of spring, the California spring that comes so early and lasts so short a time. There are patches of blue lupine, red joe-pye, and yolk yellow poppies; yuccas stand up stiffly everywhere, creamy with blossoms at their tops. Crows caw. He looks up. There are three of them. They row raggedly through the dense blue of the sky, heavy, idle, in no hurry. A meadowlark sings.

He has stood here in the middle of the curving street long enough, staring up at the house, a chill in his belly, a sense of doom in his heart. Wooden gates with massive black iron hinges stand open to a driveway. He climbs the driveway, then red tile steps that take him past sandy, cactus-grown landscaping to a broad archway under which the front door waits, made of planks like the gate, with the same kind of heavy black hardware.

Bleakly he presses a bell push and hears chimes ring inside the house, ring in a large echoing emptiness. He could turn and run. It's not too late, not yet. But he's like some little animal meeting a snake. He can't move. He laughs sourly inside. Why can't he stop lying to himself today—first that he wanted sex with Sheila, and now that he doesn't want what waits beyond this door? He presses the button again. A voice calls from a distance. "Pepito?" And it's all he can do to keep himself from turning tail and running like hell. But it's too late.

There's a rattle of bolts and chains, the door opens, and Desmond Foley stands there tying the sash of a black kimono, wincing in the sunlight, his red hair rumpled from sleep. "Dear God," he croaks, "it's you."

"I'm sorry I woke you." Nathan turns away. "I'll come back some other time."

"No, don't go." Nathan halts, despairing. Foley works up a smile. "Come inside. What time is it?"

"I don't have a watch, but it must be almost noon."

"Disgraceful." Foley shakes his head, runs a hand down over his face. "I'm ashamed of myself, sleeping so late."

"It's Saturday," Nathan says. "Everybody ought to sleep as late as they want on Saturday."

"Come in." Foley steps back and beckons him. He is barefoot. His skin is very white. Blue veins show in his long-toed, slender feet. Nathan steps inside, where it is cool. Foley closes the door and moves through a high foyer, where his voice echoes off curved white stucco walls and sleek, terra-cotta tiles. "I'm so happy you've come. I like company at breakfast." He calls into a resonance of vacant rooms, "Pepito—breakfast by the pool, please." He lays a hand on Nathan's shoulder. He points. "It's out there. You'll think there's no end to the rooms, but eventually you'll find French doors to a terrace, and stairs down to the pool. Just persevere. I'll take a quick shower and join you right away." He starts up a staircase that has wrought iron railings, calling again into the emptiness of the house, "Pepito?" This time there's a faraway shout in reply, and Foley calls, "A mimosa for my friend, please, right away?" And to Nathan, with a smile, "I won't be five minutes." And he's gone.

He's right about the house. It's very big. The rooms are like a movie set, all space and loftiness and white walls and double doorways. Deep carpets. Handsome furniture. Not much of it, just enough. The light fixtures are of the same black wrought iron as the fittings of the doors and gates. Spanish colonial, right? He thinks that's right. Or Mediterranean. Or both. He will have to read more about architecture. Writers have to know these things, the names.

Silver glints on a carved sideboard in a dining room. In another room he glimpses a white grand piano and a concert harp in a canvas cover. Here's a room with white wicker furniture, Mexican pottery, and books and magazines strewn around, not casually, really, but meant to look like it.

And there are the French doors. He goes out onto a terrace where tall spiky plants rise from stucco jars, and round white tables and white metal chairs bake in the sun. They all stand in puddles of their own shadow. He goes down the steps to the pool. It is bigger than he dreamed it to be—and he has dreamed of it often since Donald told him about it when Nathan was sick. It is as blue as in his dreams, but it is empty, and in his dreams it is always alive with naked boys. And not just swimming, either. Shoes scrape the stairs behind him, and Nathan feels his face turn red at what he is thinking. He turns guiltily.

A frail little old man with brown skin and white hair and wearing a white waiter's jacket, not unlike Frank's, gives him a gap-toothed smile, a deferential nod, and sets a tray on a poolside table. With a napkin he flicks dust off the table next to it, pulls out a chair, flicks the dust off that, and spreads the table with a crisp white cloth. He lays down folded napkins, knives, forks, spoons.

"Will the senor sit here?"

"Thank you." Nathan goes and sits and watches the man pour from a dewy glass pitcher a beautiful liquid. He fills a tall stemmed glass with this and sets it in front of Nathan. Nathan blinks. "What is it?"

"It is call a mimosa, senor," the man says.

"What gives it that color?"

Pepito chuckles. "You will know when you taste it." He turns away, turns back. "Will senor have the coffee, also?"

Nathan tastes the mimosa. Someone has done something shocking to orange juice. He swallows, nods tearfully, whispers, "Yes, please, coffee." Champagne, that's what it is. The bubbles go up your nose. The alcohol punches you in the chest. He glances up at the house. Is this how rich people start their day? Still, it's been a

long walk. He's thirsty. The sun is hot, and he welcomes the cold-
ness, so he drinks what's in the glass. He likes it. It makes him feel
happy. When his glass is empty, he rises to go get more from the
pitcher, but Pepito is back, with a silver urn of coffee, with silver
creamer and sugar bowl, spoons jingling, cups and saucers making
gentle chatter because his gnarled old hands shake a little. He fills
Nathan's glass again, pours coffee for him, lays a spoon in the saucer,
sets the sugar and cream within reach, and goes off.

Then Foley's sandals clack down the steps. He wears a tennis
visor, dark glasses, a short-sleeved shirt, white tennis shorts. The
shirt is open. He is slim but unmuscled. He draws out a chair, sits
down, shows his teeth. "Did Pepito make you comfortable?"

"Yes, thank you. Are you always so kind to strangers?"

"We'd met." Foley pours himself coffee. He lights a cigarette,
takes off the glasses, and gives Nathan a steady look. "And if we
hadn't—you and I can never be strangers."

"You didn't invite me," Nathan says. "I just came."

Foley puts the glasses back on and looks up at the house. "You
knew you'd be welcome. Didn't you?"

Nathan's face grows hot again. "Yes," he mumbles. "I guess I
did."

"See?" Foley smiles. "I don't even know your name, but I know
you. The truth is, I knew you the moment I saw you that day on
the sidewalk in front of Greiner and Tuttle."

Nathan thinks he wants to go now. He moves to push back his
chair from the table. But here Pepito comes with plates. On the
plates are red and yellow melon balls, round slices of bacon, and
heaps of scrambled eggs. In a small basket, nested in a napkin, are
rolls shaped like the moon on the roof of Moon's Café. Foley thanks
Pepito and the old man climbs creakily away up the steps. A brow
cocked in amusement, Foley looks from Nathan's face to Nathan's
plate.

Scared now, not hungry, Nathan stammers, "It—it looks delicious."

"Taste it." Foley lays his napkin on his knees. "You'll find it's as good as it looks." He watches Nathan until the boy does taste it. Then he eats a couple of melon balls himself, and butters one of the rolls from the basket. "Do you believe in reincarnation?"

"That's my mother's department," Nathan says.

Foley gives a brief laugh. "My mother's too. But I believe when we meet those we've been close to in previous lifetimes, we know it at once." He pops a chunk of the roll into his mouth, chews, nods, swallows. "I'm sure of it." He drinks some coffee. "Life has proved it to me, time and again—some of us were not meant to be strangers." A voice jeers in Nathan's memory, some boy's voice in a noisy locker room—*It takes one to know one.* Foley picks up his cigarette, draws on it, says through smoke, "Don't you agree?"

Nathan shakes his head, bends over his plate, and avoiding Foley's gaze eats desperately now, rolls, melon balls, bacon, eggs, shoveling the food in, sorry he came, wondering what's the matter with him, happy to be here, hating to be here, picturing what is going to happen next, squeezing his inner eyes shut against the vision, in love with it, made sick by it.

"You don't agree," Foley says with a faint smile, "but you came. Exactly as if I'd invited you. Which I did. Only not aloud. I simply said I'd hoped you'd be my friend."

"That's what you said." Nathan nods helplessly. "I don't understand why. I'm just a kid."

"You understand why." Foley takes the dark glasses off again. His eyes hold Nathan's. "Now, may I know your name?"

Nathan draws a breath. He can't be Frank Reed's son. Not here, not now. "The Little Animal," he says.

Foley laughs easily, and stands. "All right, Little Animal. Shall we go inside?"

THE WOMAN IN SHEILA O'HARE'S APRON THIS MORNING is overweight, fiftyish, with swollen ankles. Her hair is blond except at the roots. Her mechanical waitress's smile shows badly fitting false teeth, and a thousand tiny wrinkles in her puffy cheeks. She brings coffee, refills their cups, and rolls away, big buttocks billowing like wind-filled sails. From other tables boys wolf-whistle at her. She seems good-natured, but Nathan wonders how long she'll last. She moves out of his line of sight, and here comes Travers with a grim look on his face.

"I want to talk to you."

Nathan is bewildered. "What's wrong?" But Travers isn't answering questions. He hoists Nathan off his chair and with a strong grip on his arm steers him to the table nearest the kitchen door, and plunks him down there. He sits down opposite him. "Now—I'd like the truth, please."

"The truth about what? Did you read my play yet?"

"This week?" Travers hoots. "Be serious."

"What's so special about this week?" Nathan rises.

"Come back here," Travers says. "Where are you going?"

"Coffee." Nathan fills mugs and returns to the table with them. The one he sets in front of Travers the skinny youth ignores. He watches impatiently while Nathan dumps sugar and cream into his coffee and stirs it.

Travers says, "As you know, or perhaps you don't, the Fair Oaks Department of Health and Safety were leery of our occupying that loft with the Harlequin. It barely meets safety standards. If it hadn't been for Alex's father, we'd never have gotten away with it."

Nathan sips at his coffee. "What did he do?"

"Contributed heavily to the campaign funds of several city councilmen. But the bureaucrats won't leave us alone. They woke me at dawn last Monday with a phone call. I was to open up the Harlequin then and there for their inspection."

Nathan sets his mug down. "They didn't make you close!"

Travers eyes him. "Don't pretend you don't know."

Nathan scowls. "What do you mean, 'pretend'?"

"I'll answer you that," Travers snaps, "when you answer me this. And I want the truth, Nathan Reed, the whole truth and nothing but the truth." His look is piercing. "Why have you stayed away from Moon's for a whole week?"

Nathan says, "It's got nothing to do with you."

"Oh, but it has. And that's what hurts. You have hurt me very deeply, Nathan Reed." To Nathan's total confusion, Travers starts to cry. He fumbles a paper napkin out of the shiny square box on the table, blots his tears, blows his nose. Angrily. Impatient with himself. He wads the napkin in a bony fist. "How could you betray me so? Haven't I always been good to you?"

"Travers," Nathan says, "what's wrong with you?"

"The theater"—Travers launches a lecture—"is a place of magic and mystery, where dreams are made flesh to walk among us for a few enchanted hours every night—"

"And matinees Wednesdays and Saturdays," Nathan says.

Travers glares. "Listen to me, Nathan. To my profound regret, I have reason to believe you need to hear this. The theater began in holiness and awe, before mankind could write, perhaps before mankind could even speak. A theater holds our myths, our memories, all our history of grief and joy since the dawn of time. A theater, no matter how humble, is a sacred place, and those dedicated to the theater—the playwrights, the actors, and all the rest of us—are priests, acolytes, and vestals." Now he notices his coffee, takes a gulp of it, and bangs down the cup. "A theater," he says, "is not a whorehouse."

"Travers," Nathan says, "what are you talking about?"

"I am talking about that little tramp, Sheila O'Hare, and how she very nearly destroyed the Harlequin and all my hopes and dreams." He waits for Nathan to speak, but Nathan is too stunned. "If it hadn't been for Charlie Vorak's friends at the *Independent*, the story would have made headlines. My reputation would have been ruined."

Nathan scoffs. "How could Sheila make headlines?"

Travers says, "Stop that. You know. She told you."

"She's left town. Her family says you fired her."

The fat waitress puffs past carrying a bin of dirty dishes. Travers watches her push into the kitchen, then lowers his voice and goes on. "I certainly did fire her."

"She says it wasn't fair."

Travers hoots again. "Wasn't fair? She's lucky I didn't kill her. And since you insist you don't know, let me tell you why. When I opened the doors to the loft on Monday morning at the crack of dawn to usher the inspectors inside, what do you think met their wondering eyes? Sheila O'Hare, naked as Eve, straddling a pimply, half-clad high school boy in the middle of Donald's set for *Giants in the Earth*, while two other pimply high school boys stood by in varying states of undress and sexual arousal, cheering them on with obscenities and waiting their turns at her."

Nathan gapes. For a minute, he can't seem to hear.

Travers says, "The loft was a pigpen—hamburger wrappers, Chinese food cartons, beer bottles, stinky sleeping bags. The woman from Health and Safety stepped on a used condom, slipped, and sat flat on her ample behind. Don't laugh. It was not funny. It was one of the worst moments of my life. We are not licensed as a flophouse, an eatery, a tavern, or a brothel. We are just lucky to be licensed as a theater. Mr. Morgan is fit to be tied. We may lose Alex."

Has Nathan laughed? Why? He sure as hell doesn't feel like laughing. He feels awful. "I'm sorry, Travers."

"You're not sorry," Travers says. "You're sitting there right now thanking your stars one of those boys wasn't you. Don't deny it. The little hoyden confessed. She had a key. She'd been bringing boys up there at night for weeks. And you were one of them. That's why you've been avoiding Moon's all week. You couldn't face me, knowing I'd found out how you desecrated the Harlequin with Sheila O'Hare."

Nathan squints at him. "Did she tell you that?"

"She didn't have to. You scarcely hid your goatish interest in her that Friday. Moon remarked on it. Everyone noticed."

"That doesn't prove anything."

"Charlie says you dated her. You borrowed his car."

"All right." Nathan sighs. "We went to a movie. *The Man Who Came to Dinner*."

Travers turns his head and looks distrustfully from the corners of his eyes. "Is that a fact?" He holds up a hand. "Wait. Let me try to reconstruct this." He chews his lip, musing. "You went to a movie with Sheila. Then you stayed away from here for a whole week."

"Not to avoid you," Nathan says wearily.

"No, I see that now. Forgive me. I should have known you better. Knowing Sheila so well, I don't have to hear what happened at the movie, do I? The little slut made a pass at you, didn't she? And you weren't having any." Nathan doesn't answer, but Travers doesn't notice. He clasps Nathan's hands on the table. "It was Sheila you stayed away to avoid. Of course. Oh, Nathan, I'm so relieved." He makes his goofiest face.

"Travers," Nathan says, "when are you going to read my play?"

SCHOOLBOOKS SLANTED AGAINST HIS HIP, he hikes up Oleander Street in the red light of sunset. It's Friday. There's been a lot of work to finish at the *Monitor*. The paper goes to bed tonight, to be printed tomorrow, distributed on Monday. He's explained this to Alma, but she doesn't always remember. It makes her cross if supper's ready and he's not there. So he's hurrying. A horn beeps. A car stops in the street. He squints against the light.

Desmond Foley says, "What happened to you?"

Nathan's heart bumps. He looks back along the street. Frank walks home from Sierra Tech. He could be coming any minute now. Nathan brushes between two of the big oleanders that line the curb and steps to the car.

"What are you doing here?" he whispers.

"I've missed you. I thought you were coming back."

"I—I couldn't." Nathan glances down the block again. "Listen, I can't talk now. I'm late for dinner."

"I'd like it very much if you'd come back," Foley says. "If I forgot to say so before, I wanted you to know it."

"Oh, you said so before. Thank you. I appreciate it. But I don't think"—Nathan gulps—"I don't think I should."

"Never?" Foley frowns. "Why? We had a lovely Saturday.

Didn't we? You seemed happy when you left. Weren't you? I thought you were. I was."

Nathan says, "But it's not right. I can't do it any more. It's not—it's not how people live."

Foley gives a small, gentle laugh. "It's how some people live. You've seen my house. Is how I live so terrible?"

"No, I didn't mean—." Nathan shifts the heavy books to his other hip. "Listen, I can't talk. My father will be coming along any minute now. He'll ask questions."

Foley leans across and opens the door. "Get in. We'll go for a little ride. Plainly, we have to talk."

Nathan steps backward, shaking his head. "I can't."

"Just for a few minutes," Foley says.

"Well, okay." Nathan gets into the car quickly, sets the stack of books in his lap, and slams the door. Foley puts the car in motion. Nathan feels a surge of happiness. This is where he wants to be. All week he's ached to be with Foley again. Dreamed of it in classrooms, unable to focus on his studies, living over and over in memory that naked afternoon in Foley's wide white bed, the French windows open, the curtains stirring in the warm breeze; gone over and over it alone in his narrow cot on the sleeping porch at night. Sleep has been hard to come by. Repeatedly he's given up trying, climbed out the screen and down the honeysuckle trellis to walk the drowsing town for hours. He's wanted it and known bitterly he shouldn't want it. And now here he is with Foley and, against all common sense, all decency, wanting Foley to take him to that bed again. Now. The car pauses at a cross street. Foley turns, drives slowly along.

"I thought you'd call," he says. "Why didn't you?"

Nathan shrugs. "I guess I want a wife and kids."

Foley glances at him, brows raised. "Tomorrow?"

Nathan laughs. "I'm only seventeen."

"Exactly," Foley says. He rolls the car to the curb. Dry leaves and twigs crackle under the tires. The car halts. Foley lays a hand on Nathan's hands that are crossed on his books. "You have plenty of time. Life is long, dear Little Animal. But it's here to be lived.

And you're ready to start living. That's why you came to me last week."

Nathan frees his hands and opens the door. "But you have to start right." The books are heavy, clumsy. Getting out, he drops one. Stooping to pick it up, he says, "I could get to like it so much, I couldn't change. I better stop now."

Foley laughs bleakly. "You'll find it's not that easy."

"I have to try." Nathan shuts the door and walks away.

IT IS HOT. Sweat makes runnels in the coat of grime he's collected dusting, carpet sweeping, brooming down cobwebs from ceiling corners. He shed his shirt hours ago, before he hung the washing on the line. When it came time to iron, he shed his grubby jeans. He sits in his undershorts now, straightening up the desk so he can close it. He sorts envelopes of unpaid bills, gas, water, electricity, throwing away the old ones, keeping only the latest. Alma ought to pay them—she has the money. He reminds her, and she nods, but practicalities don't hold her attention. Here's an envelope from the county assessor. *Final Notice* it says on it in red. He laughs hopelessly and puts it in the stack, snaps a rubber band around them all, and tucks them in a corner of the desk. He alphabetizes Alma's horoscope charts, paper-clips them, puts the blanks and the pencils away, stacks the emphemeris pamphlets and tables of houses, and closes the desk. It's his last task. He starts upstairs to clean himself up, and the doorbell rings. Where did he leave his pants? He finds them in the kitchen, kicks them on, and goes to the door.

Travers Jones, in an enormous, ragged Mexican straw hat, stands on the jigsaw-work porch, the manuscript of Nathan's play in his hand. He makes a silly face. "I tried to telephone, but it's been disconnected."

Nathan groans. "My mother forgets to pay the bill." He rubs a hand in the muck on his chest. "I've been doing chores. I have to take a bath—I'm filthy."

"I'm sorry to appear without notice," Travers says, "but I've read your play, I'm dying to talk to you about it, and the Harlequin's a riot. Lighting rehearsal for *Dame Nature*—everyone shouting and running around. Alex's father tried to make her quit the play, and they had a terrible fight. She's a wreck. I thought we could talk better here."

Nathan opens the screen door. "Come in." Travers stilts inside, smelling of gin. Nathan says, "Can you give me ten minutes? I'll be as quick as I can." Travers rolls his eyes toward the parlor, shivers, and looks quickly away. The doors of the sitting room stand open. Nathan asks, "Do you want to wait in there? Books, magazines, the radio?"

Travers turns back. "If it's all the same to you, I'll wait outside. Nathan, how can you live here? It's so sinister. I mean, this house is right out of Strindberg."

"It's okay, as long as you remember to feed the bats." Nathan starts upstairs, the old carpet bristly on his bare soles. "Come on. You can wait in my room. Nothing sinister about that except me."

When Nathan comes in wearing fresh jeans and a fresh shirt, hair wet from the bath, Travers is sitting cross-legged on the floor, his back against the wall under the windows. The straw hat rides low over his eyes. He strokes the pages of *The Shotgun Flat* in his lap as he reads, and he must not hear Nathan, because he doesn't look up. Heart beating quickly, hoping and not daring to hope, Nathan sits on the chair at the typewriter. "I'm back," he says.

Travers looks up with a sad little smile. "You know what's special about your play?" He doesn't wait for an answer. "The loving. How they all love each other."

"Is it a good play?" Nathan says. "Is it even a play?"

Travers shakes the question off impatiently. "I wonder if you know how lucky you are. You don't, do you?"

"I will if you like the play," Nathan says, "if you tell me it's good enough for the Harlequin to put on."

"I'm talking about reality," Travers says crossly. "Not dreams." He closes the folder, flaps it at Nathan. "What do you need with make-believe? You have a mother and father and a wonderful aunt to love you and protect you and care about you. Why should you need greasepaint and costumes, what do you want with a glaring stage full of illusions in the dark, when you have such a lovely life?"

Nathan claps his hands to his head and wails, "Travers, I don't know. I wrote a play, didn't I? I don't know why I wrote it. I just had to. I want to be a writer, and I don't know the reason for that, either. But everybody says you're supposed to write what you know. And what's in the play is what I know." For all the sense he is making, he might as well be Joe Ridpath's barking dog. He stops and looks into Travers's thin, white, anguished face. It comes to him for the first time, and with a shock, that Travers is very young, scarcely older than himself. He asks earnestly, "What do you want me to say?"

"That you know how precious love is," Travers says forlornly. "That you know that out there in the world"—he flaps a long, pale hand at the outdoors—"there are people who, night after night, week after week, year in, year out, go to bed without having felt one touch of love the whole day long. From anyone."

Nathan says, "Moon loves you, Travers."

Travers howls. "She'd be in a hell of a fix without me. Who'd wash the dishes, carry the food, cook it when she's drunk, dump the garbage, mop the floors, order the supplies, balance the books? Love? Don't talk nonsense."

"Excuse me," Nathan says.

Travers snorts, and fumbles in his wrinkled cotton jacket, a jacket very old, too short in the sleeves, too narrow in the shoulders. He brings out a flat pint bottle of gin, twists off the cap, waves the bottle at Nathan, who shakes his head. Travers tilts the bottle up at his mouth. The gin gurgles, the skinny throat pumps. Travers caps the bottle and pushes it back into his pocket.

"She'd be dead of drink in half a year, if it wasn't for me." He smiles wryly. "No—I love Kate McCracken, that high-spirited, red-haired Irish colleen of yesteryear. I love my mother, Nathan Reed." Travers belches, wipes his mouth. His words come slurred. "But she doesn't want my love. She hates for me to give her a hug, a kiss on the cheek, even to touch her. Shudders away from me as if I were diseased." He gives a woebegone laugh. "Poor old Moon. A man betrayed her once, and she can't forget it."

Nathan sits silent. He doesn't know what to say.

Travers hiccups. "Abou and Lucille. Now, there's love between mother and son. Did you know—they sleep together in the same bed? Have done, ever since his father died, when Abou was five or something."

Nathan squints. "You're joking."

"It's the truth." Travers picks up the script. *"The Shotgun Flat* is," he says, stepping through his diction like somebody learning to dance, "a wonderful play. It made me laugh aloud. It made me shed tears. It surprised me." Nathan opens his mouth, but Travers holds up a hand. "However, it's going to be absolute hell to produce."

"Why?" Nathan's voice cracks.

"It has a little child in it. Dogs, cats, and little children are impossible."

"He's only in the first act," Nathan says.

"In the second act"—Travers licks his thumb and leafs over pages—"Nathan is ten years old. And he carries practically the whole thing." He flaps the pages at Nathan. "Side after side after side."

"There are child actors," Nathan says.

"This one will have to be Young Roscius," Travers says. "And young Rubinstein. Do you seriously expect us to find a boy who can play the piano like that?"

"He can just pretend to play," Nathan says. "Dr. Dick can play records from backstage."

"Three boys." Travers slaps his forehead. "Ages four, ten, and fifteen." He closes the script. "It's touching, it's funny, and I'd love to do it at the Harlequin."

Nathan chokes. "You would?"

Travers makes a lunatic face. "If only because you wrote it." He holds the script out for Nathan to take, then unfolds his long, bony legs and totters to his feet. He pushes the straw hat back, lifts his head, surveys the porch. "I have loved being here because this is your place."

Nathan regards the green paint flaking from the narrow boards overhead, the weather-warped shingle siding under the blowsy black screens, the gloomy old wardrobe, the crippled table and tilty chair, the faded rag rugs, the books leaning along the windowsills and stacked under the rusty cot.

"Where you sleep and work and dream," Travers says, touching the typewriter, touching the cot. "As intimate and private and 'you' as your skin, the smell of your skin." He is unsteady on his feet. "Did you know, you have a lovely smell? I'll bet no one ever told you that. You're young—you've never been that intimate with anyone, have you?" Nathan turns away, lays down the script. Travers says, "No—of course not. Neither have I." He gazes out through the screens now at the big dark pines. A breeze moves them now, bringing some coolness to the dying afternoon. Travers laughs sadly. "I have a terrible hunger for it, but no one knows that. I've never told anyone. I want to love someone very much, to hold them close, to be with them through good times and bad, shared laughter, shared tears, all the days of my life."

"I guess you should tell someone," Nathan says.

"I'd be laughed at, wouldn't I? Who'd take skinny old, swishy old Travers Jones and his silly faces seriously? I've got my theater, haven't I, my plays, my actors, my sets and lights and costumes and all of it. What more does a freak like Travers Jones expect from life?"

"Nobody thinks you're a freak." Nathan lays a hand on his shoulder. "Everyone likes you, everyone admires you, Travers. You're a very gifted, intelligent, exciting man. You know so much."

Travers laughs drearily. "I spent a long, lonely childhood reading books. I suppose I'll spend a long, lonely manhood reading books." He takes the gin bottle from his pocket, drinks again, and drops the bottle back into the pocket. "And a lonely old age too, if I live."

"You'll find somebody," Nathan says.

"I have found somebody." Travers turns. "You."

Nathan stares. Travers flings his arms around him, and kisses him on the mouth. It is a wet and gin-soaked and desperate kiss. Nathan pushes him off.

"Travers, no," he says. "I'm not the one."

Without any pause at all, Travers says, "It's a bad play. Childish. You know nothing of life, nothing." He shoves Nathan aside and careens into the hall. "You've wasted my time." He is stumbling down the stairs. "There's not an audience in the world that would sit through such infantile—." He has fallen. Nathan can tell from the thumps. He runs to the stairs. Travers picks himself up and heads for the front door. It opens, and Frank comes in. The two collide. Travers doesn't notice. He points a bony finger up at Nathan. "Go feed your bloody bats, you ignorant, overreaching child." He bumps the bewildered Frank out of his way and storms off across the porch. Frank stands staring after him. Nathan races down the stairs.

"Are you all right?"

"I guess so." Frank pats himself, checking for broken bones. "Who the hell was that?"

"Travers Jones." The straw sombrero lies at the foot of the stairs. Nathan picks it up. "He's the man who runs the Harlequin."

"Funny galoot," Frank says. "Did he read your play?"

"He read it," Nathan says.

"I guess he's not going to put it on," Frank says.

"I guess not," Nathan says.

Frank smiles, slaps his back. "Well, don't feel bad. I never did like you mixing with those people."

"They're my friends," Nathan cries.

"Not if they break your heart," Frank says.

THAT SUNNY SATURDAY NOON when he was here before, the curved street that climbs to Desmond Foley's place was deserted, not a car to be seen. Now it's late at night, yet cars are parked all along the street. Their roofs gleam in the moonlight. The tall white house stands up ghostly against the sky, every window dark. Can Foley be out? No, no—his luck can't be that bad. Not after Travers. Not in one day. He wants. He needs. Sleep it off? He couldn't. He set out to walk away from wanting, needing. But he hasn't managed it, has he? His feet have led him here. He smiles wryly to himself and climbs the driveway, the steps, the path to the door. He reaches to push the doorbell. And stops his hand midway. The door stands open.

He steps inside. Moonlight through high windows shows him the curved staircase. He closes the door behind him. Softly. Softly climbs the stairs on his rubber soles. It is strange as a movie, this. But he's not afraid. He's lighthearted. He pauses at the top of the stairs and breathes quietly. Does he hear sounds, hushed, secret? Whispers? He strains to listen. Nothing. He passes other doors to reach the door he knows, the door to Foley's big, beam-ceilinged bedroom. He will strip in the moonlight and slip into the bed where Foley lies asleep and it will all be the way it was before, the way he's tried so hard and failed so miserably to forget. And why be miserable? Why? The wrought iron latch of the door gives a little click. He pushes the door, treads stealthily, smiling, into the room. And stops so suddenly his soles squeak.

The row of French windows lets in not just moonlight but wavery blue light from the swimming pool below. It's not as bright as day, no, but it's easy enough to see. And Foley is in his bed, all right, but not sleeping, and not alone. Two boys are with him. Two. Both buck naked, as is Foley. Nathan is stunned. His knees give. He grips the door to keep from falling, and Foley sees him. He pushes the boys away and scrambles off the bed. The boys turn to stare. Nathan knows their faces. From school. He turns and runs. Foley's bare feet thump after him. Doorways open. Shadowy naked men and boys peer out, alarmed. Foley is gaining on him. Nathan can feel the heat of him. "No, wait, wait," he pleads. "You don't understand." He catches Nathan's sleeve, but Nathan jerks free and plunges down the stairs. Foley cries, "Let me explain."

Nathan reaches the bottom of the staircase and there stands Littlejohn Lemay. He has on a shirt and nothing else. The shirt is open. He is holding a cocktail glass. A gray-haired man stands close behind him, reaching around, caressing the boy's smooth chest and belly. He tilts his head in mild surprise at Nathan. Littlejohn says, "Nathan, is that you? What are you doing here?"

"Get out of my way," Nathan says, and lunges for the door. He yanks it open, and runs full tilt into the night. He is a mile down the road before he stops, panting, worn-out. He sits on a rock to catch his breath. The empty hills loom around him, the yuccas are ghost candles in the moonlight. Crickets skirr in the brush. What a goddamned fool he's been. Donald told him. *I hear he likes filling the house with good-looking high school boys on weekends.* Plain English. What in hell did Nathan think it meant? He can't claim he forgot. He remembered the part about the swimming pool, didn't he— enough to dream of the boys splashing naked there. More than once. That there were no such boys when he came here a week ago was dumb chance, wasn't it? Did he think of that? No. That things that morning went so differently from what he expected changed everything—in his mind. But it didn't change reality, did it? Didn't change the facts. *Allow me a word of caution,* Abou said. *Desmond Foley. I wouldn't, Nathan.* What a goddamned fool he is. He pushes to his feet and, head hanging, hands in his pockets, slouches on toward home.

THE BUICK COMES DOWN THE ROAD and stops beside him. Foley says, "It's not the way you think, Little Animal."

Nathan keeps on walking. "Don't call me that."

"Those boys meant nothing." Foley turns off the engine and gets out of the car. The slam of the door is loud in the stillness. He comes after Nathan on foot. "That was just fun and games. You were something else."

Nathan keeps on walking and doesn't look at Foley.

"I love you." Foley takes his arm to stop him. He looks into Nathan's eyes. "Do you understand that? It's something that doesn't happen to me often."

"I guess not." Nathan's laugh is scornful. He pries Foley's fingers off his arm. "Not with so many to choose from. Why bother? Leave me alone, please." He walks on.

"That's not fair. Surely if I'm willing to bare my soul, you can take a minute to listen."

"Go back to your fun and games," Nathan says.

"Loving can cause a lot of pain," Foley says. "I avoid that kind of pain when I can. With you it wasn't a matter of choice, I knew I loved you the first time I saw you." He walks beside Nathan again, not touching him, but close. "When you didn't return my smile, when you turned away, I thought I'd been spared the pain. And I was relieved. Then there you were at the play, and I couldn't help myself, I had to speak to you. And you turned away a second time. And I thanked whatever gods may be, and tried to forget you."

Nathan laughs grimly. "And then I came to your door."

"Exactly," Foley says. "And there was no hope for me."

"And now there isn't any hope for me," Nathan says. "I felt wonderful that Saturday. Like you said. Wonderful, when I left. You don't know how hard it was for me to—make up my mind to come see you. You don't know what it meant to me, the beautiful way you treated me, made—made love to me." He looks at Foley and is angry because his eyes are full of tears like a hurt child's. "It was all so right and fine, when I'd expected it to be"—he moves his shoulders—"I don't know. . . ."

"Disgusting?" Foley submits.

Nathan nods. "Yeah. Disgusting. Like tonight."

Foley barks a little laugh. "Because it wasn't you?"

"You know what I mean." Nathan moves on. "Or maybe you don't. I'd like you to leave me alone now, please."

"Come back to the car. I'll drive you home."

"Thank you," Nathan says. "I'd rather walk."

"It's very late," Foley says. "You never know what time it is. Little Animal, damn it, stop." Something desperate in his voice turns Nathan back. "Take this." Foley is holding out a wristwatch. Its gold and crystal glint in the moonlight. "So you won't think badly of me."

"You mean so I won't talk about what goes on up here on Sunday nights?"

"Why would you do that? Have I hurt you so badly you want to destroy me? Over a romp with a couple of nameless, faceless—"

"That's what we all are, isn't it, really?"

"No, I tell you, you were different, you were special."

"Keep the watch," Nathan says, and tries for a smile. "It's all right—I won't talk. Don't worry. What would I talk about? I wasn't here tonight, Mr. Foley." He turns and goes on down the road. "I wasn't ever here."

WHEN NATHAN OPENS THE FEEBLE OLD SCREEN DOOR and steps into the clatter and chatter and coffee and bacon smells of Moon's, Hotchkiss grins, waves a hand, and calls out:

"Buenos días, Señor Reed. ¿Qué pasa?"

Buddy sings, " 'Where did you get that hat?' "

Peg and Charlie throw Nathan in the straw sombrero token smiles, but they look as if they were sore at each other.

Nathan sets his stack of books on the windowsill. "I'm returning it," he says. "Be back in a minute." He heads for the kitchen door, dodging the billowy waitress on her way to the tables with plates of breakfast. He pushes the swing door, puts his head into the heat and sizzle. "Moon—where's Travers?"

"Drunk." Moon casts a savage glance at him. "Oh, it's you, is it?" She turns over pancakes with a spatula, drops it, comes at him, wiping her hands on a soiled apron. "I want to talk to you. What's that?"

"He left it at my house yesterday."

"And what was he doing at your house?" Moon demands.

"Talking about the play I wrote. Didn't he tell you?"

"He jabbers all the time," Moon growls. "I don't pay any attention. I've got more important things to do. What's the matter with your play? I never knew a play to put him to bed with a bottle for the whole night and refuse to get up in the morning and help his mother." Her fists are on her bony hips. She leans her sweaty, red face close to him. "What happened—and on a Sabbath day of all days—to put him in such a black mood? He doesn't like your house, you know—he says it's haunted. What went wrong?"

"It's not haunted." Nathan lays the hat on top of the refrigerator. "I don't know what's the matter with him."

"Listen to me, Nathan Reed." She catches his arm. "I love that boy with all my heart and soul. He's quare and contrary, and full of dreams as a schoolgirl, but he's life to me. He's all I've got. I won't have anybody hurting him, understand? Not you, with all your beauty, nor Sheila O'Hare with all her sex, nor anybody." She shakes a raw, red fist under Nathan's nose. "I'll protect him to the death."

"Why would I hurt him?" Nathan says. "He's my friend."

"Well, somebody knocked him into a dark pit yesterday," Moon says, scowling. She gives a start, gasps, "Saints and martyrs!" and hurries back to the stove to snatch down plates and scoop the pancakes onto them. She throws him another glowering glance "Who was it, if it wasn't you?"

Nathan wants to tell her the truth, but he can't, can he? "Maybe it's about *Dame Nature*. Alex—maybe they're losing Alex. Ask him."

"He's dumb as a post." Moon lays bacon strips beside the flapjacks and sets the plate in the service window. "He won't utter so much as a curse at me." She turns back to the stove, cracks eggs into a pan. "He'll only lie curled up in his bed like a hurt dog, and drink, and weep."

"Sometimes dogs run into traffic," Nathan says.

Moon snorts. "Oh, you're a philosopher now, are you? Get out of my kitchen."

Hotchkiss has made hats for himself and Buddy out of newspapers. Now he points make-believe pistols at Nathan. "You're outnumbered, Pancho Villa."

Nathan feels glum about making Travers so unhappy. But he grins and holds up his hands. "I surrender. Too many Napoleons." He sits down. And sees the reason for the hat making. Hotchkiss has wanted to keep busy while Peg and Charlie fight. Now Peg, looking furious, makes to get up. Charlie tries to push her back down. Knocking away his hand, she stands so abruptly that her chair falls over. Donald Donald appears and picks it up. Peg grabs her purse and heads for the door, where Dan waits, leaning back, arms folded, smug. Charlie rises, takes two steps after Peg, turns back scowling, sits down again, and shifts his chair so he won't face the window. Dan's Packard gleams at the curb in front of Moon's, its top down.

Nathan asks Charlie, "What's wrong between you two?"

"I've got a summer job offer," Charlie says. "City desk at the *Independent*."

"But that's great." Nathan peers. "Isn't it?"

"Not to Peg." Charlie gives a rueful laugh. "We were going to Mexico and live in a village on tortillas and beans and write a novel together. Paradise."

"Where would the money come from?"

"Peg's mother. Naturally, Peg didn't tell her she'd be taking me along—but two can live as cheaply as one."

"Tortillas and beans could get boring," Hotchkiss says.

Buddy trills, " 'Sweethearts can live on love alone. . . .' "

Nathan looks out the window at Peg and Dan getting into the car. "What's she going to do, then—invite Dan to Mexico?"

Charlie jerks around, scowling. "Over my dead body."

"Can Dan write a novel," Buddy asks, "half a novel?"

"Dan can hardly write his name," Charlie says. "She's just trying to make me jealous." He stops looking. "Well, it won't work. I can't turn that job down. And she isn't going to trade me off for Mexico."

"I hope not," Nathan says. "I like you two together."

Donald sets coffee in front of Nathan and sits in Peg's chair. "Nathan, you promised me *The Shotgun Flat* so I can draw up the designs."

Nathan nods. What else can he do? Tell Donald it's no use, a waste of time, that Travers isn't going to put on the play? He frowns and sips the hot coffee. He can't do that. Not without explaining why. And Donald would run smirking to tell everybody. Nathan won't do that to Travers, no matter what. Without a word, he pulls the script from his loose-leaf binder and passes it to Donald.

Outside, the Packard roars off down Sierra Street.

FRANK IS CARRYING AN OLD B-FLAT TENOR SAXOPHONE in a ratty black case. He follows Charlie and Peg along the edge of a high sea cliff. Nathan trails after. Below lies the Munroe beach house. It is night. Light pours from the house onto the sand, and its nimbus touches the surf that foams around ragged black rocks. Charlie locates a wooden staircase to take them down the cliff face. Wind blows off the sea, smelling of fish and iodine. It dislodges Frank's hat. Nathan doesn't understand why Frank, proud of his thick white hair, has chosen to wear a hat tonight. Maybe because when he last played in a dance band, ten years ago, all men wore hats. The hat blows into Nathan's hands, and he passes it down to Frank. At the foot of the stairs, they follow a duckboard walk to the house, which has decks all around. From inside come voices, laughter, the thump of a string bass tuning up, practicing riffs, a trumpet running scales.

Inside, woven grass rugs have been rolled up and wicker furniture has been pushed against the bare-board walls of a big room to make space for dancing. In a corner, near a baby grand piano, wooden folding chairs and music stands are grouped. Buddy in his wheelchair is the trumpeter. A squat boy with greasy hair, who seems to be smiling at some secret joke, is setting up drums and cymbals. The thumper of the bass fiddle is a gangly kid in thick glasses. Frank heads that way, Nathan beside him. Buddy turns his wheelchair, sees Frank, smiles and waves a small, crippled hand.

"Mr. Reed. Glad to see you."

"We'll see," Frank answers. "Been a long time." Buddy introduces Frank to the bassist and the drummer. Frank takes the saxophone from its case, sits on a chair with it, and bends forward to study the charts on his music rack, nervously wetting and softly honking on the new reed he put on the mouthpiece at home in the attic. He runs barely audible scales. Buddy does the same, but keeps breaking off to look at his watch and then at the door, where more and more guests keep arriving. He tugs Nathan's sleeve.

"Go try to find Luke Bando, will you? We're going to be in great shape without a piano player."

"What does he look like?"

"A cherub who's losing his hair."

Nathan makes his way through knots of young people, chattering and laughing, drinking sodas. The girls wear formals, the boys black bow ties and white jackets. He knows many of them from classrooms and campus. Others, those with suntans, must be neighbors. This will end up as a first-night party for the Harlequins, but *Dame Nature* won't be over for an hour, and since Dan is in the cast, his big, bluff father and tiny, chirpy mother are acting as hosts.

A long table loaded with food stands at the room's far end. Nathan swings past it, shakes Mrs. Munroe's fluttery little hand, loads a paper plate with ham, roast beef, cheese, and potato salad, remembers a fork, then starts for the door to shout for Luke Bando. But there's no need. Bando comes in a side door. Nathan knows this because Buddy Challis cheers and calls the piano player's name. Nathan goes to a corner of the deck, sits on the rail, and eats. He's almost finished when the band starts playing.

People exclaim and applaud. Frank must have had his timid way. The opening tune is not loud and upbeat. It's "Way Down Yonder in New Orleans," taken at a sleepy tempo. The porch trembles under him as, inside, people start to dance. Buddy's trumpet rings clear and saucy with the melody line. Frank's saxophone sounds tentative. Nathan takes his empty plate inside. How does Frank look? Pale and uncomfortable. He wonders if he was right to argue and josh him into taking Buddy's invitation to be part of his pickup band tonight. Now the time comes for Frank to take his solo. Habit gets him to his feet all right, but he doesn't look at the crowd, he looks as if he wishes he were somewhere else. He does two indifferent choruses and sits down almost before the last note fades and Luke Bando takes up the tune. Frank reads his chart with dull eyes. Nathan hopes he'll cheer up.

He's thirsty. He gets rid of the empty plate and takes a bottle of beer from a washtub of chipped ice under the buffet. Peg and Charlie are dancing, Charlie looking determined, Peg as if she were far away in her thoughts—just going through the motions. Nathan has never learned to dance. Why? He never asked himself before. But it's no mystery. Dancing involves girls, doesn't it? And he's never given a thought to girls. He throws Charlie and Peg a smile, pries the cap off the beer bottle, and goes back outside. "The Shiek of Araby" follows him, but it has grown faint by the time he reaches the edge of the tide.

He sits on the sand, sets the bottle on the sand, and peels the cellophane off a pack of cigarettes, the first he's ever bought. He sets a cigarette in a corner of his mouth, like Humphrey Bogart, puts the pack back into his shirt pocket, and tries to light a paper match. The wind blows it out. He tries cupping the match in his hand as he's seen Bogart do, but he only burns his fingers. Finally he turns away from the wind, pulls his jacket up around his ears, and gets the cigarette lighted. The smoke makes him cough. He tries the beer. It's bitter, isn't it? Sure. It's for grown-ups. Sweets are for kids.

He inhales carefully from the cigarette again. And he doesn't cough this time. He'll learn. He has to. You can't be a little boy forever. He turns down his collar and sits smoking, drinking, gazing out at the dark, restless ocean. From the house, the sound of the band, the sound of voices drift down. It's nice. He likes being out here all alone. It makes him feel the way his night walks used to. Before life got so complicated. How come there's so much to keep secret, suddenly? What's happening to him? He hears himself tell Littlejohn that weird morning in the rain, *It's nature—biology, physiology, chemistry.* He smiles to himself. Really? Is that all? He doesn't want to think about it. Maybe when he finishes his beer, he'll strip off his clothes and go swimming. Maybe he won't swim back.

A TIMID VOICE CALLS, "NATHAN?"

He turns, frowning. It's pretty dark out here. He can only make out a silhouette.

"It's me—Sheila." She comes to him, huddling in a pale coat too small for her—her mother's? "I wanted to say something to you."

Nathan can't believe this. "How did you get here?"

"I'm living with my parents now, in Santa Monica. It's not all that far from here. I knew about *Dame Nature* opening at the Harlequin. There'd be a party, wouldn't there—like before?" She glances wistfully up the sand toward the glowing windows of the house, the dancing figures, the music and the voices. "I was at the first one—remember?"

"I remember," Nathan says numbly.

"And I figured you'd be here," she says.

"I'm here." Nathan wonders if this is a dream. But his dreams of Sheila always involve those half-naked boys Travers described, waiting their turns at her in the early-morning loft. And in his dreams, Sheila fades, and the boys take care of one another. He stands up, brushing the sand off his pants. "I'm here, Sheila. What do you want?"

"Travers told you, didn't he?" She sounds bitter. "About me and those other boys?"

"Was he lying?" Nathan says.

She takes the cigarette from his fingers, sucks smoke from it, hands it back to him. It has lipstick on it. He flicks it into the surf.

She says in a small voice, "No, he wasn't lying. But"—she lays a hand on his sleeve and peers up into his face, pleading to be believed—"they didn't mean anything. I mean, I get lonesome. I wanted . . . I like sex a lot, don't you, doesn't everyone? But those boys—I didn't care about them, they weren't friends, understand? Friends?"

It's Desmond Foley all over again, isn't it? How many times is he going to be asked to listen to this? "I know what the word means." He drinks from the beer bottle.

She withdraws her hand. "You hate me," she says.

"I don't hate you, Sheila," he says.

Her shadowy face lights up. "Oh, good. Oh, good. Because I love you, Nathan." He hears the same words in Desmond Foley's voice. What the hell do these people mean by love? Up at the house, Frank plays "Melancholy Baby" on the tenor sax, hoarsely, with a big, wobbly vibrato. Nathan knows what love is. He loves Frank. Sheila keeps talking, urgent, breathless. "You're not like the rest. You're special. There's something intelligent and sensitive about you. I kept telephoning your house to tell you, but you were never home, and you never called back."

"I know. That was rude of me. I went to Roz and Ruby's to apologize. On Saturday. But you'd moved out by then."

She stands tiptoe and kisses his mouth. "That's sweet." She hugs him. "You read books and you think a lot and you're—talented. And I could never live up to you." She gropes for his hand. "But I could be loving all the time, Nathan. I'd love that, going to bed with you every night, waking up beside you every morning." She starts to lead him along the sand. "I'd never look at any other boy again."

Nathan halts. "Where are we going?"

"I know a cove where no one will see us. Come on, Nathan. It won't be like at the movie. This will be real. Like it's supposed to be."

He pulls his hand away. "No, Sheila. I can't."

"Why not?" she cries. "Because I'm a cheap little tramp, like Travers says?"

"No," he says, and slings the beer bottle in a long, high arc out to sea. "Because I'm queer."

STRANGERS, MEN, WOMEN, SLEEPY CHILDREN, straggle out of the dark by ones and twos and threes to stand in a ragged assembly on the sand, gazing up at the house, listening to the music. Nathan no longer has the beach to himself. Grumpily he climbs down off the rock where he's been perched and hikes back up to the party.

The band finishes off "Two Sleepy People." Buddy and Frank, Luke Bando, the gawky bassist, and the drummer with the secret smile shuffle their music. The dancers stand motionless, the thud and splash of the sea reaching into the house for a strangely solemn moment. Then Buddy, trumpet to his lips, nods a brisk tempo, the drummer begins a military snare drum beat, Buddy blows a bugle call, and the band is off in full cry with "Zulu Parade."

The dancers whoop and begin to jitterbug, arms and legs flying. It isn't Charlie that Peg dances with now—it's Dan Munroe, flopping around like an outsize kindergartener, and laughing at himself. Pudgy Charlie sweats to keep up with Alex Morgan, who wears slacks and, surprisingly for her lanky build, dances like a professional. Nathan watches. From the sidelines. What's he doing in here? He goes to the tub, crouches for another beer, pries off its cap, gets to his feet, and Abou Bekker stands there, saying sternly:

"I've been looking for you. Come." He walks out. Nathan follows. People are on the porch. Abou goes down to the sand, avoids the crowd, stops in the dark at the water's edge. Nathan goes to him and holds out the bottle, but Abou shakes his head. Nathan takes out his cigarette pack and offers that. Abou doesn't want a cigarette, either.

"I'm not here to socialize," he says. "I want a straight answer to a straight question."

Nathan puts the cigarette pack away. "What question?"

"Were you at Desmond Foley's house Sunday night?"

"Jesus." Nathan nearly drops the beer bottle. "Who told you that?"

"Never mind who told me. Is it true?"

"I asked you first," Nathan says.

"You wouldn't know him," Abou says. "Or I hope not. An actor I once worked with. He knows you're a friend of mine. He was there. He saw you."

Nathan looks away. "If you believe him, why ask me?"

"Because I don't want to believe him. I think you're too fine for that. Tell me it isn't true."

Nathan wishes that sometimes someone had taught him how to lie. He drinks beer and says, gloomily, "It's true."

"You're joking. Child, this is not a laughing matter."

"I'm not joking," Nathan says. "I wish I were."

"But I warned you to stay away from Desmond Foley."

Nathan digs with his shoe at a seashell in the sand. He mumbles, "I wanted to see—what it was like."

Abou clutches his hair and keens. "You stupid boy."

"Don't get excited," Nathan says, "I'm not going back."

" 'Don't get excited'?" Abou yelps. "Nathan, I care about you. You are a beautiful, gifted person. And getting mixed up with that crowd could destroy you." With shaking hands, he takes the cigarette pack from Nathan's pocket, waits for the wind to take a breath, lights a cigarette. "Desmond Foley is getting careless. Rumors are all over town about his house and the men who go there, and what they do with the boys who go there. Sooner or later, the police are going to hear about it. It's inevitable."

"I won't be there," Nathan says. "Why don't you tell your actor friend he mistook me for somebody else?"

"I already did." Abou puts the cigarette pack back into Nathan's pocket and gives it a pat. He smiles. "Of course."

A voice comes drifting across the sand. "Bob-bee?" They turn and look. Lucille Bekker is on the porch, a round figure against the light. She beckons.

Abou takes the bottle now, drinks from it. "Buddy says you've finished your play. When do I get to read it?"

"Donald's got it," Nathan says.

"I hope I'm next," Abou says.

"It's time to go ho-o-ome," Lucille calls.

"Coming." Abou hands back the bottle and goes.

HE HAS SAT ON A ROCK AGAIN FOR A LONG TIME ALONE. Now the beer is gone and his ass hurts and he climbs down and heads back to the house with the empty bottle. The band is playing "Chinatown," up-tempo, ricky-tick, and some of the young party watchers on the beach are dancing now, laughing, kicking up sand. Around them, middle-aged people, old people applaud. Three very small children try to dance and end up falling down, giggling. Nathan climbs the steps, crosses the porch, goes into the light and the loud music.

And stops. By the buffet table, Dan is forking slices of ham, beef, turkey onto a plate. He's the host. That's all right. It's who is holding the plate that shakes Nathan. It's Gene Woodhead, in his cadet's uniform. His hair shines golden in the light. He is more beautiful than ever, and he is giving Dan a sly, sexy smile. Dan plops a big helping of potato salad on the plate, hands Gene a fork, hurries to get him a beer. At the beer tub he meets Nathan.

"Ah, Nathan, good." He uncaps the beer. "Don't go away. It's important." He hurries off. "I'll be right back." Nathan uses the opener on his own bottle, and stands watching as Dan says something to Gene, and Gene turns sharply and gives Nathan a surprised look. He grins, and they come over together. Dan says, "Gene tells me you two know each other."

"We used to be neighbors," Nathan says. "What are you doing here?"

"My school's only a mile up the road," Gene says. "Dan and I found we had something in common. We swim in the same ocean." The short, rosy girl who plays the lead in *Dame Nature* plucks Dan's sleeve and draws him away. Dan looks over his shoulder and mouths "Wait for me" at Nathan.

Gene steers Nathan into a corner. "I heard something wild about you." He stuffs his mouth with food. "From Littlejohn."

"Don't tell me," Nathan growls. "Desmond Foley's."

"I thought you were the one who wasn't queer."

Nathan makes a face. "I was surprised to see Littlejohn there. Last time I saw him, he thought Jesus would roast him in hell for jacking off."

Gene raises his golden eyebrows. "Didn't you send him to me to get straightened out? That's what he said."

"I guess so," Nathan says glumly. "You mean it was you who took him to Foley's place?"

Gene smirks. "I thought he'd fit right in."

"How come I didn't see you there on Sunday?"

"I don't go anymore." Gene wags his head. "All those naked guys stumbling around fumbling with each other—I get to laughing so hard I can't do anything."

Nathan says, "I'll never go back. It was a mistake. Gene, don't go telling everybody, okay?"

Gene studies him with his blue, blue eyes. "You going to be friendly to me next time?" He pushes potato salad into his mouth. Mayonnaise shines on his chin. "No more 'little kid stuff' shit?" Nathan doesn't speak, and Gene seems to take this for agreement. "Good." His hand brushes Nathan's crotch. "Don't worry—I won't tell anybody."

Dan comes back, throws Gene a smile, says to Nathan, "Get your play multigraphed." He flips the tail of his white jacket, pulls a wallet from a hip pocket, slides bills from the wallet. "Use the place around the corner from the post office. They're the fastest."

"I can pay for it myself," Nathan says.

"No, this is Harlequin money. It's a business matter. We'll settle the royalty rate later. Get at least ten copies." He pushes the bills into Nathan's hand. "And be sure to save the receipt."

"Dan, Travers hates the play."

"That's why you have to act fast." Dan touches Gene's hand. It's a caress, really. "Excuse us for a few minutes?" Gene nods, and Dan leads Nathan out into the sea breeze. "Travers and I have been friends practically from the cradle. We made our stage debut together in kindergarten, as a fairy and a bunny rabbit." He leads Nathan up the beach. "Moon was our cook, in those days. I know Travers Jones."

"At first he loved the play," Nathan says.

"I believe you, but he'll never admit it, not now."

"What's he been saying?" Nathan asks.

"You don't want to know, but he's venomous. What did you do to him?"

"What makes you think I did anything to him?"

"I know when his feelings are hurt. What happened?"

"It's private," Nathan says. "I can't talk about it."

"Oh, dear," Dan murmurs. "So that was it, was it?" They leave the light from the house. Nathan walks into the dark gratefully. His shoe strikes a stone. He kicks the stone along ahead of him, white in the starlight.

Dan says, "I knew he fancied you. I've seen it before. But he rarely makes a move. He hates rejection, and he imagines everybody, everybody in the world, is going to reject him." Far off now, the band begins to play "Harbor Lights." The sand crunches softly under their shoes. Dan says, "And the handsomer they are, the more timid he is. Yet he made an honest-to-God pass at you, did he?"

"Let's talk about something else," Nathan says.

Here, a high wall of rocks crosses the sand and reaches out into the surf. Dan climbs up on the rocks. "Whatever happened, if your play wasn't good, he wouldn't savage it so. Wayne and Buddy love it, Charlie and Peg, even Donald—"

"They don't matter." Because of the beer bottle, Nathan can

only use one hand for climbing, but he climbs. "The Harlequin belongs to Travers." He digs into his jacket and reaches up, holding out the bills. "Take back your money, Dan. You'll only be throwing it away."

"The Harlequin doesn't belong to Travers. He's only the manager." Dan goes off seaward, teetering across the rocks. "He can't make any decisions without a vote of the board. We put up the funds. Or our parents do."

Nathan gets to the top of the rocks, stops, takes a swallow of beer, heads out after Dan. Dan halts, sits down, reaches up for the beer bottle. Nathan hands it to him. Dan drinks. For a time, he gazes down at the waves crashing on the rocks below. He drinks again, and passes back the bottle. He pats the breast pocket of his jacket.

"Calls for a cigarette," he says loudly.

Nathan gives him one, takes one for himself, and they spend time and matches and take strange, knee-scraping positions before they get the cigarettes lit. Dan stands up.

"Let's go all the way out to the end," he shouts.

"These shoes are too slippery," Nathan calls, but he goes after Dan anyway.

"They're meant for dancing," Dan howls. "Why weren't you dancing tonight?"

"Nobody asked me," Nathan yells.

They get to the far point, where the rocks step down into the tide. They stand, waves breaking at their feet, spray in their faces, and laugh and pass the bottle. Nathan ought to speak to Dan about Gene, about hurting Peg. He hasn't the nerve. Then the beer is gone, and they teeter back along the spiny ridge of rock, and scramble, slipping, down to the sand, and head back toward the house, a tiny box of light in the immense darkness of sea and sky.

Dan says, "We have to prevent Travers getting a majority on his side and rushing another play into rehearsal to spite you. You get those copies made."

"It's got three young boys in it," Nathan says.

"I know—impossible to stage," Dan says. "Shut up."

After a silence, Nathan says, "Donald has the script."

"Get it from him," Dan says, "first thing tomorrow."

THEY REACH THE HOUSE. The piano is playing alone. "In a Mist." Footsteps sound on the cliff stairs. Up on the road, people call good-night to each other, and car doors slam. The crowd on the beach has straggled off. They've left a bonfire. Dan kicks sand over it, the coals wink out. When they walk into the big room, the overhead lights still glare. A Mexican man in a white coat finishes clearing the long table. Everyone else has vanished, even the band members and their instruments. Peg and Charlie must be waiting in the car. The table is bare. The caterer wheels his cart out into the kitchen. Dan switches off the overhead lights. Under a rosy bridge lamp, the piano player is Frank. Nathan wanders across to him. Frank looks up.

"You're some party boy," he says. "Haven't seen you all evening. Where you been?"

"I could hear better outdoors," Nathan says.

"Nathan, will you close that side door, please?" Dan walks over to the baby grand, laughing with pleasure. "Mr. Reed, I'm Dan Munroe. I want to thank you for coming down tonight. Everyone told me how much they enjoyed your music."

A wicker chair holds the door open. Nathan moves it, swings the door, and just before it closes, he sees, off in the shadows of the deck, holding each other close and rocking from side to side to some slow romantic tune only they can hear, tall, bony Travers Jones and short, curly-headed, snub-nosed Tommy Burns, who plays the schoolboy hero in *Dame Nature*. Nathan very softly shuts the door.

IN THE BACKSEAT OF CHARLIE'S CAR, the saxophone case between his knees, Frank says, "You've started smoking."

Nathan says, "It makes me feel insouciant."

Frank laughs, pulls his hat down over his eyes, and falls asleep.

NO ONE ANSWERS THE PHONE AT THE DONALD HOUSE. Nathan walks there. Dew wets the legs of his jeans when he cuts across the lawn. On the flat, broad rail of the porch, the jacket of a book has dew on it. He pushes the doorbell. No one comes. He pushes it again, keeping his thumb on it. It's bad manners, waking up a household like this, but he has no choice. It's seven in the morning. Where the hell can the Donalds be?

There's a rattling at the door. It opens, and Malcolm squints at him. He is in pajamas. His hair is tousled. His perky little cock sticks out of his buttonless fly. He doesn't even notice. He blinks grouchily at Nathan. "Reed. What do you want?"

"I have to see Donald," Nathan says.

"Try Arroyo Hospital." Malcolm winces at the morning light. "Jesus, Reed, I didn't get to bed till four."

"I'm sorry I woke you. Is he very sick?"

"He's always very sick." He shrugs. "It's nothing new. My folks are with him." He starts to shut the door.

"Wait. He borrowed the play I wrote, the only copy. I need it back. I wouldn't bother you, but it's important."

"Okay." Malcolm unhooks the screen door. "Come in." He turns away, yawning. "Only don't ask me to find it. If I go in his room when he's not there, he thinks up things to do to me." He pads off toward the rear of the house and waves a sleepy hand. "That's his room. Help yourself."

It's a big room, white, cheerful, with many windows. The bed is open. A stethoscope lies on the sheets. Forgotten by some doctor in a hurry? Or a fixture here. Donald has a bad heart. Maybe he listens to it, alone in the dark, counting the beats, wondering when it is going to quit on him. Nathan doesn't want to think about it. Magazines lie on the nightstand by the bed, and on the floor within reach of the bed. He looks these over. No sign of *The Shotgun Flat*. Donald's desk is piled with textbooks, his loose-leaf binder, drawing pads, paints and brushes, a T square, French curves, art books, paperback books. *The Shotgun Flat* isn't among them. He sits and opens drawers. He hates doing it, but the play has to be here someplace.

He stops. In a bottom drawer lie folded tabloid newspapers. Like the *Monitor*. Exactly like the *Monitor*. Only they aren't the *Monitor*, are they? They're printed in French, and they're old. The paper is yellowing at the edges. He peers at the dates: 1936, 1937. The headings are in the same jaunty brush lettering Donald used to win the design contest back in January. Kenneth Stone says, *There's something familiar about it. I'd almost swear I've seen it before, but damned if I can remember where.* In Europe, right? Grimly, Nathan digs a manila envelope out of Donald's wastebasket and pushes the papers into it.

"Is this what you're looking for?" Malcolm appears in the doorway, flapping Nathan's script. "Hey—are you all right? You don't look like you feel too good."

"It's nothing." Nathan stands quickly. "Morning sickness. I'm pregnant." He takes the script. "Thanks. Where did you find it?"

"Bathroom," Malcolm says. "I had to pee." He turns and goes off down the hallway. "It's hard to sleep when you have to pee."

THE ELEVATOR IS CROWDED and everybody seems to hold flowers wrapped in rustly green paper. The confined space is damp with the sweetness of the flowers. And Nathan understands what Frank meant that time when he said, *If you knew how I hate the smell of cut flowers.* The smell of sickness and death. Well, he hasn't brought any, not he. He's brought those lousy French newspapers. He is going to make Donald eat them. The elevator bumps to a stop. The doors slide open. He gets out. He is going to make Donald take them to Wayne Hotchkiss, and the head of the art department, and Dean Staat, and confess what he's done, and the prize is going to the student who came in second. He barges down the hallway, dodging floor moppers, meals on carts, nurses with hypodermic needles on trays. The door to room 306 stands open. He yanks the envelope from under his arm and barges in, waving it. "Donald, you cheating son of a bitch——." That's as far as he gets. A young woman in starchy white jumps up from a chair and charges at him. "Quiet. Be quiet. Are you crazy?" She grabs his wrists and struggles with him. She is not very big, but she is strong. She hisses, "This is a sickroom. This patient is critically ill. Get out. Get out of here this instant." While Nathan tries to fend her off, Mrs. Donald, clutching a Bible, rises and scowls at him from beyond what he takes to be an oxygen tent. It's of heavy white cloth. There's a window cut in it, covered in celluloid. Nathan gets a quick glimpse of Donald flat on his back. His eyes are closed. His skin is a weird clay color. His lips are blue. He looks dead. That's all there's time for. The little nurse propels him backward into the hallway and closes the door. It has a sign on it. OXYGEN NO SMOKING. He carries the envelope down the long backyard under the brooding branches of the pines to the incinerator, a rig of flat cement slabs with a cast-iron door and a blackened stovepipe chimney. He burns the papers. The acrid smoke blows toward the house. And in a moment, Alma looks out the back porch screen door. It's early, not nine o'clock yet, but she is dressed to receive clients. She calls crossly, "What are you doing?" Nathan answers, "Sorry. It'll be over in a minute." And it is.

TOM DAWES HAS BEEN ASKING NATHAN to write sports stuff lately. His one staffer, Rupe Ewing, got mad about something and quit. And there's a lot of sports stuff going on this spring. Tom can't handle it alone. So Nathan stays late today in the *Monitor* office, writing up an interschool swimming meet, then doing his own weekly piece for Buddy, dumbbell dialogue he overheard sitting with the baseball team in the dugout during a game. If he doesn't do it now, it may never get done. But he's aching to talk to Frank. And he takes a bus out Sierra Street to get him home faster.

The house is hushed in the sunset light. Alma doesn't answer when he calls, and he remembers she said something about eating supper with Mrs. Gregory and her veterinarian son, Roland. She long ago gave up trying to rope Frank in on these things, but she still tries with Nathan. "Such a nice young man. Not one of those freakish young people you run with." Nathan demurred. "I've got a lot of homework." He peers into the sitting room, the parlor, the kitchen, calling Frank's name and getting no answer. He runs up the stairs, sets his books in his room, opens the door to the attic. "Frank?" No answer. He climbs the stairs, and stops.

He can't believe what he sees.

Frank doesn't come home. Nathan rings the Atheneum. They say he left on time. They don't know where he is. Nathan goes out on the lacy front porch and stands there in the gathering dusk, looking down the brushy street, wondering what to do. He sits on the steps until it's dark. His stomach sends him signals, and he goes back to the kitchen, switches on the light, slices breast meat from a roast chicken, makes himself a sandwich. He drinks a glass of milk and eats the last piece of lemon pie. Washes the day's dishes. Goes up to the sleeping porch to study. An hour later Alma comes home. He hears her, goes to the stair head, calls down to her. She comes without even taking off her hat, and he leads her up to the attic. She gives a cry and reaches out to prop herself on a barrel marked China.

"His instruments." She pleads up into Nathan's face. They're all gone. Brasses, reeds, drums, gongs, fiddles—even his beloved cello. Only the piano is left. "Nathan—where are his instruments?"

"I don't know. He hasn't come home."

Now, suddenly and without warning, she turns on him in a fury. "Oh, you wicked child. You see what you've done? I knew the minute you brought that crippled boy here, he'd bring bad luck." She walks among the desolate-looking trunks and crates and cartons, wringing her hands. "No, I didn't say anything, of course. I know how you feel, you and your father. You think it's superstition." She faces him, her jaw set. "But it is the wisdom of the ancients, Nathan, and tonight"—she gestures at the place—"you can see what comes of closing your mind against it."

"Buddy's not bad luck," Nathan says. "He had bad luck. He got polio. It could happen to anyone, Mother. It could happen to me."

She shakes her head stubbornly. "Never. I know your soul as well as I know my own. For lifetime after lifetime you have been treading upward toward the light."

"It could have happened to me," Nathan says again.

"Dear pilgrim, think. Use your mind. What sort of previous life do you suppose a person like that is paying for, all twisted up that way? A life of evil and cruelty, Nathan—to be expiated by suffering in this lifetime. Karma, Nathan, karma."

"Mother, he thought Frank would enjoy playing in a band again. He's a kind, good-natured kid. He loves music and people who play music. I thought it would do Frank good."

"You were wrong, and I knew it, but of course, I held my tongue. What's the use of arguing? It's always two against one in this family." She brushes past him, and her heels clunk down the bare wooden stairs. "But I knew how it would be—he didn't sleep a wink after he'd agreed to do it. He tossed and turned and ground his teeth."

"I'm sorry," Nathan calls after her. "I'm very sorry."

She stops at the stair foot and looks back up at him. "You will have less to be sorry for in this life, young man, if you don't meddle with other people's destinies." She marches off, a one-woman parade of righteousness.

Nathan laughs. Her whole life is dedicated to meddling with other people's destinies. But his laughter doesn't last. He looks at the sad attic and wants to cry. Frank loved fooling with all those instruments, loved having them around to pick up when he felt like it. Alma is right. Nathan has done a terrible thing. He goes miserably down the stairs, switches off the light above, and closes the door.

A HAND SHAKES HIS SHOULDER. He opens his eyes. His head rests on his folded arms on an American history book open on the table by the typewriter. He has been dreaming of soldiers in the Civil War, all those young boys. He has walked in a smoking field where they lie dead. Their open-eyed faces stare up at him. Each of them is Donald Donald. The light of the desk lamp glares in his eyes. He winces, coughs, sits up. Frank stands over him. "It's late," he says. "You belong in bed."

"Where have you been?" The clacking old alarm clock reads one thirty. "I've been waiting to talk to you."

"I haven't been anywhere." Frank sits on the side of the cot. He looks worn out. "Just walking."

"What did you do with all your instruments?"

Frank shrugs. "Borrowed the Atheneum station wagon. Hauled them over to Sanchez School. Kids can use them. Piled them up in the breezeway there. They'll find 'em in the morning."

Nathan stands. "Let's go get them back."

Frank shakes his head. "I don't want them anymore."

"Why not? What do you think—you were bad, playing with Buddy? You were good."

"I was awful and you know it," Frank says. "I never felt so ridiculous in my life. All those kids—what in the world was an old man like me doing there?"

"Playing a great tenor sax," Nathan says.

"The hell you say." Frank's laugh is wintry. "Reading the notes, I was barely passable. Improvisations? Nathan, I was lousy, out of practice, out-of-date, a real honker."

"When you played, people danced closer."

Frank laughs, reaches out, pulls Nathan to him and hugs him hard. "You sure as hell know how to turn a phrase."

"What are you going to do without your instruments?"

"I should have got rid of them fifty years ago. It was a silly conceit of my silly mother's—this curly-headed baby genius of hers, playing any instrument you put into his tiny hands, able to play back any tune he heard." He pushes up off the bed and goes to stare out at the night. "I was a freak, a sideshow attraction. A musician? I couldn't read a note. Why should I? I had a perfect ear. God, she was ignorant."

"Frank—you learned to read."

"Enough to get work." Frank turns to face him now, bracing himself against the ledge of books, arms folded across his chest. The lamp on the table shines its light downward, so his face is in shadow. "I was lazy, Nathan. It came too easy. I never took it seriously. I never in my life worked at it. I was a grasshopper in the sunshine. Ask your mother."

"She's terribly upset about this," Nathan says.

"She wants me to be happy," Frank says. "And I've taken advantage of that, shamelessly. When I married her, I knew she'd never drive me. I shied from the sort of woman I ought to have married, somebody to kick my ass, push me, nag me, make me study and practice and work. On one instrument."

"You didn't even keep the cello," Nathan says.

Frank smiles and shakes his head. "It's too late now."

"I feel awful when you say that," Nathan says.

Frank laughs, moves from the windows, ruffles Nathan's hair. "That's because you're young. Life is still all hellos for you." He goes to the door. "Later on, you'll learn that sometimes it's a relief to say good-bye."

"IT'S BEEN SUCH A WARM SPRING. I've never had strawberries ripen so early." In the dark little kitchen, Lucille Bekker brushes back a wisp of hair from her damp forehead. Her cheeks are flushed. She stirs juicy chunks of berry into a galvanized can of heavy cream, eggs, and sugar. Nathan totes it outside. Lucille follows and drops with a sigh onto the porch swing. "Now, the rest is up to you boys."

Abou sets the can in a green wooden bucket, pours ice and salt around it, and assembles the beaters, the lid, and the rigging to turn bucket and beaters by. Then he sits on the porch steps with the bucket at his feet and begins to crank. Nathan sits beside him and grins.

"You're doing physical work."

"Not for long. I'm simply showing you how."

"Do it some more," Nathan says. "I'm a slow learner."

"Hah." Abou's elbow digs him in the ribs. "You'll crank this like a galley slave or you'll get no ice cream."

The swing creaks. Lucille says, "You promised I'd like your play, Adonis, and you were right. I love it. I laughed and laughed."

Nathan turns his head, surprised. "You read it?"

"Of course I read it." She beams. "Bobby and I share everything."

"You did more than laugh"—Abou grunts with the effort of cranking the freezer—"you used up half a box of Kleenex, wiping away tears." He stops cranking. "We'll let it sit a few minutes now. Then it will be your turn." He nudges Nathan playfully again. "And I want to see you put some muscle into it."

Nathan says, "What did you think of my play?"

"That you have a very strange family." Abou stands, takes a folded handkerchief from a hip pocket, and wipes the sweat from his face. "What do they think of it?"

"They haven't seen it." Nathan glances back at Lucille. "We don't share everything. I guess we're all sort of private." He winces up at Abou against a very bright blue sky. "Maybe that's what makes us seem strange. My father goes along with his music, my mother goes along with her fortune-telling, and I go along—." He laughs. "Maybe I haven't started yet."

"You've started." Abou goes past him up the steps to sit beside his mother on the swing. "You've written a play like no play ever written before."

"Saroyan," she says. "*My Heart's in the Highlands.*"

"Saroyan is sentimental." Abou corrects her sharply. "*The Shotgun Flat* is as unsentimental as its title."

Nathan stands up, startled and concerned, and frowns at them.

"In fact," Abou says, "it's a shotgun blast." His amused brown eyes run Nathan up and down. "It's no wonder you haven't shown it to your family. You have no mercy."

Nathan feels attacked. "Is that what you think writing's supposed to be? An act of mercy?"

"Don't take offense," Abou says. "You've shown yourself no mercy, either."

"It's not a question of mercy," Nathan says. "That's your word." He sits down angrily on the step and begins cranking the freezer. Hard. Putting muscle into it. "I wouldn't be mean to them. I love them." The freezer clunks and squeals. Ice and salt fly. "It's only the truth. That's what writing is supposed to be—the truth."

Abou muses, "Who was it who said, 'What is truth'?"

"All right." Sweat runs down Nathan's ribs. Sweat runs out of his hair into his eyes. He cranks as if his life depended on it. "But is it any good? I told you Travers—"

"Travers is drinking himself into madness, exactly like his mother. They'll both go to early graves—you watch."

"He told Buddy the other day it was 'static.' "

"Yes, he's right about that." Abou pushes up off the swing, sits beside Nathan on the step again, pulls the freezer to him, begins to crank. "It lacks one element no play can be without—something the central character wants from the first moment, struggles for all evening, and gets, or fails to get, or ceases to want when the play ends."

"But my central character's only a child."

Abou lays a hand on his arm. "Don't be alarmed. It can be fixed. Easily." He smiles with his beautiful teeth. "I've jotted down some notes. If they make sense to you, the repairs should take no time at all." He bends forward, heaves at the crank again. It turns grudgingly. He tells Lucille, "It's starting to resist."

She waddles down the steps as Abou disassembles the rigging and lifts the lid. She peers. "Almost," she says. "Keep at it. I'll be back." Abou screws the mechanism down, and Nathan takes up cranking again. It's a stiffer job now. He is going to have blisters.

"Dan says Moon used to be the Munroe's cook. He and Travers grew up together."

"Till they were nine or ten. The Munroes tolerated her drinking for a long time, but finally they had to fire her. The shock of being without work with a small boy to raise sobered her up. They asked her back, but she wanted to be on her own, so they lent her the money to open Moon's."

Nathan says, "I guess that's why Dan's so confident Travers can't stop *The Shotgun Flat*."

"Dan's not very grown-up, you know—as witness his hare-brained scheme to elope to Mexico with Peg after graduation and get married." Abou slides the freezer to himself and cranks for a while. "Travers has paid back every penny he borrowed. He's filled those sixty pitiful seats almost every night. There's no arguing with success. We're going to have to fight hard for your play."

Nathan's heart jumps. "You're going to direct it then?"

Abou gives up cranking. "Travers is wrong about child actors." He brings out the handkerchief and wipes his face and neck again. He doesn't smell of sweat. He smells of cologne. "It's their mothers who are poison."

Lucille warbles, "Here we are," and the screen door creaks as she comes out with spoons jingling in bowls.

"After the ice cream," Nathan says to Abou, "can I please see your notes?"

FRANK SAYS, "WILL STONE BE AT THAT MOON'S PLACE for breakfast tomorrow, you think?"

Mouth full of meat loaf, Nathan nods. "Probably."

"Will you give him a message for me? Tell him Dr. Schoenwald leaves on the sixteenth."

Nathan swallows, cocks his head. "Sounds mysterious."

Frank stiffens. "Nothing mysterious about it. When Stone got me the job at the Atheneum—"

"You got the job yourself," Alma says.

"Well, all right, when he told me about the job, and they hired me, he asked me to, well"—Frank turns a little red, clears his throat, drinks some water—"kind of keep an eye on Schoenwald."

Nathan spoons mashed potatoes onto his plate and ladles gravy onto them. "Who is he?"

"Special guest lecturer on rockets. From Germany. Came in January. Going back there now."

It was January when Stone arrived to teach at FOJC. Nathan blinks at Frank. "You think that's the reason he got you the job? To spy for him?"

"What? Spy?" The newspaper lies beside Frank's plate. He fumbles with it, turning pages noisily. "I don't know what you're talking about. Simple favor, was all." He glances at Nathan over the paper. "You've been seeing too many movies." He folds the paper small again, lays it down, eats, looks at Nathan. "You won't forget to tell him, will you? He said it was very important. The man wasn't to leave, without my telling him."

"I suppose you've tried phoning him?"

"He's always out," Frank says. "Of course, if it's too much trouble—"

"It's no trouble," Nathan says. "I'll tell him."

"Good." They all eat in silence for a while. Then Frank says, "Here's a Bible banger with a new angle. This one bills himself as Lightning Smith." He pushes the paper at Nathan. "Look at that picture." Nathan looks. The ad it illustrates takes up a quarter page. In the picture, the evangelist stands on a platform with his arms spread wide while jagged bolts of lightning fly out of his splayed fingers. IF MAN CAN MAKE MIRACLES, WHY CAN'T GOD?

Nathan gives the paper back. "Scientific," he says.

"Beulah Land Church," Frank says. "Isn't that where that friend of yours goes—what's his name, Robin Hood?"

"Littlejohn," Nathan says. "That's the church, all right, but I don't think he goes anymore."

" 'Lightning Smith,' " Frank reads, " 'has brought more than one million sinners to repentance. This powerful, inspired preacher, this dynamic man of God, will startle and amaze you in ways you will never forget. For three electrifying nights—.' " Frank snorts and turns the page.

"It's all so misguided," Alma says, shaking her head.

NATHAN MEETS STONE COMING OUT OF MOON'S, picking his teeth. "Ah, Nathan. I haven't had a chance to tell you how beautiful your piece was about the swimmers. A poem." He chuckles. "And on the sports page, of all places. Buddy was fit to be tied."

"Tom Dawes needed help." Stone is moving on. "Wait." He stops, turns back, working with the toothpick, blinking those white lashes of his in the hard morning sunlight. Nathan says, "My father asked me to give you a message."

"Oh?" Stone tilts his head.

"Dr. Schoenwald is leaving on the sixteenth."

Stone goes motionless. His thick, freckled hand has poked the toothpick well back into his mouth. His mouth is wide open. There's something grisly about the picture.

"Are you all right?" Nathan says.

Stone gives a start. "What? Yes, sure, fine." He tries for a smile. It's not a success. He looks stunned. "Thank—thank your father for me." He seems surprised to find the toothpick in his hand, and he tosses it away. "As he may have told you—I've been waiting for that news." He glances at his watch. "Thank you, Nathan. I must run now." He doesn't run, but he walks away fast.

Inside the noisy café, Travers at the cash register is deep in conversation with Tommy Burns. Their heads are close together. They are almost holding hands. When Travers notices Nathan, he doesn't make a horrible face. Nathan wishes he would. Strange, but he's going to miss those. At the table under the Acme beer sign, he lays his stack of books on the windowsill and sits. Buddy grins at him.

"That column about the baseball players is the funniest thing you ever wrote."

"Now you're even with Tom Dawes," Nathan says.

"Of course, the baseball players don't think it's funny," Hotchkiss says. "They've been phoning in threats."

Nathan stares. "You're kidding."

"S'truth." Hotchkiss nods solemnly. "I told them to tell it to Dean Staat."

"When I answered the phone," Buddy says, "I told them they couldn't scare you. You'd fight them, day or night, anywhere, their choice of weapons."

"You'll get me killed with your sense of humor."

Buddy shrugs. "You wrote it. I didn't."

"They'll cool off," Hotchkiss says. "How's your play?"

"I'm making changes. I'll show them to Abou Saturday."

Peg says, "Dan's worried about time."

"So am I." The old waitress comes with coffee for him, and Nathan orders, and she rolls away on her swollen ankles. Nathan says, "I'm working as fast as I can."

"Our side has lost a vote," Peg says.

Nathan feels hollow. "No. Who?"

Buddy says, "Alex. She got a movie contract. Remember the guys with the plaid jackets that night at *An Inspector Calls*? Talent scouts. Paramount."

"They talked to Abou," Nathan says.

"Not screen tests, they didn't. They talked screen tests to her," Hotchkiss says, "such stuff as every American girl's dreams are made on."

"And ever since, they've been sending her flowers."

"But can't she still be on the board?" Nathan asks.

"She's got to be trained—dancing, singing, posture, grooming. At the studio. She has to polish her graces at parties and premiers. It's a twenty-four-hour-a-day regimen."

Nathan tastes his coffee. "She's too tall to be a movie star." He lights a cigarette, and understands Hotchkiss in a new way. The combination of tastes—coffee and cigarette smoke—is glorious. "She'll make all those million-dollar heroes look like midgets."

"Nevertheless," Peg says, "it's true. She's aglow."

"I'm not," Nathan says. "We needed her vote."

"She'd have left anyway," Peg says. "Her father's been raising hell about the Harlequin. Something went wrong there. Something about mad midnight sex orgies. Mr. Morgan wouldn't tell Alex, and Travers won't tell me. But Mr. Morgan was shocked out of his mind, and wasn't having his little girl mixed up with that Harlequin crowd anymore." She looks closely at Nathan. "Ah-hah." She plunges a hand into her big shoulder bag and comes up with pencil and notebook. "You know something, don't you, genius? 'It's a reporter's job to know.' Speak, Nathan."

"Dean Staat wouldn't let you print it," Nathan says. "Besides, do I look like the midnight sex orgy type to you? I wasn't there. And hearsay isn't news."

"I don't want to print it," Peg says. "I just want to know. And yes, you do look like the midnight sex orgy type to me. At least a midnight sex orgy I'd like to be at."

"Be serious. Moon and Dr. Dick will vote with Travers. Against you and Dan and Abou. That's a tie. What happens?"

Buddy looks at Peg. "Tell him," he says.

Peg looks blank. "Tell him what?"

"About Tommy Burns."

"He's short. What else is there to tell?"

"Didn't you hear? His parents paid the performance royalties for *Dame Nature*. That puts Tommy on the board."

Hotchkiss snorts and throws a disgusted look toward the cash register. "Board and bed, I'd say." He frowns at Nathan. "How did you manage to make Travers your enemy? I'd have said he was very—uh—fond of you."

"I can't tell you," Nathan says glumly. "It's private." His breakfast arrives. He stares at the eggs, sausages, and potatoes for a bleak moment, and pushes the plate away. He looks from Hotchkiss to Buddy to Peg. Tears sting his eyes. Their faces are blurs. He tries for a joke. "Well, now you know how *The Shotgun Flat* ended."

"Don't cry," Peg says. "Abou is on your side. And he's one person who can turn Travers around all by himself."

HOTCHKISS LEANS ACROSS AND OPENS the passenger door of his faded blue 1938 Dodge sedan for Nathan. The car's roof, hood, and fenders are strewn with leaves and twigs from that driveway where he parks it so he can write his novel in the garage—if there is any novel. Nathan gets in. The air in the car is thick with cigarette smoke. Hotchkiss says:

"Sorry to take you out at night, but Charlie's working graveyard at the *Independent,* Joanie wouldn't understand if I took Peg, and I need a witness with me."

"It's okay." But Nathan is scared. What will he be witness to? Twenty minutes ago, on the phone, Hotchkiss said that Stone is missing, has been missing for days. "I can spare the time. It's pointless to go on trying to fix that play."

"Dean Staat should be doing this," Hotchkiss grumbles. "But he's chickenshit, isn't he? 'You're the man's closest friend,' he says, and when I don't jump, he adds, 'you're his drinking buddy—everyone knows that.'" Hotchkiss jams the car in gear and they drive down Oleander under streetlamps scrimmed by tree branches. "You ever hear of a veiled threat, Nathan? Well, that's a veiled threat."

"Does the dean think Mr. Stone is sick?"

"He doesn't know what to think. He hasn't called in sick, but he also hasn't taken his classes. Not Monday, Tuesday, or today. He doesn't answer his telephone. He hasn't been at Moon's. He hasn't been at Laughing Jack's."

GLOOMY OLD CEDAR TREES FLANK THE DOOR of the apartment building. Hotchkiss pushes a button, the door lock buzzes, Hotchkiss opens the door, they step inside. They face a long, sullen hallway of doors dark with varnish. A hunchback comes out of the first of these. He doesn't look welcoming. "I'm not keen on this," he says. "But since it's the college that's asking, I guess it's all right. Mr. Stone's a very private man, you know."

"Have you seen him since Monday morning?"

"I don't spy." The manager goes at a crooked, spidery walk up a staircase with railings as thick with old varnish as the doors. "I respect my tenants." In an upper hallway as cheerless as the one below, he raps on a door numbered 9. "Mr. Stone?" he calls. "People from the college here to see you." No answer comes. He cocks a doubtful look up at Hotchkiss, checks Nathan with skeptical eyes; then with a headshake he unlocks the door and pushes it open.

The room is grays and browns, cheap carpet, overstuffed easy chair and couch, fabric worn thin, cushions sagging, a coffee table strewn with books, magazines, student papers, mail. A cracked pottery table lamp, a spindly metal floor lamp, a bookcase mostly empty. Nathan thinks of those books Stone left behind in Germany.

"Ken?" Hotchkiss calls. He crosses the room, reaches through a doorway, and switches on a light that shines on a small white kitchen—cupboards, stove, refrigerator, dishes in the sink. He switches the light off, goes to another door, works the light switch there. It's the bedroom. He steps inside. Because he is so afraid, Nathan forces himself to go as far as the doorway. The bed is made. A pair of trousers hangs over the back of a chair, belt drooping. The closet door is closed. Nathan opens his mouth to tell him not to open it, but no sound comes. Hotchkiss opens it.

"He can't have gone far," he says. "His clothes are all here." He shuts the closet, lights a small bathroom, steps in, looks around, steps out again. "Nothing."

The manager says, "If you don't need me, I'll get back to my place." He smiles radiantly with large false teeth. "I'm expecting a long-distance call." He crab-walks to the door. "My daughter's about to make me a grandfather."

"Congratulations," Hotchkiss says.

"Door will lock itself when you leave," the man says.

Hearing him hitching down the stairs, Nathan bends and picks up envelopes from the coffee table. The stamps have Hitler's picture on them. The printed return addresses appear governmental. He blinks at these an ignorant moment, lays them down, picks up envelopes with American postage. These were sent by Stone to various addresses in Germany, and have been returned rubber-stamped. What do they say? Gone—No Forwarding Address? He expects so. Stone writing to friends, trying to trace his wife and daughter—the friends now gone too? He feels sick, lays the envelopes down, and sees Hotchkiss standing in the bedroom doorway.

The journalism instructor looks stunned. In his hand lies a gun. From the movies, Nathan knows what it is. "A Luger," he says. "Where did you find it?"

"Under his pillow." Hotchkiss hefts it, gazes at it in amazement. "What the hell does a man like Ken Stone want with a thing like this?"

CARDBOARD CARTONS ARE PILED BESIDE THE PORCH. Lucille Bekker, in a faded housedress, a dish towel wrapped around her hair, comes bumping out the screen door, carrying a carton loaded with towels, sheets, pillowcases. The white shines in the sun as she stumps down the short steps to set the carton in the weedy driveway. Nathan, walking toward her with the script of *The Shotgun Flat* in his hand, wonders what is going on. Lucille straightens up and sees him, and doesn't smile. She looks frazzled.

"Adonis? What are you doing here?"

"It's Saturday," Nathan says. "Abou wanted changes in my play. I made them. He was going to look at them today—remember?" The wooden-sided station wagon is not in the driveway. "Where is he?"

"In Hollywood," Lucille says. "With the books."

"What books?"

"All the books." Lucille gestures with a short, plump arm at the house. "We're moving, can't you see?"

"I can see, all right," Nathan says. "Why? What about me? What about *The Shotgun Flat*. He promised—"

"Oh, Nathan, don't, please." She picks up an empty carton and climbs the steps. "I've got too much to do here to worry about you right now." The screen door bangs behind her. "There's no time."

"I guess not," Nathan says to himself. He goes onto the porch, stands among the potted plants, and calls inside, "Why are you moving?"

"They've hired Bobby at Paramount studios," she calls from the kitchen. Tinware rattles. "It's a sort of apprenticeship arrangement. For gifted theater students. He'll be working under directors. During shooting. On the sound stages. Learning the craft."

Nathan steps into the living room. It's empty, except for dust in corners, scraps of paper. The old gray furniture and rug are gone. The bookcase. Even the piano. "That's pretty exciting," he says. "I don't blame him for forgetting about me."

Lucille pushes through the curtain in the kitchen doorway, a carton of pots, pans, ladles, baking tins in her arms. "He didn't forget about you. He tried to ring you and explain. But your phone was disconnected."

"My mother forgets to pay the bill," Nathan says. He takes the carton from her and carries it outdoors. "None of the kids at Moon's knew this. They'd have told me."

"He didn't have time to tell anyone," Lucille says. She is holding open the screen door. "Hand me another carton, will you?"

He does. "It certainly was sudden."

"I guess that's how they do things in the picture business." She goes off with the box. Nathan follows her to the kitchen. "They proposed this months ago."

"He didn't mention it months ago," Nathan says.

"In case nothing came of it," she says. "It sounded too good to be true. And that was how it seemed to be turning out. He'd given up hope." She takes down cans from shelves. "Then, all of a sudden, on Sunday, they called and asked him to be at the studio Monday morning."

"That's why nobody's seen him," Nathan says.

Stacking the cans in the carton, she nods. "He's worked every single day from six in the morning until late at night. It's exciting, but very exhausting."

"He won't be directing any plays for a while, then."

She throws him a sympathetic smile. "I'm sorry, Adonis." She finishes filling the box with soup and beans, flour and sugar, rice and spaghetti—turns, pats his cheek. "But it's very good. Surely somebody will put it on."

"Not the Harlequin." Nathan picks up the carton and carries it through the curtain. "Abou was my only hope for talking Travers into it."

She follows him. "There are other theaters."

"Not that would look at stuff"—Nathan nudges the screen door open with his foot—"by a seventeen-year-old boy."

THE BIG CLEAN WINDOW OF THE OWL CAFETERIA glares with light, as it does all night every night. The inside of the place is white tile, the tabletops are white, so is the floor that somebody is forever mopping. Charlie Vorak sits at a table with a mug of coffee, and a notepad on which he is feverishly scribbling. Nathan pushes inside, collects a mug of coffee, and sits down across from Charlie, who looks up.

"Childe Nathan. What are you doing out so late?"

"Walking. I walk at night a lot."

Charlie slurps coffee. "I remember. When you can't sleep, you walk. What's the matter?"

Nathan tells him.

"Jesus," Charlie says, "that's too bad."

"It's good for Abou," Nathan says.

"Movies?" Charlie makes a face. "Maybe."

Nathan tries the coffee and lights a cigarette. "What are you doing out so late?"

"Covering the police blotter for the *Independent*."

"That's supposed to be a boring assignment."

"Not tonight." Charlie grins, and taps the notebook. "Tonight a scandal's broken that's going to rock this town." He gulps off his coffee, pockets his pencil, picks up his notes, and rises. "What a scoop." He heads for the door.

"Wait." Nathan's coffee is too hot to gulp. He leaves it to dash after Charlie. "What kind of scandal?"

"S-E-X." Charlie pushes outside. "Arrests galore."

"Galore?" Nathan trots after the editor, through the pools of lamplight on the deserted sidewalk. Charlie is moving as fast as his short legs will make his chunky body go. "Will you explain?"

"Doctors, lawyers, brokers," Charlie says, "you name it." He rubs his hands and chuckles. "Nathan, kid, every paper in the nation will reprint this story. And I've got an exclusive. None of the L.A. papers has anyone at Fair Oaks City Hall on weekends. I'll be famous." He hustles across Euclid Avenue. "You can say you knew me when."

"I don't understand. Sex? All those people?"

"Not just people—important, respected, well-off people. At a fancy mansion in the hills." Charlie laughs grimly. "And not just sex—perversion. Reputations are going to smash like statues at the sack of Rome."

Nathan's heart shrinks. He stops, catches Charlie's arm. "Are you talking about Desmond Foley's?"

Charlie squints. "How did you know?"

"There's been gossip," Nathan says.

"That he corrals teenage boys there for debauching by Fair Oaks' finest citizens, churchgoers, married men, family men with kids?"

" 'Debauching'—that's quite a word, Charlie."

Charlie barks a laugh. "I'm broadening my vocabulary for this special occasion."

"I thought you knew everything that goes on in Fair Oaks," Nathan says. "How come you never heard what I heard?"

Charlie makes a face. "Some circles I don't move in." He walks on, heading for the *Independent* building at the next corner. It stands up white against the night sky, a few lonely windows alight.

"Who told the police?" Nathan asks.

"It's not for publication, but I'll tell you, if you don't repeat it. It was a kid who's been going there, and suddenly got religion. There's this evangelist in town. Lightning Smith. Fire and brimstone. 'Repent, ye sinners, for the day of judgment is at hand.'" Charlie bellows this, flinging out his arms. The words echo down the deserted street. He grins at Nathan. "And at tonight's meeting, the kid repented, and ran straight from Beulah Land Church to the police department. He gave them the names of everyone involved."

Nathan feels sick. "Littlejohn Lemay?"

Charlie frowns. "You do know a lot about this."

Nathan shakes his head. "I know Littlejohn. We went to junior high together. I know about that church of his. And I know he was messed up with Desmond Foley."

"We can't print his name," Charlie says, "or the names of any of the kids. Just the men." A police patrol car glides past. Charlie jerks a thumb at it. "They're out rounding all of them up for questioning right now—men and boys." He looks at his watch. "Oh, Christ. Gotta hurry."

"Wait. Charlie, is your car here? Can I borrow it? I have to see somebody right away."

Charlie peers. "You mean warn somebody?"

"Unless you kill the story. Charlie, you killed the one about Sheila O'Hare and the sex at the Harlequin."

"This one's too big to hide," Charlie says.

"Nobody's killed," Nathan says, "nobody's wounded."

"Look, Nathan, if it's not in the *Independent* today, it will be in the L.A. papers tomorrow, anyway." He sighs, digs his keys from a pocket, lays them in Nathan's hand. "I'm sorry. You better go warn your friend, whoever he is."

HE LEAVES CHARLIE'S RICKETY CHEVY behind Dan's flashy Packard up on the silent coast road. He runs down the cliff steps. The beach house is dark. He tries the side door. It's locked. The front door. It's open. He stands in the big room, where the grass rugs are down now and the wicker furniture is in place. Nobody's here. He peers into the kitchen. No one. He softly climbs the stairs. All four doors up here stand open. He halts and listens, hoping to hear Dan breathing in his sleep, but the wind off the ocean and the thud of surf are too loud. The house creaks like a ship. It's not totally dark. He can make out the shapes of furniture, but not whether anyone is in any of the beds. Timidly he raps a door frame. "Dan?" No answer. Damn. Why is his car up on the road if he's not here?

Then footsteps thump the deck. He hears Dan's chortle, Peg's exuberant laugh. The door opens. The footsteps cross the big room. There's the clunk of the kitchen door. He runs quickly down the stairs and outside. He wades in sand around to the side of the house where light falls from kitchen windows and a pane in the kitchen door. He climbs wooden steps and raps the door.

"Dan? It's me—Nathan."

Peg gives a shriek. And through the glass Nathan sees her, her wonderful black cloud of hair pinned loosely up, dash long-legged for the swing door. She is naked. The door flaps closed behind her. Nathan hears her fleeing up the stairs. Dan is naked too. He grabs a sandy beach towel off the floor and knots it around his hips. He yanks open the door. "Nathan, it's three in the morning. What's the meaning of this?"

"There's trouble," Nathan says, "very bad trouble."

"Are you all right? You're so pale."

"I'm not all right," Nathan says, "and neither are you."

"What do you mean?" Dan steps back, holding the door open. "Come in. What kind of trouble?"

"I'm sorry about the time." Nathan swings a chair out from the table and sits down. His legs seem unable to hold him. He nods at the opposite chair. Eyeing him warily, Dan sits. Nathan says, "But I only just found out." Without mentioning Charlie's name, he tells

Dan what Charlie told him. "The police have the names of everybody involved."

Dan acts bewildered. "What's that got to do with me?"

"Maybe nothing—directly." Nathan lifts his head and listens. The shower is running. He hears the water going through the pipes. Just the same, he leans across the table and keeps his voice low. "You never went there?"

"Certainly not."

"Well, Gene Woodhead did," Nathan says.

Dan blinks. "Gene who? Ah, that boy in the cadet's uniform, the night of the party."

"Come on, Dan. Don't play games. This is serious. The boy who went to the police is a friend of Gene's. It was Gene who introduced him to Desmond Foley."

"Nathan, I really don't understand you. I hardly know Gene Whitehead."

"Woodhead," Nathan says. "You know him right down to the skin."

"Did he tell you that?" Under his suntan, Dan is pale. "Then he's a liar."

"He didn't have to tell me. I know him. I used to do sex with him myself. One whole summer. And the way he was looking at you and you were looking at him, fawning over him, fetching him food and drink, it was obvious as hell."

Dan is shaking. "Nathan—I am not that way." He stands up. "And anyone who could come here and charge me with such rotten things is not my friend. I'll have to ask you to leave." He turns his back, chin raised, arms crossed on his chest. As if this were a play. "Now, please. I'm sorry our friendship had to end like this."

"So am I." Nathan gets up and goes to the door. "But don't wait for graduation, Dan. Be all impulsive and crazy in love and take Peg to Mexico tonight, and get married tomorrow morning." He pulls open the door. "So when the police scare Gene Woodhead into giving them your name—"

Dan turns sharply, almost losing the towel. "He wouldn't. Gene wouldn't do that to me. He and I are—"

"Strangers?" Nathan says. "Good night, Dan." He goes out into the dark, and closes the door.

THE THUMP-A-THUMP OF THE WASHING MACHINE wakens him. Downstairs. Directly below him on the back porch. He raises his head to peer groggily at the clock. He rubs his eyes and looks again. Has it stopped? No, he hears its tinny tick. Nearly one. Broad daylight. Hot. He is sweaty. He totters down the hall to use the toilet, splashes himself awake with cold water, then kicks into jeans, and goes numbly down the stairs. The kitchen is vacant, breakfast dishes still on the table. Also the *Independent*, folded into the odd shapes it always takes when Frank has read it through. Nathan finds the front page.

ACCUSATIONS OF MISCONDUCT
HIGH SCHOOL BOY LINKS
FAIR OAKS PROFESSIONAL MEN
TO SEX RING
By Charles Vorak

Nathan swallows in a dry throat. He reads quickly down the gray column. "District Attorney . . . fourteen arrests . . . confessions confirm boy's sordid story of shocking sexual . . . free on bail this morning . . . Desmond Foley, musician at whose secluded . . . Harvey M. Coldbrook, M.D.; Chase Milligan, of the brokerage firm of Hyde, Rouche and Wendt; Philip M. Steck, attorney-at-law; Roland Gregory, veterinarian; Municipal Court Judge Lester . . ."

"Didn't I tell you Desmond Foley would get into trouble?" Frank stands in the doorway, wet wash in his arms.

"You were right," Nathan says.

"You want to step out here and see what's wrong? I've made a mess of this." He has. The sheets he is holding are supposed to be white, but they are pink. Nathan steps past him out onto the porch, plunges an arm into the soapy water of the Maytag, feels around, and comes up with a red shirt. The one he bought to take Sheila to the movie. The one he wore that morning to Desmond Foley's. Taking it off him tenderly in that breezy noontime bedroom, Foley had said it made him too beautiful to bear looking at. Nathan holds it up dripping for Frank to see.

"Damn," Frank says. "How did I miss that?"

"Whites with whites," Nathan says, and tosses the shirt aside. He finds a dusty bottle of bleach, pours half of it into the water, takes the sheets from Frank and pokes them back into the water, lays the lid on the machine, and starts it churning again. "They'll still be pink, but maybe not quite so pink. Frank, why are you doing this? It's my job."

"You needed sleep. You were out all night." Frank goes into the kitchen. "Coffee?" He takes a mug from a cupboard, fills it from the old blue enamel pot on the stove, brings it to Nathan at the table. "What was it all about?"

He hates lying to Frank. "A crisis with my play."

Frank goes back to the stove to fill his own mug. "How many does that make?" He sits down and pushes the newspapers aside. "First your newspaper bunch didn't let you finish reading it to them, then this Travers Jones took against it, then the fat Arab said you had to rewrite it. Now what?"

"He's not 'the fat Arab,' Frank," Nathan says hotly. "He's as American as you are, and his name is Abou Bekker."

Frank holds up placating hands. " 'May his tribe increase,' " he says. "Sorry. No harm intended. You're touchy today. Maybe you ought to go back to bed."

"Excuse me," Nathan says. "I guess I'm hungry." He fetches cornflakes, milk, a bowl, and a spoon, and sits down again. "They've given Abou a job at a movie studio." Nathan fills the bowl with cornflakes, spoons on sugar, pours on milk. "So he won't have time to direct the play."

"That's a shame," Frank says. "But I still don't know what kept you out all night."

"I had to go to the beach." A shred of the truth.

" 'Heard the mermaids singing,' did you?"

" 'Each to each.' No, I thought Dan might direct it." How can he be so glib? It's disgusting. "He's going to be in it, anyway." Nathan stuffs his mouth with cereal, chews, swallows. "And the beach house doesn't have a phone, so I borrowed Charlie's car and drove down there. To ask him."

"What was the hurry?"

"He leaves for Mexico tomorrow—today."

Maybe Frank believes him, maybe not. He lets it go. "All right. But now that we've got a telephone, I wonder if you couldn't jingle it once in a while when you're out late, to let your mother and me know you're all right?"

"I'm sorry you were worried," Nathan says, "but it was already late when I decided to go, and I didn't want to wake you up." He bends over the bowl and shovels in more cornflakes. "I was all right."

"Good." Frank pushes back his chair. "I'll get on with the damned wash."

Nathan yelps, "Please, Frank, don't. You go to the park, okay? Play chess. Swap stories with your friends." He puts his hands together prayerfully. "Please?"

It's plain Frank is relieved, but he pretends to be wounded. "Only trying to help."

"Don't feel bad," Nathan says. "I promise to call you the minute I need anything dyed pink."

THE SUN IS HOT, splintering down through the pine branches, and there's a good breeze. He tests the wash flapping on the line. Not dry yet. But soon. He climbs the back steps, pulls open the screen, crosses porch and kitchen, pushes into the hall, and hears a car stop out front. It's not a car whose sound he knows. He halts, and stands waiting for fate to strike. He's been expecting it, dreading it, ever since he woke up.

But the steps crossing the porch aren't those of police officers.

He knows those steps. Alma's come home. His heart lifts, he starts for the door to meet her, then waits, alarm jumping up in him again. Something's wrong. There's no spring in her step. Pushing the door shut behind her, she comes out of the entryway at an old woman's gait. Usually, the Sunday meetings at the Spiritualist church buoy her up and send her home happy. She looks anything but happy. He feels like running up the stairs before she can see him, and escaping down the trellis.

She speaks. "Where's your father?" Her voice is dull, her usually lustrous eyes clouded.

"The park," Nathan says. "What's wrong?"

"A terrible thing has happened." Alma goes into the sitting room. "A simply terrible thing." Her voice drifts back, sepulchral. "And to the most wonderful woman in the world." Nathan is able to draw a shaky breath. Whatever the terrible thing is, it's not to him it's happened. Not yet. He goes into the sitting room, where she sits limp in a wing chair, staring at nothing. "What is it?"

"Mrs. Gregory's son has been arrested," Alma says. "Some wicked boy has told the most awful stories to the police, the most disgusting lies."

Nathan sits cross-legged on the floor at her feet. "I read about it in the paper."

That gets her attention. She looks at him startled, as if seeing him life-size for the first time. "Yes, of course. Your father and I can't protect you anymore, can we? From the squalid side of life." She bends forward and strokes his hair. "If I could, I would. Forever."

"Roland is his name," Nathan says. "A veterinarian."

She nods. "Just as I did with you, his mother taught him the laws of reincarnation and karma as a little boy. He's the gentlest, kindest young man. He knows that in each of the creatures of this earth there dwells an immortal soul that one day will inhabit human form. These poor beings can't speak about their pain. Can you think of nobler work for a man to dedicate his life to?"

"I guess not," Nathan says.

"And now this." Alma's face darkens, her hands make fists on the chair arm. "He's ruined. Of course, it's all a mistake. There's no truth in it. I stood and heard him swear to his mother, with tears streaming down his face, that there is not a shred of truth to it."

"He'll be all right, then," Nathan says.

"Never." Alma stands up and begins to pace. "Even when the lies are shown up to be exactly that—nothing but vicious lies—suspicion will cling to him for the rest of his life. The newspaper should never have printed it."

Nathan wants to tell her he asked Charlie to quash it, but he can't, can he, can't tell her or Frank anything, not about this, not about most of his life—not anymore. He wishes he were a child again. He gets to his feet. "I'll fix you a cup of tea."

"Mrs. Gregory is so precious to me, so precious to so many of us." Alma wrings her hands. "I'm frightened for her, Nathan. I offered to stay. Several ladies did, but she shut us out. She's like I've never seen her before. I'm afraid her nerves may give way completely."

"Did you call a doctor?"

"She doesn't believe in doctors. She believes in the healing spirit of the Universal Mind."

Nathan starts for the kitchen. "She'll be all right, then, won't she? You try having some faith, yourself."

She comes along after him. "Yes, of course, you're right. How much like Dr. Fuller you sound, sometimes."

Filling the kettle at the sink, he throws her a smile. "Shall I grow a little white beard?"

She smiles wanly back at him. "Not just yet, please."

POLICEMEN STAND AROUND HIS COT. He wakens with a cry, dives for the lamp, and switches it on. Nobody. He is in a sweat and breathing hard. Trembling, he opens the door to the hall—the house is pitch dark, dead asleep. He yanks into his shirt, pants, socks, and shoes, switches off the lamp, and climbs out the window and down by the honeysuckle vine. He is so shaken he loses his footing, and damn near falls. Oleander Street is empty and hushed under its trees. To the south glow the neons of Sierra Street. He heads north into the sleeping neighborhoods.

Gradually his heartbeat slows, his breathing eases, he cools off. He smiles wanly to himself. Walking is still the best medicine. How far has he come? He doesn't know or care. But he's on a street lined by old date palms that now and then shed long, dried fronds. And behind him one of those fronds rattles. As if someone had kicked it. He turns to squint back through the shadows. Nothing. He waits. But the dry scraping doesn't come again. His nerves are shot. He's imagining things. He turns and walks on.

He's going west on Guava Street when he hears brush crackle, and a muffled curse. He whirls. A crouched figure darts across the streetlight-mottled sidewalk into darkness. He was right before. He's being followed. By whom—the baseball players? He'd better get back home. He turns in at an alley and begins to run. From the end of the alley, he starts eastward on Loquat Street, but down the block figures stand waiting. He turns back, heads west toward Arroyo Avenue, and on Arroyo heads north again. Going where? There's only one place. Joe Ridpath's nursery.

He glances back. Nobody's coming. Maybe no one ever was. He slows to a walk, but he keeps going. He'll make a wide circle before he heads home. What's that? The low thrum of an engine. He turns. There are no curbs, no sidewalks up here. A car comes creeping along the road edge with its lights off. It's not a police car. It's not any car he knows. He stands undecided a moment. But only a moment. It's after him, all right. He turns and runs. As hard as he's ever run in his life. Block after block. But dark and relentless, the car comes crawling after. His legs are giving out. He's gasping for air. Then pain stabs his side. He grabs his side, staggers, can't keep his feet. He sprawls in weeds and gravel.

"Now we've got him." The car stops, its doors open, howling figures lunge out. He can't tell who they are. It's too dark. The doors slam. He has to get up and run again. He pushes to his hands and knees. "Kill the son of a bitch." And they are on him. A foot jolts him in the ribs. Someone lands on his back, flattening him, beating his head with fists. "You chickenshit sneak." Nathan covers his head with his arms. But that doesn't protect the rest of him. He's being kicked and punched all over.

He's dragged to his feet. "This will teach you to run to the cops." Some one holds him from behind, pinning his arms. Three of them come at him. He kicks at them. It's no good. A knee slams up into his crotch. He bends forward with the pain. The knee crashes into his face. Bone crunches. Blood spurts from his nose. "It wasn't me," he gasps. "It wasn't me." Blood chokes the words into a gurgle. "Let me go." He tries to yank free. His arms are wrenched upward. It hurts. He screams.

And suddenly a dog is rushing around them, barking, snarling, snapping. A voice bawls, "What in hell's going on here? You trying to kill that boy?" There's a flash, a loud bang, a whoosh in the air. "Clear off now, you hear? Clear off, or I'll buckshot your ass." The gun goes off again.

"Oh, shit." The kicking stops, the hands holding him let go. He can't stand on his own. He drops to the ground. Voices cry, "Don't shoot, mister! Don't shoot!" The boys scramble for the car, falling over each other. The car roars off before its doors even close. Nathan tries to get up but he's too dizzy. He groans, and lays his face in the grass and grit. The pain makes him sick to his stomach. The dog whimpers in his ear, noses his hair. A hand rolls Nathan over. Joe Ridpath crouches beside him. "Well, I'm damned. It's you again."

"Yes sir." Nathan's mouth is swollen. It's hard to speak. "Sorry to bother you so late." He sits up, wincing. "Home was too far." He tries to wipe the blood off his face. "I didn't know where else to run to."

"No bother," Ridpath says. "Friends of yours?"

Nathan wants to laugh. Instead, he faints.

THEY COME OUT THE BACK DOOR OF THE HOSPITAL into a half circle of light that shows white ambulances waiting, and be-

yond them lightless buildings and a wide night sky. He can see
these things, though his eyes are swollen nearly shut. His face is
bandaged. Gauze and tape are tight around his rib cage. Nothing
hurts anymore. But the pills that have killed the pain have left him
dopey. Joe Ridpath helps him up into his rusty pickup truck, slams
the door, goes around to the other side, and climbs in behind the
cracked steering wheel. He starts the clattery engine.

"All right if I take you home now?"

Nathan has refused to go home, refused to let Ridpath call
Frank and Alma, pretended to the emergency room people Ridpath
was his father. "No. Where I want to go is twelve-twenty-one Bar-
ranca Lane." He looks into Ridpath's fretful face. "You don't have
to take me. I can walk."

"You couldn't hardly walk across this here lot," Ridpath says.
"What's so important? You're hurt, boy."

"I don't care," Nathan says. "I have to go there. I'll pay for the
gas."

The truck jounces out of the parking lot, and Ridpath points
it north. "This got something to do with them that beat you up?"

Nathan nods. "Everything."

"Going to be more trouble? Because if there is—"

"No more trouble," Nathan mumbles, and falls asleep.

"WHAT'S THAT?" RIDPATH SLOWS THE TRUCK. Nathan
blinks awake. Ahead, along a street of brushy old eucalyptus trees,
firelight casts a fitful glow. "Looks like trouble to me."

It's a big bonfire, in the front yard of a house midway up the
block. Figures surround it, a lot of figures, men, women, children.
The windows of Ridpath's truck are down. Nathan hears jeering,
hooting, chanting. A sign stops Ridpath at a crossroads.

He turns the wheel. "I'm going to take you home."

"Let me out here." Nathan fumbles for the door handle. "I'll
walk."

"Your crazy old man would kill me," Ridpath says.

"I won't get mixed up in it," Nathan promises. "Turn left here. There's an alley. I'll go in the back way." The alley is unlighted, but Nathan knows the gate. He used to go through it often. "Stop here." He works the cranky door handle and climbs down. It's painful. He nearly faints again. He slams the door. "I'll be right back."

He goes through the gate. The rear windows of the house are lighted up. The rear door opens and a man comes out, lugging suitcases. A woman hurries after him. They make for the side door of the garage. The man's breathing is quick and angry. The woman whimpers. They disappear into the garage. Car doors open in there.

Nathan limps across the lawn and in at the back door. And there, in the kitchen, stands Littlejohn, holding a carton stuffed with clothes, not folded, tumbled every which way, sleeves and corners hanging out. In his surprise, he almost drops the carton.

"Nathan. You're all bloody. What happened?"

"Four kids from Desmond Foley's jumped me in the dark and beat me up." Nathan is dizzy and weak. He drags out a chair and sits. "They think I was the one who told the police. If somebody hadn't come along, they'd have killed me, Littlejohn. Next time they will."

"No." Littlejohn looks ready to cry.

"Yes. Now, God damn it, you call the *Independent* right now and tell them you were the one who snitched, just you, and nobody else—and you want it printed tomorrow. Littlejohn Lemay—in large type, so nobody can miss it."

"Nathan, I can't." He jerks his head to indicate the uproar at the front of the house. "Beulah Land Church already knows, and look how they're acting."

"I don't care fuck about the stupid church."

"They've burned 'Sodomite' in the lawn with gasoline. How do you think my parents feel?"

Nathan pushes up off the chair and wobbles to an inner doorway. "Where's the phone?" He turns and knocks the carton out of Littlejohn's hands. The clothes scatter on the shiny linoleum. "You go make that call. Now."

Littlejohn backs away, shaking his head. "What do you want? For those boys to kill me? Be fair, Nathan. I didn't give your name to the police. Not yours, not Gene's. You're my friends. I protected you. Don't make me—"

Footsteps scrape behind Nathan. He turns. Mr. and Mrs. Lemay look shocked when they see the blood and bandages. "Nathan Reed? What in the world—?"

"I had an accident," Nathan says. "Where you going?"

"I don't know," Mr. Lemay says. "But if we try to stay here, they'll burn us out."

Sirens wail in the distance. The police are coming. Does Littlejohn understand what that means? It hurts his mouth, but Nathan grins at him. Littlejohn understands. He looks sick. Nathan mumbles, "Excuse me," edges past the elder Lemays, and steps out into the darkness. He hobbles across the lawn and opens the gate. The truck is waiting. Flinching at the pain, he hauls himself up into it, slams the door, sighs and shuts his eyes. The sirens grow louder. Ridpath starts the engine.

"Did you get what you come for?"

"Not yet—but I will." Nathan tries to laugh, but it hurts his ribs. "That's the police. We'd better go."

Ridpath grunts, and the truck clatters into the dark.

A WEEK HAS PASSED. He's back at Moon's.

"The barbarians haven't changed," Charlie says. "Not in two thousand years. They still go for the noses."

Nathan has taken off the bandages. His eyes aren't swollen shut anymore, but the flesh around them is still black and blue. His nose is flattened.

"Also the genitalia." Hotchkiss lights a cigarette from the butt of another. "How are your genitalia, kid?"

"They used their knee on those too," Nathan says.

Charlie says, "That will teach you to insult baseball players in the public prints." He looks at Buddy.

Buddy turns red and says, "Jesus, I'm sorry, Nathan. I didn't think they'd take me seriously."

Hotchkiss says, "You mean it was really them?"

"Who else?" Nathan shrugs and forks scrambled eggs into his mouth. The cuts inside have healed. The teeth that were loose are tight again. "My father wanted the police to lock up the whole team, but I talked him out of it. There were only four, and I couldn't see their faces. It was too dark." He washes down the eggs with a gulp of coffee, and asks Charlie, "You going to get a Pulitzer Prize for your big sex-scandal story?"

"All the news unfit to print?" Hotchkiss says.

"The follow-up about the Beulah Land Church crowd was hilarious," Buddy says. "Here's this kid confessing all to get right with Jesus, but are the dwellers in Beulah Land grateful to him for exposing Desmond Foley's little Sodom in suburbia—do they take the repentant prodigal to their bosom and kill the fatted calf? They do not. They descend on him with torches and anathemas."

"And the police come to break it up, and into the public prints goes the scrupulously concealed name of Myron and Hester Lemay's darling boy—Littlejohn."

"I hope he's run a long way." Buddy looks thoughtfully at Nathan. "If the ones he squealed on ever catch him, the same thing could happen to him that happened to you."

Hotchkiss eyes them both puzzledly for a second, then changes the subject. "What's going on with your play?"

"Abou's left town. He's taken a job at Paramount."

Hotchkiss's eyebrows go up. "And that's that?"

"Oh, no," Nathan says. "George Abbot's going to do it at the Shubert Theatre on Broadway." Suddenly he's lost his appetite. He lights a cigarette and looks away. And here comes Donald Donald, thin, his paleness underscoring his pimples. He gives the table a grin, grabs a chair from the next table, sits on it with his arms resting on its back.

"Young Lazarus," Hotchkiss says.

"I wasn't sick," Donald says. "I was faking it." He takes Nathan's coffee cup and drinks from it. "If I didn't stage my Little Nell act once in a while, nobody would put up with my being such a louse, would they?"

"I went to the hospital. I saw you. You convinced me."

Donald seems really surprised. "You did?"

Charlie says, "So did I—with Buddy."

"What for?" Donald drinks more of Nathan's coffee. "Were you afraid I might live?"

"You old sentimentalist, you," Charlie says.

"A regular Edgar A. Guest," Hotchkiss says.

"Peg was there," Donald says. "She brought flowers." He looks around the noisy café at kids hunched over food and drink and books, yelling at each other, laughing at each other. He asks Charlie, "Where is Peg?"

Charlie gets up. "Gotta go. See you all later."

Donald blinks after him. "Did I say something wrong?"

"Peg and Dan Munroe ran off to Mexico last weekend," Buddy says. "To get married. They're going to stay all summer. Peg is going to write that novel. Dan is going to learn Spanish from the natives. It says here."

"I heard about the plan." Donald drinks more of Nathan's coffee. "But the personnel changed, didn't it?"

Nathan asks Hotchkiss, "Did Mr. Stone ever come back?"

"He was on a bender. He's teaching his classes again, but he's not eating breakfast—not here, anyway. I've had a drink with him. But he's quiet. Something's worrying him."

Donald jerks his head at Nathan. "You know, Reed once threatened to beat me up. Fact. What happened, Reed—you pick on somebody your own size?"

"It was a team effort," Buddy says.

Donald says, "They quit too soon—he's still beautiful."

"An inner sweetness shining through," Hotchkiss says. He pushes back his chair. "Buddy, you ready to go?"

Donald moves to set the coffee cup in front of Nathan again and knocks it against the edge of the table, dumping coffee into Nathan's lap. "Oh, sorry, Reed. Guess I'm still a little weak."

Nathan jumps to his feet, snatches paper napkins, and blots up the coffee. "You shit, Donald." He slams the wet brown wad on the table. "You could have died in that hospital. You weren't really trying."

Buddy is shocked. "Nathan!"

Hotchkiss is shocked. "Take it easy."

Donald only smirks. "I was thinking of you, Reed. You need me. Life is too easy for you." He gets off the chair and sets it back in place. "You were born with it all—looks, talent, brains. You live in heaven. I can show you what it's like in hell. Isn't that what friends are for?"

Nathan opens his mouth to ask him about the French newspapers. But he doesn't. He sits down again. "You'll never know," he says.

ALMA'S EYES FILL WITH TEARS WHENEVER SHE LOOKS at him. He hopes this will pass, as he hoped his going back to school would reassure her. But now, as he stands in the hallway, looking into the sitting room, she is wistful and damp-eyed again. "Poor Nathan. It was your father I was worrying about." She sits at the drop-leaf desk and taps her pencil on a horoscope chart. "Transiting Mars is just about to oppose his natal Saturn. I've been so afraid for him, I didn't even look at your chart."

Nathan walks in and gives her a hug. "It's all right."

"But it's here, plain as day." She waves the scribbled chart at him in dewy-eyed contrition. "Sudden and mysterious assault—Uranus squaring Mars on the ascendant. A scar on the face you'll wear for life."

"Forget it," he says. "It doesn't hurt."

"I'll never forgive myself," she cries. "I could have warned you. It's my doing, Nathan. I'm responsible."

"No. That was four other fellows."

She studies him, head tilted. "The doctors can work wonders these days. You had such a beautiful nose."

"Just like my mother's." He kisses the top of her head. "I really don't mind, Alma." He heads for the hall and the stairs. "It's a lot of trouble—being beautiful."

IT'S LATE. HE'S WORN OUT FROM STUDYING, trying to catch up the week's homework he missed. He straightens his shoulders, leans back in the chair, raises his arms in a long, weary stretch. And hears Frank and Alma coming up the stairs. The chattering clock says eleven. There must have been a late show on the radio. He pushes back the chair, rises, goes and opens the door. Alma has gone into the bathroom. He calls to Frank.

"Can I talk to you?"

Frank stands in the weak, watery light of the hall ceiling fixture. "Depends what you say."

"You haven't spoken to me for a week."

"What did you expect?" Frank comes to the doorway. "I trusted you. You lied to me. You got pretty high and mighty with me here a while back when I told you I was looking for work and I wasn't. Well, now the shoe is on the other foot." He comes into the room. "Did you think I asked you who beat you up just to pass the time of day?"

"No, Frank." Nathan shuts the door.

"I asked because I care, Nathan. You'll be a father someday and you'll understand how much I care." He sits on the side of the cot. "I hated to see you hurt that way, hated the ones that did it to you."

"I'm not crazy about them, either," Nathan says.

Frank looks up at him. "Then why protect them?"

"I wasn't protecting them." Nathan sits on the chair again. He doesn't look at Frank, he looks at the pages of the open book by the typewriter, shining in the lamplight. "I was protecting you. Trying to."

"Me?" Frank scoffs. "From what?"

Nathan still can't look at him. He mumbles, "Something you wouldn't like knowing."

"You mean something you're ashamed of," Frank says.

"You could say that." Nathan gets up, goes to stand at the screens, gazing out at the black shaggy shapes of the pines against the night sky. "How did you find out?"

"I went to see Joe Ridpath," Frank says.

"What?" Nathan spins around. "That 'redneck son of a bitch'? You were so mad that night when I told you he was the one who brought me home, you ranted and raved."

"I got over it." Frank sits on the bed. "He saved your life. I didn't. He was there. I wasn't. He took you to the hospital. I couldn't. Don't have a car. I'm not totally unreasonable, you know."

"I never thought you were." Nathan sits in the light at the book-strewn table. "You just hate Joe Ridpath, is all. I understand that."

"He did the right thing," Frank says. "I'm grateful. And the next morning, I drove the Sierra Tech station wagon over to the nursery and thanked him." He smiles glumly. "Ignorant hillbilly bastard."

"And he told you about the side trip we took after the hospital," Nathan says. "Is that right?"

Frank nods. "Said you told him it connected to the beating you took. I didn't bother you with it because you were in such pain, it was better for you just to take your pills and sleep it off. I still believed you—that it was the baseball players from school. But then came the evening paper. Now, Joe Ridpath didn't know what that bonfire on the lawn up there in Foothill meant. You didn't explain it to him. The paper explained it to me."

He raises his shaggy gray head in the dim light and looks at Nathan. "I can also put two and two together. It was Littlejohn Lemay you went to see. And he was in hot water over that sex mess at Desmond Foley's. So it was about that they beat you up—pretty much had to be, didn't it?" He gives his head a sorry shake. "You'd lied to me. And it made me feel terrible. It changed everything between us. You wanted me to talk to you?" He laughs sadly. "Not half as much as I wanted you to talk to me."

"I couldn't see their faces," Nathan says. "It was too dark. But you're right—they were from Desmond Foley's. They thought I was the one who told the police."

Frank stares. "Why would they think that?"

Nathan sighs. "I went there once and made trouble and they saw me."

Frank's face twists. "Went there? What in hell for? Didn't I warn you about Foley? Didn't I tell you to keep away from him?"

"Yes, and it was good advice, but I didn't take it, did I? I kept hearing talk. And I"—he turns to the windows again—"was curious. I wanted to see for myself."

Frank snorts. "There are things in life it's better not to poke your nose into."

Ruefully, Nathan rubs his nose. "I know that now."

"What kind of trouble?" Frank asks.

"It wasn't intentional." Nathan comes back into the light, stands looking down into Frank's face. "I didn't act morally superior, or anything like that, Frank. But that must have been how they took it."

"What do you mean, you didn't act morally superior?" Frank's tone is appalled. "You weren't part of it?"

"What Charlie called the debauchery?" Nathan shakes his head and sits down again. "No. Look, I'd like to leave it now, okay? It's past. Can we forget it, please?"

Frank starts to object, stops himself, sighs. "I guess so. I wish it hadn't happened. But I expect you've learned your lesson." He pushes to his feet, heavily, an old man. "You don't need sermons from me."

"Wait." Nathan bends and pulls from crackly brown paper under the table one of the multigraphed scripts of *The Shotgun Flat*. He lays it in Frank's hands. Frank blinks at it. Nathan says, "It's my play. Will you read it, please?"

Frank opens it. "I was wondering when you'd ask me."

"I wanted you to see it on stage. But I don't suppose that will ever happen now. Frank, it's got you in it, and Alma, and Aunt Marie. I thought it was loving and funny. But Abou says it's merciless."

Frank flips over the pages. "Bad as that, is it?"

"I don't want to hurt your feelings." Nathan reaches for it. "I can just put it in the incinerator. That's what I've been thinking I should do."

"After all that work?" Frank holds it to his chest. "It took you months. Hell, you almost killed yourself to finish the damn thing."

"It was probably a mistake," Nathan says. "I'm making a lot of mistakes lately."

Frank opens the door. "I'll take it downstairs and read it now. I don't feel like sleeping."

WHEN HE GETS HOME FROM SCHOOL THE NEXT DAY, the script lies beside the typewriter. Fastened to the cover with a bent paper clip is a badly typed note. *Very good*, it says. *I don't recognize the fool who plays all the instruments, but I suggest you not show this to your mother. She might.*

EXCEPT FOR THE SPORTS PAGE, the *Monitor* is ready to put to bed. Supplied with a hamburger and French fries from across the street, and a large paper cup of coffee, little Tom Dawes stays behind at his littered desk to take the out-of-town game reports over the phone when his stringers call them in. Nathan holds the door so Charlie can push Buddy's wheelchair out. They go down the empty corridor and out through the clattery bronze-and-wired-glass building doors. The air is heavy. Sudden gusts of wind turn the leaves of the trees. It's not a cold wind. It's warm and damp. The sky is cloudy, the color of his bruises. When they reach the parking lot, which is mostly empty because it's so late in the day, rain starts to fall. Fat, heavy drops.

"Come on, Nathan," Charlie says, "I'll drive you too."

The stuttery old windshield wiper of Charlie's Chevy is having a tough time with the downpour when they reach Oleander Street. Nathan ducks and runs to the porch, but his hair is soaked by the time he reaches it. He keeps his head down, and almost collides with two youngish men standing there in hats, fly-front raincoats, and polished shoes. Have the police come for him after all? The front door is open. Alma is framed in the door. She's been seeing clients. She wears one of her costumes for that purpose—black dress with silver trim, silver headband with a white plume, lots of thin silver bracelets. She looks pale and scared.

"Nathan, thank God." She steps out and hugs him. "Something's happened to your father."

"Nathan?" One of the men holds out his hand. "Arthur Prior. Army intelligence."

Nathan shifts his stack of books and shakes the hand.

"Your father's had an accident. He's in the infirmary at Sierra Tech. He's asking for your mother and you. We've come to drive you there."

"What kind of accident?" Nathan says.

"He'll be all right," Prior says.

"Why isn't he in the hospital?" Nathan says.

"The institute has fine medical facilities," Prior says. "And we'd like to keep the incident as quiet as possible."

The other man says to Alma, "You'll want a coat, Mrs. Reed. Can I get it for you?"

" 'Incident'?" Nathan says. "What does that mean?"

Alma says, "Why won't you tell us what happened?"

"It's a national security matter, ma'am." The man steps inside to the hat rack and lifts down Alma's purple cloth coat. He helps her into it. "It involves another country. It's a touchy diplomatic situation."

Alma is scornful. "Oh, what rubbish."

The man smiles faintly. "You may be right. But we don't know yet. Foreign scientists come to Sierra Tech, important men. We're responsible for their safety."

"Well, Frank Reed is no foreign scientist, for heaven's sake—he's just a porter."

"And he'll tell you what happened," Prior says to her, and to Nathan, "You want to leave your books here?"

Nathan takes the books to the staircase and sets them there. And a small olive-skinned woman with dyed black hair peers from the gloomy living room into the shadowy hall, wide-eyed, anxious. She says in a timorous voice to Alma, "Perhaps I'd better come back another time?"

"Oh, Mrs. Hoffman," Alma cries. "Forgive me. It's my husband. He's had an accident."

"Oh, dear." Mrs. Hoffman, clutching coat and handbag, scuttles past them. "I do hope it's not serious." And she flees into the rainy dusk.

SOLDIERS STAND GUARD AT THE DOORS to the infirmary. At the end of the hall of open doorways and empty hospital rooms down which Prior and the other man lead Alma and Nathan, another soldier stands by a closed door. Prior taps the door and opens it. "Mr. Reed, here's your family." He ushers Nathan and Alma inside, steps out, and closes the door after him.

"Frank." Alma rushes to the high bed. She bends to embrace him, then sees that his shoulder is bandaged. Her hands flutter. "Oh, dear, are you in awful pain?"

Frank shakes his head, reaches for her hand. "They've doped me up. I don't feel a thing." He smiles at Nathan. "Don't look so worried. I'm all right." But the hand he gives Nathan feels cold and weak. "Get your mother a chair."

Nathan gets the chair, sets it beside the bed, and she sits and takes Frank's hand again. "What happened, Frank? Colonel Prior wouldn't tell us a thing. Only a lot of piffle about secrecy and security guidelines and the tense situation in Europe."

"What happened is, I got shot." Alma gives a cry she stifles with a hand. She's white, and her eyes are very wide. Frank says, "Now, now. Don't carry on. It was only three times."

"Frank, don't try to be funny," she says.

"Fact," Frank says. "Shoulder, side, thigh." He touches the places. "None of them fatal."

"I tried to warn you, every day," Alma says.

"I'll listen next time," Frank says.

"There must never be a next time. Frank, what in the world? A shooting? Here? This always seemed to me the most peaceful place on earth."

"How did it happen?" Nathan leans on the windowsill.

Frank says, "I'd loaded the station wagon with his luggage. To take him to the airport for a flight back east. His ship sails from New York tomorrow. He put up his umbrella, came down the Atheneum steps, I opened the door for him, and before he could get in, some maniac opened fire from the bushes." Frank wags his head and laughs a laugh that stops in pain as soon as it starts. "Not at me—at him."

"Was he hit?" Nathan asks.

"You'd have thought so," Frank says, "from the way he yelled. But no. He wasn't hit. He's up above the clouds right now, safe and sound, winging his way to New York."

Nathan thinks he knows, but he asks, "Who is he?"

"Dr. Schoenwald," Frank says. "The German."

"But who was it who shot you?" Alma asks.

"Nobody knows. In all the excitement, he got away. I was down. There was a lot of blood. Schoenwald was under the car, screaming about Jewish plots. Till Colonel Prior arrived on the scene, nobody did anything but run around waving their arms. Catching the shooter was the last thing anyone thought of." He snorts amused disgust. "Academics. Worse than musicians. Nobody even saw him."

"They didn't call the police?" Alma says.

"No. Prior's in charge. Army intelligence. Government doesn't want anybody to know this happened. That's why the doctors here patched me up. No police records, no hospital records. Schoenwald threatened Ribbentrop would be writing to Cordell Hull about this. Probably bullshit, but if Hull isn't in a position to deny it, all hell could break loose." He pushes back his shaggy hair. "Meantime, I get kept here."

Alma says, "Then they'll have to keep me here too. I'm not leaving you alone in this place." She gets up and goes out into the hallway. "Colonel Prior?" she calls, and the door swings shut behind her.

Nathan says, "You know who it was, Frank."

"Sure, I know. But I haven't told Prior. Prior would have to send him back to Germany. The Nazis would demand it. And you know what they'd do—they'd hang him. And I'm not going to be responsible for that. He was a friend to me. He never meant me any harm." He cocks his head. "Why Dr. Schoenwald?"

"I guess Schoenwald had to be the one in Germany that betrayed him, didn't he? Stone arrived in Fair Oaks at the same time as Schoenwald. He must have traced him through a news story or something. He owned a gun. But the way he hated killing, I guess he couldn't bring himself to use it until the last possible moment."

"He got out of Germany safely," Frank says.

"But not his wife, not his daughter, not his friends."

"No. You told me. The Gestapo took them."

"He was trying to avenge them," Nathan says.

Frank laughs grimly. "I wish he'd practiced up on his marksmanship."

RAIN DRIPS ON AN EXTRA CAR parked in the shrubby driveway, but it's not Stone's car. Darkness has fallen. Nathan's shadow, cast by a streetlamp, goes before him down the path of sunken flagstones to the crouching house. He shelters under a little outcrop of red tile roof above the door, and thumbs the bell push.

Beyond the door, he hears children wailing. And Joanie's voice. Shouting. Does she ever just talk? A weak bulb goes on over the door. The door opens. The knot of Hotchkiss's tie is dragged down, his collar is open. A cigarette burns in his fingers. He glares at Nathan.

"What the hell do you want?"

"Kids sick again?" Nathan says. Fumes of VapoRub reach him. A child coughs croupily. Another child whines. "I'm sorry. I tried to phone, but it's always busy. I'm hunting for Mr. Stone. He isn't home. Is he here?"

"That would be all I need," Hotchkiss says. "Forgive me, Nathan. But this is not a good time."

Joanie yells from somewhere, "Who the hell is that?"

"A student," Hotchkiss calls.

"Will you come back here, please?" Joanie appears in a far doorway, light at her back. "The doctor thinks Scott may have to go to the hospital. Wayne?"

Hotchkiss says to Nathan, "He's at Laughing Jack's." He squints at his wristwatch. "Or he was, an hour ago. Till I took the phone off the hook. He kept calling and calling. I had to come talk to him. Matter of life and death."

"You should've gone. You're the only friend he's got."

"Married men can't have friends." Hotchkiss takes a last drag from his cigarette and tosses it into the dark. "He's drunk, Nathan. I know him when he's drunk. Everything's a matter of life and death. He probably wanted to debate some point in Schopenhauer."

Nathan starts to say, "But what if this time—"

"Wayne Hotchkiss." Joanie comes to the door. She sees Nathan. "Oh, no. Not the genius playwright. Go away." She grips Hotchkiss's arm. "The doctor says they may have to put a hole in Scotty's throat and stick a tube in so he can breathe. Do you hear me?"

Hotchkiss nods. "A tracheotomy." He lays his hand on hers, and says to Nathan, "I told him to go home and sleep it off, I'd see him in the morning at Moon's. Excuse me now. I've got sick children here." He closes the door.

THE RED NEON TUBING THAT SPELLS LAUGHING JACK'S spits and sizzles in the rain. Nathan pushes a black door into air thick with tobacco smoke and the fumes of liquor. The only light seems to come from the bar, where eight or ten drinkers sit clutching glasses, looking morose.

"Hey kid, you gotta be twenty-one to come in here."

It's a big man back of the bar who speaks. Nathan goes to him. He wears an apron like Travers Jones's. His hair is cut close around his crumpled ears. His face is battered. Since he doesn't look as if he's ever laughed in his life, Nathan figures this must be Laughing Jack. Nathan tells him, "I'm looking for Kenneth Stone."

"You're too late." The man moves off to take a glass from a patron and dump ice and whiskey into it and return it. He comes back. "He left about an hour ago."

"Was he all right?"

"You mean drunk? I've seen him in worse shape."

"I meant—did he seem, well, upset?"

"He sure as hell did. He wasn't reciting no limericks tonight." The man's tiny eyes under scarred brow ridges study Nathan. "You a fighter?"

"I was jumped by a bunch of kids in the dark."

"You got a nice build on you, make a classy-looking club fighter. I could introduce you to a good trainer." He gestures at faded photographs framed above the back bar. "I was in the fight game myself. I still got contacts."

"Thank you. Right now, I'm worried about Mr. Stone."

"He come in here very shaky, very pale. What he done first was knock back a double scotch. Then he kept going to the telephone back there and trying to call somebody. Then he give that up and asked me for paper to write on. I keep it here. You never know." His massive shoulders shrug. "And he sat over there at that table writing and drinking White Horse. Long time. Then he needs a envelope, doesn't he? And a stamp. Think I was a goddamned post office." A man and woman come in out of the rain, whooping and wheeing and shaking out their hats. Laughing Jack goes to wait on them. When he comes back, he says, "And he addresses the envelope, stamps it, says thanks and good night, Jack, and he's gone."

"He didn't say where?"

"Nah. Something crazy about this weather. You ever know it to rain here this time of year? I been here twenty years. I never did."

"It's a tropical storm. They usually stop in Mexico."

Laughing Jack's tiny eyes flicker along the bar. "He probably went home, didn't he?"

Nathan shakes his head. "It's too far," he says.

THE GUARDRAIL IS BROKEN, and a car is down in the brush with its lights on. He stumbles and slides in mud down to the car. It is Stone's. He thought it would be. He pulls open the door and squints inside. Stone is not here. The car is at such a tilt that when he stretches an arm to open the glove compartment, he loses his footing and sprawls on the seat, bruising his sore ribs on the gearshift. He grunts and opens the glove compartment. It is filled with road maps and Life Savers and other junk, but no flashlight. He was afraid of that. He worms his way backward out of the car and stands in the rain, looking around. But the car lights make seeing into the night impossible. He reaches in and switches them off. The canyon looms up, ragged blackness against blackness. He can't climb it in the dark. He'll only get lost, or break his neck. He gets into the car and closes the door. He's so tired he aches. He sits shivering in his wet clothes, nodding asleep, waking. It's no good. He searches and finds behind the seat a dusty lap robe. He strips, wraps the robe around him, lies on the seat, and in a minute he's dozed off.

IN THE RAINY MORNING LIGHT, Stone appears to be asleep. He lies under the rock ledge. Across the way, the waterfall splashes. The old pines tower above, tatters of mist caught in their branches. A Chinese painting. But Stone is not asleep. The Luger is in his hand. And the top of his skull is blown away.

AT HOME ON OLEANDER STREET, he bathes and shaves and puts on dry clothes. It's no longer raining. The clouds are breaking up. Off to the south, shafts of sunlight strike through. It's okay to wear his best slacks, best jacket, best shoes. And fifteen minutes later, without knocking, he walks into Prior's office at Sierra Tech.

Prior stands up behind his desk. "What is it, Nathan?"

"Somebody has to get his body," Nathan says. "You don't want the police in on this, so I guess you'll have to do it."

"Sit down," Prior says. "Whose body? Where?"

Nathan sits on a stiff oak chair and tells him. "If you check the gun, I expect you'll find it fired the bullets that wounded my father."

"You want to explain?"

Nathan explains. It takes a long time.

"You knew this last night, and didn't tell me?"

"Schoenwald wasn't hurt. Why would you want Stone?"

"Wouldn't you want him? He shot your father."

"Not on purpose. Frank knows that."

"And you're telling me this now—why?"

"So you'll know Mr. Stone was just settling a private matter. He was only after justice. Germany would never give him that. He had to do it himself. It was a brave thing." Nathan takes a shaky breath, blinks back tears. "And—he was my friend, and I don't want the coyotes to eat him."

Prior muses. "I'm told those canyons are dangerous."

Nathan nods. "They are."

"He could have fallen to his death."

"You going to ask the police to record it that way?"

"For the present," Prior says. "You know why?"

"Frank told me." Nathan pushes the telephone across the desk. "Please send them for his body now, will you? Or it will be dark before they can get back down."

THROUGH A WINDOW WHERE RAIN HAS MADE STREAKS in the dust, Nathan sees Moon mopping the floor. She wears a wraparound apron, and her fiery hair is covered by a dish towel. The chairs are upended on the tables. He wanted to be here early, and he's too early. He turns away, but Moon has seen him. With loud rattlings she unlocks the door and pulls it open. Her face is redder than ever.

"By all that's holy," she says, turning away, going back to her bucket and mop, "if opening time was four o'clock somebody would be standing out here hungry in the dark that's always darkest just before the dawn, wondering why the place wasn't open at three." She lifts mop from bucket, streaming water, splashes it down, and pushes and pulls it with long motions of her skinny arms. She throws him a glance. "I wish Travers kept your hours. He'd be breaking his back at this, and not his cherished mother, for whom, to hear him tell it, no sacrifice is too great."

Nathan takes the mop from her. "I'll do it."

"That boy"—she sets a chair down and plumps herself onto it, untying the towel from her hair, wiping her face—"will sleep through the last trump. He'll be late at heaven's gates when the dead arise incorruptible."

"Will they?" Nathan hefts and squeezes dirty water from the mop. "Do you really believe they will?"

"You're not a Catholic, or you wouldn't ask."

Nathan swings the damp mop in a wide arc now, to soak up the soapy water. "I wish I were," he says. "It would be nice to believe we'll all see each other again someday. In a happier place."

"Ah, you're talking like an old man," Moon chides him. "You've got the greatest gift of all—you're young. Be happy in that, Nathan Reed. Young and beautiful, with all of life before you. Stop thinking about dying."

"I'm thinking about Mr. Stone," he says.

"What are you saying? Surely you don't mean he's dead."

"It's in the *Times* this morning." Nathan wrings the mop again and swabs another section of linoleum. "He was hiking up in Harrow Canyon. Fell and broke his neck."

"Ah, no," Moon mourns. "Sure, and I'm graved to hear it. He was a wonderful man. Sad, you know. He understood too much. Whole libraries stored away in his brain."

Nathan sees Stone's shattered skull, and shuts his eyes. Moon takes the mop from him.

"Here, are you all right?" She leans the mop in the bucket and hurries to draw coffee for him. He trails after her, dazed. She puts the coffee mug into his hand. "Sit down. You're white as a ghost." She takes a chair off the table under the Acme beer sign and helps him clumsily onto it with anxious red hands. "You care too much." She sets a second chair down and puts herself on it. "It won't do. Life doesn't single us out, Nathan. It hurts us willy-nilly. If you care too much, it will drive you to drink."

"Thank you, Moon." He gives her a pale smile.

"I'd rather you didn't call me that," she says. "It was never a name meant kindly. 'Twas meant to mock my round, red face, which is my cross, and I try to bear it cheerfully. I know they call me Moon behind my back, so I put it on the sign. But I'd like it if you'd call me Kate."

"Thank you, Kate." He smiles again.

"Ah, well—thank you for spelling me with the mop." She pats his hand. "Now—your color's coming back—that's good." She rises. "I'll just finish up this floor, then I'll fix you one of those big, brutal breakfasts of yours. It will get the blood out of the part of you that thinks, and into your belly, where it can do you good."

HE WAS TOO TIRED TO EAT LAST NIGHT. Now he devours a slab of ham, a mountain of potatoes, three eggs, and half a loaf of toasted bread. Travers, looking pale and shaky, has arrived and is waiting tables. A different breed of customers comes so early—truck drivers after a long night's drive, milkmen just off their routes, scruffy down-and-outers in secondhand clothes and beard stubble with a nickel for a cup of coffee, and no more. Travers fills Nathan's cup and collects Nathan's plate—all without a word, certainly without a funny face. Nathan lights a cigarette.

And the first spate of laughing, scuffling students bursts in, skirmishing for favorite tables, slamming down books, knocking over sugar jars and ketchup bottles, yelling at Travers for attention. Watching the scrimmage, Nathan almost overlooks the entrance of Hotchkiss, unshaven, necktie knot hanging, shirt buttoned crookedly, the wounded scarecrow. He flaps toward the table where Nathan waits. His bloodshot, baggy eyes scarcely notice the boy until he's pulled out a chair and sat down. He blinks.

"It's the crack of dawn. What are you doing here?"

"Waiting for you," Nathan says. "How's Scotty?"

"They didn't have to do the tracheotomy," Hotchkiss says. "But they're keeping him in the hospital." Travers brings him coffee. Hotchkiss orders poached eggs on toast. He says to Nathan, "Nice of you to ask."

"Why don't you ask me about Mr. Stone," Nathan says.

Lighting a cigarette with shaky hands, Hotchkiss frowns. "What about him?"

Nathan takes a folded page of the *Times* from his pocket. Kenneth Stone's death didn't make headlines. The story is only two paragraphs long, and tucked away in a lower corner of page five. Nathan lays it in front of Hotchkiss. "What's this?" He gropes his broken reading glasses from a breast pocket, puts them on, picks up the paper, squints at it, and blanches. "Oh, my God." His tobacco-stained fingers lose their grip. The page falls. He grabs for it, lays it on the table with shaking hands. He takes off the glasses and glares at Nathan. "Thank you, very much."

"I'm only the messenger," Nathan says.

"I don't understand." Hotchkiss wobbles the hot coffee to his mouth, burns himself, rattles the cup into the saucer. "Why didn't

I hear about this? Dean Staat knew we were friends. Why didn't he call me?"

"Maybe your phone was off the hook," Nathan says.

Hotchkiss coughs smoke. "What's that supposed to mean?"

"Isn't that your way of dealing with bad news from Mr. Stone? 'With him, everything is a matter of life and death'—isn't that what you said?"

"I don't like your tone, Nathan. Let's remember who we are, here, shall we? Man and boy? Teacher and student? Ken Stone was my friend, and I am in pain, and I don't need you adding to the pain."

"There's more." Nathan puts out his cigarette and taps the paper. "I hate disillusioning a journalism instructor, but newspapers don't always print the truth."

Hotchkiss narrows his eyes. "What do you mean?"

"The story's a fable." With Hotchkiss's Laughing Jack's matchbook Nathan lights a fresh cigarette. "Stone knew that canyon. He wouldn't have fallen. Not even in the dark."

Hotchkiss gapes. "The police gave out a lie?"

"One part is true—that the body was found by a hiker." Nathan drinks some coffee. "You know who that hiker was?"

"You? How? Why?"

"He wasn't home, he wasn't at your place, he wasn't at Laughing Jack's. That left the canyon. He took me there once, remember? Told me how he loved it. Away from the world, he said. I guess that's where anybody'd go in trouble, isn't it—away from the world, if they could."

"Trouble? What trouble?" Hotchkiss asks.

"I can't tell you. I'm—not allowed."

Hotchkiss scoffs. "You're bullshitting me."

"No. The police weren't allowed, either. But it was the trouble he needed to talk to you about when he rang you up, and you wouldn't go."

"Scotty was sick. He could have died."

"The doctor was there, Joanie was there. How many people does it take to get one little kid to a hospital?"

"You saw how upset Joanie was," Hotchkiss says.

"Not half as upset as Mr. Stone," Nathan says. "He killed himself, Mr. Hotchkiss. With that Luger you found under his pillow the night you and I went to his place."

"Killed himself?" Hotchkiss begins to shake all over. His color is muddy. His mouth trembles. When he reaches for his cigarette, it sticks to his lips. He burns his fingers trying to pull it away. He spits the cigarette out, shakes his fingers, staring at Nathan. "Killed himself?"

"The man in charge of army intelligence at Sierra Tech ordered me to keep it secret, but I had to tell you. Up there alone in the dark, he put the barrel of the gun in his mouth and blew his brains out." Tears start down Nathan's face. "You should have seen it, Mr. Hotchkiss. You should have been with me yesterday morning up that canyon in the rain. You'll never see anything so sad in your life."

Hotchkiss has been shaking his head, shaking his head. Now he pushes back his chair and runs staggering between the tables, where kids stop eating to stare at him. He plunges out the floppy screen door. Travers stands at Nathan's side, holding a plate of poached eggs on toast.

"What happened? Is he coming back?"

"I doubt it." Nathan blows his nose on a napkin.

"Well, what am I going to do with these?" Travers says crossly. "Nobody eats poached eggs on toast at Moon's."

HE HAS LEFT THE LETTER WITH COLONEL PRIOR. He found it in the mailbox on the filigreed porch this afternoon when he got home from school. It surprised hell out of him. It was addressed in pencil. To him. Nathan Reed. Not to Wayne Hotchkiss. It made Nathan miserable to realize he was the only person left in the world Stone could reach out to. He sat on the porch steps and read the letter. A scrawl, drunken, meandering, repetitive. He stuffed the pages back into the envelope, put it into his pocket, left his books inside, and walked to Sierra Tech. Now he nods to the soldier posted at Frank's door and pushes into Frank's room. Alma has got a little table from someplace and is reading cards on it. Frank is picking at his supper on a steel tray on his lap. He appears not to like it much. They both smile at him. He must look grim. Their smiles fade.

"Mr. Stone thought he killed you," Nathan says.

"What? Oh, no. That was why he shot himself?"

Nathan says, "He wrote me a letter. It only came today. I think Colonel Prior wishes I hadn't read it, but since I did, he says I can tell you what was in it—only we all have to keep it secret. It's like a Greek play, Frank. He begs me never to forgive him for killing my father—to hold his name in contempt forever, a lot of stuff like that."

"Oh, what a rotten shame." Frank pushes away the tray.

Nathan can't hold back the tears. "I could have told him you weren't dead. I couldn't find him. I was too slow."

"You did your best." Alma gets up and takes him in her arms. "All night, in the rain. What other boy—?"

"That wasn't the only reason he did it." Nathan gives her a hug, wipes his eyes, and turns to Frank. "I shouldn't have come in here saying that. He had other reasons, older ones. It's a pretty mixed-up letter."

"This the one he wrote at the barroom?" Frank says.

"Laughing Jack's," Nathan says. "For one thing, he blames himself for what happened to his wife and daughter."

"Himself?" Frank's eyebrows rise.

"For staying in Germany too long. He should have left when Hitler began jailing politicians, harassing the Jews, rewriting the laws. Way back years ago."

"Why didn't he?" Frank says.

"He had a good position at the university. He was respected in

the community. He wasn't political. He didn't even vote. A model
German citizen. He kept looking the other way, even when his colleagues got hauled off in the middle of the night. It wasn't till 1938
he figured he might be next."

"He grieved for his wife and children," Alma says. "Of course
to me he never talked about anyone but you, but a person could tell.
He was terribly lonely."

"He wrote to friends in Germany, associates, but the letters just
came back unopened, those that weren't from the government, saying
they had no record of any such persons, couldn't trace them."

"My guess is," Frank says, "all he lived for was to kill Schoenwald. And when he botched that up, he figured there was no point
in going on."

Nathan nods dully. "Still, if I'd climbed up the canyon after
him, if I hadn't waited till daylight—"

"You'd never have made it," Frank says.

Nathan starts to cry again. "But he shouldn't have died thinking nobody cared."

Alma brushes away his tears with her fingertips. "He knows
now," she says. "He knows you cared." She turns up to Nathan one
of her awful spirituelle smiles. "And they're together now. He isn't
lonely anymore."

Nathan says, "Sure."

"You don't believe me." Sadly Alma lets him go, returns to her
chair, and sits, hands folded in her lap. "I'm so sorry. Life is going
to be unbearable for you, Nathan, until you accept that there's a
divine plan behind everything that happens, a purpose beyond our
poor understanding."

"It's what I understand that's unbearable," he says.

"You mustn't joke about sacred things," she says.

"I'm not joking," he says.

FRANK SITS IN THE GENERAL GRANT BED in his and Alma's
room; the coverlet is strewn with books, oddly folded sections of

newspaper, smeared plates, cups, glasses, silverware. Nathan has left his schoolbooks on the sleeping porch. Exams are almost over. Soon he won't have to carry books anymore. He wonders how long it will take him to keep his balance walking without them. He stops in the doorway to his parents' room and shakes his head.

"What happened to Alma?"

Frank grimaces. "Off on a higher spiritual plain, I guess. Hardly got a word out of her. She fixed me a good breakfast, and then I didn't see or hear her till lunchtime. And when she brought that, she was all dolled up, and she forgot to take away the breakfast stuff."

"She's not even home, Frank."

"Probably at that Gregory woman's," Frank says, and makes a jotting in his crossword puzzle. Nathan gathers up the dishes, sets them on a tray on the dresser, and refolds the newspaper, which he lays on a chair.

"How'd you get to the bathroom?"

"On my own. Used the cane. It wasn't too painful. Good for the scar tissue to stretch it a little, anyway."

"You want me to help you there now?"

Frank laughs. "I thought you'd never ask." Nathan lifts books off the bed onto the chair so he can lay back the covers and Frank can turn. He helps him sit up in those ragged pajamas of his, and get his feet to the floor. Frank keens under his breath at the pain. Nathan asks, "You been taking your pills?"

"Hell." Frank puts an arm over Nathan's shoulders and the boy heaves him to his feet. "They make me woozy. Might as well knock off a pint of rye and get some"—he halts for a minute this side of the door, shuts his eyes, bites his lip—"pleasure out of it."

"I haven't got a pint of rye." Nathan leads him haltingly, one slow step at a time, down the hall to the bathroom. "I could try to buy one for you"—he opens the bathroom door—"but I'm afraid I look too young. Laughing Jack thought so." Nathan chuckles. "When he saw my nose, he said I should be a prizefighter."

"Man's an idiot," Frank says. "I'm all right now."

"Yell when you want me." Nathan goes out and closes the door. And the bell on the front door jangles. He runs down the stairs. An underfed kid in khaki and puttees stands on the porch. His bicycle lies against the steps. He holds out a yellow envelope. "Western Union," he says.

FIRST SPIRITUALIST CHURCH OF FAIR OAKS the sign reads. In gilt on a black background. *Meagen St John Gregory, Pastoral Guide.* The uprights of the signboard stand deep in grass. Maybe Roland, the veterinarian son, used to mow the lawn. Where is he now? There's been no news of him and the other disgraced friends of Desmond Foley lately. Charlie Vorak could tell him what became of the story that was going to make him famous. But Nathan never sees Charlie now. He avoids the *Monitor* office. He hasn't been back to Moon's. What's there to go back for?

He sighs, pushes a wrought iron gate, and goes up a walk to a porch spiffy with new paint but as giddy with jigsaw work and spoolery as Aunt Bessie's. The double front door has frosted panes etched with serpentine fern patterns. A sign hangs off the doorknob, handwritten, with flourishes: *In Communication with the Spirit World. Please Do Not Disturb.* He frowns. The telegram in his hand reads, "Alma you should pay your phone bill have had a fall and broken my hip bedridden need you come at once love marie."

Mrs. Gregory is only dealing with the dead. They're not going to get any deader. Aunt Marie is more important. Nathan opens one leaf of the doors and steps into a hushed, high-ceilinged hall, where a stiff stairway climbs, and coats and hats—his mother's among them—hang off curved brass hooks on a papered wall. To one side, sliding doors stand open on a vacant dining room. To the other side, the sliding doors are closed.

From beyond these he hears a voice. The hair on the back of his neck stirs. It's Kenneth Stone's voice, complete with Iowa accent. Nearly perfect—just a little too deep. Nathan softly slides the doors open a crack. The voice says, "Listen carefully, Wayne, my friend.

This is what you've been wanting to know." And the voice tells about the bungled shooting of Dr. Schoenwald at Sierra Tech, and the reason behind it. "Don't blame yourself for not coming to Laughing Jack's that night. You had a sick child to worry about. It's more important to look after the living. I was already a dead man. And I'm with my beloved Ursula, now, my dear Gerda. I'm happy again. Believe that, Wayne—believe—"

Nathan slams open the doors. The room is dark, the windows covered by curtains of heavy black velvet. There's only a weak glimmer of light from candles on the mantelpiece. Seated on small carved chairs at a black-velvet-draped table are Alma, Wayne Hotchkiss, Charlie Vorak, and a big, bosomy woman with a puffy white face. Their hands clasp each other's on the tabletop. Their faces turn toward Nathan, mouths open, eyes wide. Except Mrs. Gregory's. Her eyes remain closed. She moans. It's moan enough to haunt a dozen houses. Nathan gropes the wall beside the door frame, finds switches, punches them. Light floods the room.

"Nathan," Alma cries. "What's the meaning of this?"

"Outrageous!" Mrs. Gregory heaves to her feet. There is a lot of her. She ought to make at least two wraiths when she passes to the other side. Her voice is a bull roarer. It makes the walls shake. "Leave this sanctuary at once, or I shall call the police."

"Go ahead," Nathan says, "and I'll tell them you're a fraud, using my poor, silly mother to help you stage a phony séance to pick this man's pocket." He looks through tears of fury and despair at Alma, who is standing, holding on to her chair's back. "The shooting was a secret, Alma. Everything I told you was a secret. Damn. The one person Mr. Stone didn't want to see or hear anything about that letter was Wayne Hotchkiss." Hotchkiss, pale, trembling, stands, and fumbles trying to light a cigarette. "Do you know what he said about you, Mr. Hotchkiss? That you denied him three times that night—the same as Peter did to Jesus."

"Child," Alma says, "you're saying things you'll be sorry for when you've had time to think."

Nathan stares at her. "Are you sorry for this?"

"You don't understand." She comes toward him, reaching out. "We must be kind to one another." She tries to touch him. He puts a chair between himself and her. She is hurt, but she goes on. "Mr. Hotchkiss was in torment. He couldn't sleep till he knew what it was Kenneth Stone wanted to tell him that night. And I knew, didn't I? Nathan—how could I refuse to help? If Mr. Stone could speak for himself, do you suppose he wouldn't—to give his earthly friend peace?"

"If Mr. Hotchkiss wanted to know"—Nathan glares at the journalism instructor—"he should have gone to Laughing Jack's when Mr. Stone phoned him, and found out. Too late is too late. You're supposed to be an intelligent man, for Christ's sake. Did you really think this"—he waves an arm at the huffing, sputtering Mrs. Gregory—"this fat faker could coax Ken Stone off his slab in the basement at city hall, so you could apologize to him?"

"I'm leaving." Hotchkiss strides for the hallway. Charlie is right behind him. He gives Nathan a sheepish look. "Professional curiosity is all, kid. Thought I ought to see a séance for myself."

"Well, don't write it up," Nathan says, "not unless you clear it first with Colonel Prior, army intelligence. At Sierra Tech."

Charlie's eyes light up with curiosity. He wants to ask a question, but "Right" is all he says. Then he hustles off after Hotchkiss. In a moment, the house door closes.

Alma says, "Nathan, this was very wrong of you."

"It wasn't what I came for." He holds out the telegram. "I came to bring this."

Alma turns the envelope over in her hands. Telegrams terrify her. Sometimes Frank would send them when he was on the road, to let her know where he was booked next, with what band, to play what speakeasy, nightclub, roadhouse. She would never open them herself, always hand them to Aunt Marie. This one she gives back to Nathan, pleading with her eyes. "I can't. You read it to me."

He reads it to her.

YOU READ IT TO ME. Are these the last words she's ever going to say to him? Her looks are dark and angry. Old suitcases from the attic, dusted off, lie open on the bedroom floor. While Frank dozes in the bed—she's made him take those pills he hates—she stuffs the suitcases with dresses, blouses, skirts out of the wardrobe, underwear, corsets, and stockings from dresser drawers. When Nathan offers to help, she gives no answer, doesn't even look at him.

He loads the suitcases into the trunk of the taxi, and sits in the backseat with her on the trip to Los Angeles and the new Union Station. It's a long way, but the whole time she looks out the window and says nothing. At last, the cab swings up the curved drive and stops outside the station doors. Nathan hoists the bags from the trunk while Alma pays the driver.

She holds open a heavy door so Nathan can carry the bags into the splendid place—somebody's gilt-and-crimson fever dream of an old Spanish palace. But she still says not a word to him. She buys her ticket at a carved counter. And down at the end of a long room of tiled floors, massive benches, lofty stained-glass windows, and painted rafter beams, they stand and wait in line before locked doors for the eight o'clock train. Children laugh, cry, run around. Hundreds of voices echo in the room. Not Alma's.

At last, the doors open and Alma and Nathan follow the line of travelers out onto a platform cold in shadow beside tracks where empty freight cars, flat cars, and tanker cars wait. Those farthest off shine dewy in the morning sun. Alma and Nathan and the others walk and walk along this platform. Finally the travelers clump together beside Pullman coaches, where they wait some more. Not a word from Alma.

Doors bang open on the coaches. Black men in red caps seize baggage and begin passing it up to white-coated black men in the coaches. Step stools clatter into place, and passengers begin to climb aboard. At last it's Alma's turn. Nathan takes her elbow to help her up. She puts a brief, cold kiss on his cheek. "Look after your father," she says, and disappears inside. He waits on the platform, smoking cigarettes. A bell clangs. Steam hisses. Men shout along the platform and wave faded signal flags. The train begins to move. He sees her through a window. He lifts a hand to wave, but her face is turned away.

FRANK SAYS, "EVERYBODY ELSE HAD A DARK BLUE suit. Why didn't you say you needed a dark blue suit?"

"I didn't. It wasn't one of the requirements."

They sit side by side on the Sierra Street bus. It is evening. Dressed-up people stroll the sidewalks, looking into lighted shop windows. Neon signs smile the names of stores. In a glassy ice-cream parlor, graduates gobble sundaes with their friends and families. Nathan holds his diploma in his lap. Fake parchment. He slips off its purple ribbon, unrolls it, looks at it. Someone labored to ink his name in perfect Gothic letters. It still doesn't seem much reward for four years' drudgery. He thought it would never end. Now he wonders where the time went.

"Didn't I look all right?"

"Best-looking boy in the bunch." Frank takes the diploma. "I wanted to tell everybody that was my son—the handsome one in the tweed jacket." He studies the diploma a moment, lets it roll itself up again, and passes it back to Nathan. "I'm proud of you."

Nathan slides the ribbon back onto the diploma.

"Your friends got to wear caps and gowns," Frank says.

"They did two years of college," Nathan says.

"Sure poured the honors on Charlie Vorak," Frank says. "Lucky he had his girlfriend there. He could never have carried all those scrolls and plaques by himself."

Nathan was astonished to see Peg, a mortarboard perched on her wonderful smoky cloud of hair, the dark roses in her cheeks, her eyes shining. "I thought she was in Mexico."

"Doing what?" Frank says.

"Writing a novel. Living in a palm-thatch hut on the beach, married to dashing Dan Munroe."

"You never told me that," Frank says. "It was Charlie and Peg this, Charlie and Peg that."

Nathan shrugs. "Things happen—people change."

"And change back, I guess," Frank says. "Nice to see Buddy again."

"He's the best of the bunch," Nathan says.

"He got you writing for the paper," Frank says.

"He thought I was better than I am. I guess I handle words well—people say so—but I'm no writer, Frank." He sighs. The bus is crowded with happy graduates and their smiling parents, younger brothers and sisters. If he knew what they were so happy about, maybe he could feel that way too. "Writing's more than typing up what you see and hear."

"It's knowing what makes people tick," Frank says. "You're young, and it beats me where you got it, but by God you know. I admit that play of yours stung a little—"

"I didn't mean it that way," Nathan says.

"But it's good. You got the way we talk and act down to a tee. You think about it—if writers spared everybody's feelings, there wouldn't be any plays, or books either."

"Not good ones," Nathan says.

Frank slaps his knee. "Damn right. Nathan, don't be like me. Don't find excuses to waste your talent. Use it."

"Oleander Street's next." Nathan gets up and stands in the aisle of the swaying bus. Holding on to the seat back, he reaches across, above Frank's head, and pulls the signal cord. "Got your cane?"

IT'S THE FIFTEENTH OF JUNE. The boys assembling on the damp, early-morning grass beside the city hall could be waiting for buses to take them to a school baseball game in a neighboring town. They aren't. They're waiting for the door at the foot of those white-walled basement stairs over there to open. They're going to do something they've never done. They're going to sign up for the draft.

The war is eight thousand miles away. Planes aren't strafing the roads into Fair Oaks. The ground isn't shaking with exploding shells from heavy artillery in the hills. Squadrons of tanks aren't snarling their way across the dusty cabbage fields of Arcadia and Monrovia. All the same, the United States of America is getting up an army of kids to fend these dangers off.

Nathan leans against a tree, lights a cigarette, and looks at them. There are hundreds. All the boys in Fair Oaks due to turn eighteen this year are either here now or will be soon. *They have no doubt that it is a damnable business . . . they are all peaceably inclined. Now what are they? Men at all?* Last night he dug out and read again the books Stone lent him months ago—Emerson, Thoreau. *Whoso would be a man, must be a nonconformist.* Nathan smiles wanly to himself. He's here, isn't he? Brave Nathan.

IT WAS A LONG, DRAWN-OUT PROCESS. It's past noon now, and he is hungry. Half a meat loaf waits in the refrigerator. He pictures in his mind the sandwich he's going to make with slices of that meat loaf on thickly buttered bread slathered with ketchup, all washed down with cold milk. He can almost taste it as he hops down off the bus, and he can't just calmly walk up Oleander Street. He trots. Until he reaches Villa, where he stops and stares.

What has happened? What is all that stuff out in front of Aunt Bessie's house? He breaks into a run. It's the furniture, all of it. The wing chairs, the radio, Alma's fortune-telling table. The beds, his typewriter, even the Maytag in its film of dried white soap scum. Giant cardboard cartons overflow with clothes, blankets, sheets, towels. It makes a wall along the parking strip.

He turns. Boards have been nailed across the downstairs windows of the house. Boards form an X across the front door. A notice is posted beside the door. He runs up the walk. A board at the top of the steps blocks off the porch. He climbs over it and reads the notice, but he can't seem to take in the words. He wanders up and down the porch, trying to understand. Then a man in suntans comes up the walk. A badge glints on his chest. A gun hangs at his hip.

He is a thick man with a belly slung in a belt. From under the bill of an officer's cap, he squints up at Nathan.

"Something I can do for you, son?"

"I live here," Nathan says. "Who are you?"

"County marshal's office. You've been dispossessed. Back taxes. Three years is the limit."

Nathan recalls that envelope in the bill-choked desk where Alma did her horoscopes. *County Assessor's Office.* And in red, *Final Notice.*

"But what are we going to do?" Nathan says.

"You got all kind of warnings." The man holds out a metal clipboard thick with papers. He licks his thumb and turns over the sheets. "Lookee here." Nathan climbs down to peer at the carbon copies of forms the man shows him. But it's pointless. The man's got all that makes the world turn on his side. Alma thinks the world stands still. And Frank—whether it turns or not doesn't concern him.

Nathan says, "My mother has a savings account. We can pay it now, can't we?"

"Afraid it's too late. To get it back now, you'll have to buy it off the bank. Ten thousand dollars. You got ten thousand dollars?"

"You're joking," Nathan says. "It's falling down."

"It's a double-size lot," the marshal says. "I expect they'll raze it and put up apartments." He kicks leaves on the walk and squints upward. The magnolias are in bloom, creamy white, big as dinner plates. "Get these messy old trees out of here, for a start. It's the land they want."

"Where's my father?" Nathan says.

"That your father, was it? Thought it was your grandfather. He argued with me for a while. Then he didn't want to stay out here any longer with his traps and calamities for all the world to see. He said you'd know where to find him."

———

FRANK SITS ON A BENCH UNDER A PEPPERTREE in Cordova Street Park. His cane leans beside him. A wax paper bag of potato chips is in his hand, and pigeons peck around his feet. He crushes potato chips in his hand and listlessly tosses the crumbs to the birds, who hustle around on their red feet, making *prutt-prutt* noises and rustling their feathers, each one trying to get all the bits of potato chip for himself. Frank looks hunched, shrunken, hollow-eyed. Nathan sits down beside him.

" 'In disgrace with fortune and men's eyes,' " Frank says.

"It's not your fault," Nathan says. "Alma held the purse strings. She was supposed to pay the bills. I kept reminding her. Didn't do any good, did it?"

"Few hundred dollars," Frank growls. "California. No place for people like us. Thing like this could never happen in Minneapolis, you bet." He crushes a last handful of potato chips, flings them to the birds, crumples the bag, and tosses it into a wire mesh trash basket. "What are we going to do now?"

"On my way here, I used Baumgartner's pay phone," Nathan says. "Morgan Moving and Storage will pick the stuff up this afternoon and hold it for us. No charge."

Frank squints at him. "Why would they do that?"

"Alex Morgan was one of the Harlequins," Nathan says. "She liked me. Kept pretending she wanted to marry me. I phoned her in Hollywood and asked her to put in a word with her father. He does whatever she wants. Just about, anyway. She's very pretty. Going to be a movie star."

Frank grunts. "No point in living out here unless you're a movie star. Or a queer. That was a weird bunch you took up with at that Harlequin."

"They're through with me," Nathan says.

"I'm glad to hear it."

"You want to go home, Frank?"

Frank nods heavily. "I miss your mother. She's only been gone a few days. Feels like a year already. No reason for me to stay here.

They're not going to take me back at Sierra Tech. Sent me a check for a month's pay. Said I'd understand." He sighs. "I'd have to hunt for another job, and you know how good I am at that. In Minneapolis, there's always some church or other. And the snow. Sounds ridiculous, I suppose, but I miss the snow. Weather's always the same here, day after day. I'm tired of it."

Nathan studies him a moment. "You want me to have Morgan's ship the stuff to Aunt Marie's, then?"

Frank brightens. "Would they?" The brightness fades. "Naw. That would cost an arm and a leg."

"Alma can pay it," Nathan says.

"I'll pay for our train tickets," Frank says.

Nathan takes a breath. "Only one. I'm not going."

Frank tilts his head. "You mean now—or never?"

"I'll be eighteen next month," Nathan says. "I want to be on my own."

Frank says, "We're on our own a long, long time in life. I'd stick with my family while I could, if I were you."

"I hurt Alma's feelings at that séance," Nathan says. "I don't think she's ever going to forgive me."

"Ah"—Frank turns his mouth down, waves a dismissive hand—"she'll get over it."

"I won't," Nathan says. "Frank, she's so dishonest."

"She means well," Frank says. "You know that."

Nathan shakes his head. "I'm staying here."

"How will you eat?" Frank says. "Where will you live?"

Nathan doesn't think it would be smart to speak Joe Ridpath's name, so he says, "Somebody promised me a job, free room and board. If I'm ever broke and out on the street, I'll write to you." Frank looks so doleful that Nathan puts an arm around him and a kiss on his stubbled cheek. "I promise. Cross my heart."

Frank finds his cane. "Hope there's a train tonight." He stands up, and the birds fly away.